Never Again, No More 3:

Karma's Brew

Never Again, No More 3:

Karma's Brew

Untamed

www.urbanbooks.net

Urban Books, LLC
300 Farmingdale Road, NY-Route 109
Farmingdale, NY 11735

Never Again, No More 3: Karma's Brew

ISBN 13: 978-1-64556-175-0
ISBN 10: 1-64556-175-5

First Trade Paperback Printing January 2021
Printed in the United States of America

10 9 8 7 6 5 4 3 2 1

Distributed by Kensington Publishing Corp.
Submit Orders to:
Customer Service
400 Hahn Road
Westminster, MD 21157-4627
Phone: 1-800-733-3000
Fax: 1-800-659-2436

Dedication

To all of my firsts:

First and foremost, to my mom, Mary, the first person to believe in my talents and challenge me to pursue them. My hubby, Chris, my first and biggest fan. My first readers, Sabrina, Ms. Kathy, Jessica, thank you for reading my work even when my story was little more than words on paper.

Acknowledgments

Giving honor and thanks to my Lord and Savior Jesus Christ. I am humbled and grateful for this gift you've instilled in me. Thank you for your continued blessings as I travel down my destined path and for all things that you would have me to do.

To my husband, Chris, my best friend and the love of my life: You were my first fan and my biggest fan, and the one who always . . . like always . . . keeps it real with me. Thank you for your honest feedback, even when I don't want to hear it. Thank you for loving me so unconditionally.

To my children: My Angel, who watches over me, I love you always. Kam, Ki, and Christian, as you grow, I see your talents bloom and manifest. Always believe in yourself and always follow your dreams. And keep your mom on her feet. Gotta stay young in these streets! LOL

To my dad, who never fails to showcase all of my accomplishments: I love you. Thank you for always making me FEEL like a real star ☺

To my girl, Diane Rembert: Honey, thank you for everything—and I do mean EVERYTHING! God connects people for a reason, and I know you were meant to be a part of this lifelong journey with me.

To N'Tyse: As long as we have each other and King Jesus, miracles happen! Being on the winning team with you is simply heaven sent. Thank you!

Acknowledgments

To my family and friends who've supported this journey and loved me from the cradle or the A1: My gratitude to you knows no limits. I love you all.

To my readers and fans: Thank you for your continued support of my work. I promise you all fuel all of this Untamable greatness. I'm going to keep pushing. Stay with me!

So, how about we jump on this Untamable ride and see where these *Never Again . . . No More* characters are gonna take us now?

Disclaimer: This work of fiction may contain sensitive subject matter.

Chapter One

Trinity

Although it was a bit breezy and chilly, I leaned against the rail of my terrace in my silk pajama set. My long, silky hair hung loosely, lightly caressing my face as it blew with the morning air, and the sheer serenity of the moment brightened my mood. My arms were riddled with chill bumps after a crisp but refreshing winter breeze kicked up, so I rubbed some warmth into them with my hands as the sun began to peek out beyond the horizon. I never grew tired of admiring the morning sun bursting onto my beautifully landscaped back yard, especially not from the terrace of my estate home in Evanston on the North Shore of Chicago, which was one of the most elite areas, if not *the* most elite area, in all of Illinois. Even after six months, the view still amazed me, just as it did the first time I had seen it.

We were a hell of a long way from the hood-nigga lifestyle we had been living. Our renovated Victorian-style mansion was a house that I could never even *dream* of having. It was situated on six acres of land. Terrence had purchased the eight-bedroom, six-bathroom home with family in mind. Aside from the normal features of our home, it boasted amenities such as a theater room, a library, an office, a small home gym, a basketball court, a pool and pool house, and a four-car garage. Our neighbors were CEOs and high-powered executives, and our kids were in private school with their kids. Career-wise, I'd enrolled in an online college and opened up my own art gallery, where I sold a lot of my own personal sketches as signature collections, and Terrence became a real estate investor.

"Good morning, Mrs. Kincaid," I heard as I felt two arms wrap around my waist.

I took a moment to enjoy the feel of being in Terrence's arms, then turned around. "Good Morning, Mr. Kincaid," I replied and kissed my husband.

"How is my lovely wife doing this morning?"

"Why, I'm *lovely* as always." I beamed.

"Do you ever get tired of watching the sunrise?" Terrence asked, pointing out into the horizon.

Lifting my arm up, I wrapped my fingers in Terrence's dreadlocks. "Nah," I said as he kissed me again.

"Keep pulling on my locs like that, li'l mama, and I'm gonna take you back to bed and give you a reason to hold on to them," Terrence said suggestively.

"I don't have a problem with that. I love to please my husband."

Our passion took over as we kissed on the terrace. Soon, both our pajama pants were down around our ankles, and Terrence lifted me up to make love right there on the ledge.

"Fuck! I want you so fucking bad, li'l mama," he moaned.

Freeing his thick erection from his boxers, I slid my hand up and down. "Take it," I commanded him.

Terrence wasted no time, sliding my lacy panties down. Just as we were about to connect, I heard a familiar sound. "Wanhhhh!"

"No, no, please no," Terrence whined as he buried his face in my chest.

"I'm sorry, boo. The baby calls."

Standing, I pulled up my underwear and pajama pants. While Terrence regained his composure, I walked into our bedroom to turn the baby monitor off and then, he joined me in the hallway, and we walked across the hallway to our baby's nursery.

"Hey, son. You couldn't wait just five more minutes, huh?" Terrence said, picking up our two-month-old baby boy, Tyson.

"And if that was all you were gonna give me, then my li'l Ty-Ty did his mama a big favor." I laughed as Terrence stood there rocking the baby.

He leaned over and kissed me. "I'm a heavyweight. All I need is one good punch and you'll be knocked out," he joked.

I burst out laughing as I grabbed the baby's blanket and turned off the monitor in the nursery. "Your cocky ass is too much! Come on. Let's head down to the kitchen so I can warm up his bottle. Your son's appetite is increasing."

As we walked out of the nursery to the kitchen, I couldn't help but stare at Terrence as he held our son. I couldn't believe just how much Tyson looked like Terrence. Our other two children, Brittany and Terry, were split down the middle between Terrence and me, but not Tyson Jahmal Kincaid. He was definitely his daddy's spitting image, so I was so thankful that I had gotten away from Pooch before he was born. One look at Tyson and Pooch would have known, without question, that his son was really Terrence's son.

Part of me thought of Pooch and felt sorry for what he was going through. I'd been following his case via the news and learned that he'd gotten double life without parole. That seemed like far too long for any man to pay for his transgressions. Don't get me wrong, Pooch did some fucked up shit. Selling death on the streets to little kids' mamas and daddies and people's children was low, but at the same time, you had to blame the junkies, too. None of these niggas in the street would make money if people just said no to that ignorant shit. One thing a drug dealer never had to do was beg for a customer, recession or not.

Then, I thought about his sleazy ass with those skank-ass strippers. That wasn't illegal or anything, but it did degrade women. He even had my homegirl Lucinda dumb in the head enough to be employed at his establishment. What kind of man would hire your best friend to strip at his club? I'll tell you what kind, a nigga like Pooch. Now, that was low, but it didn't constitute prison time.

There was other shit, too, like murdering those young cats and only God knows who else over the years. Nobody's life was worth taking for any reason. My theory is if you didn't give them life, then you don't have the right to take it. Yet, in a way, I still felt sorry for Pooch because he was never one of these thugs that fucked with anybody as long as you didn't step to him or his family or mess with his money. So basically, any dude bad enough to tangle with Pooch was gambling on cheating death.

Maybe that's why I insisted that we live in a gated community and permanently change our last names to Kincaid. When Terrence and I moved from Atlanta after bringing down Pooch and his organization, Terrence wanted to take on his dad's last name of Warren, but I refused out of fear. I just knew Pooch would track us down. So, we ended up taking on Terrence's maternal grandmother's last name of Kincaid. I didn't want any mishaps. Even though Pooch was safely situated behind bars in federal lockup, I still felt unsafe at times. It's almost as if I could hear him taunting me from inside the prison. Sure, I was a long way from Atlanta, in a neighborhood that his ghetto ass would never think to look for me, with a different last name, yet I still worried about Pooch catching up with me—us.

Terrence sat down next to me at the breakfast table as I fed Tyson.

"What's on your mind?"

Looking up at him with a smile, I fibbed, "Nothing."

"Liar." He chuckled.

"I'm just happy—"

He interrupted me. "You were thinking about Pooch again, weren't you?"

"I can't help it, Dreads. I feel so disconnected with the world back home. We left everyone and everything we knew and loved in Atlanta. Even though I know Pooch is locked up, I feel like I'm still a target. It's what I don't know that bothers me."

"Well, I'll tell you what I know," Terrence said, pulling his chair in front of me and placing his hands on my knees. "I know that I will never allow anyone or anything to hurt you or our children. So, you don't have to worry about Pooch or nobody else. I got you, and when I say I got you, I mean it."

"I know. It's just—" I began just as our nanny, Consuela, arrived.

"Buenos días, Mr. and Mrs. Kincaid," she sang, halting our conversation.

"Good morning, Consuela," we greeted her in unison.

"I see little Tyson is up early for his feeding." She smiled as I placed him on my shoulder to burp him.

"Ain't he always?" I laughed. "This boy ain't missing no meals."

"He's a growing boy. He needs all the meals he can get," she said. "Well, I am about to start breakfast for the other kids. Would you like anything in particular for yourselves?" Consuela asked.

"Actually, no. I am going to treat my wife out to a special day of shopping and relaxing, so we'll get something while we're out," Terrence said, smiling at me.

"Dreads! You didn't tell me that we were doing anything today."

"I know. It was a surprise."

Consuela smiled at us. "I love to see two young people so much in love. You have a wonderful husband, Mrs. Kincaid."

"Aww thanks, Consuela," Terrence said as he hugged her. "Well, we should get the kids dressed so we can drop them off at school. I'll send them down for breakfast as soon as they're done, Consuela."

"No problem, Mr. K. Breakfast will be ready when they get down."

I put the baby back in his nursery and turned on the monitors. On my way to the kids' rooms, Terrence grabbed my arm, pulled me in our bedroom, and locked the door in one swoop.

"What are you doing? I have to get the kids dressed."

"It's only seven o'clock. They don't have to be to school until eight-thirty."

"So?"

"*Sooo.*" He chuckled, pulling me by the waist and pressing my body close to his rising erection. "Let me show you how good my five-minute bout is," he joked.

I bit my bottom lip and kissed him. "This better be one powerful punch."

In one swift motion, his pants were at his ankles, and his luscious member was standing at full attention. "I'm already ready to knock it out the box," he said with a seductive grin, and that is exactly what he did—in a record four minutes!

Moments like this made me forget the hell I had endured while living with Pooch, and I was determined that I would never go back to that life again. It was a hard decision, but I decided to let go of my fear so that I could fully enjoy raising my kids and being Mrs. Terrence Kincaid. Terrence had proven over and over again that he would take care of me, and now it was time to breathe, relax, and enjoy all my new life had to offer. For the first time, I could honestly say I loved my life! And that was the shit I would remember from now on.

Chapter Two

Pooch

I was going fucking insane! I hated this damn place. Couldn't eat in peace and couldn't shit in peace. Now, I couldn't even sleep in peace. Who wanted to listen to these damn shit-packing muthafuckas in the cell next door moaning and groaning on each other? It made me sick to my muthafucking stomach! How in the hell did two grown, rusty-ass men find pleasure in fucking and sucking on each other? I was cool with one of them dudes at first. I mean, he was a real thug-lookin' nigga. Swole like a muthafucka. I'm talkin' about a real cock diesel nigga. His cellmate was kinda quiet, an average-size nigga who liked to read a lot. You never would've thought those two was on some ol' secret lover bullshit.

And that cock diesel nigga had a damn dime-piece-ass woman! I mean, that chick . . . whoo! That's a bad bitch! Cock Diesel would be all up on her during visitation like he just loved her so much, slobbing her down as if he loved pussy so much. I bet if she knew those same lips were on some dick right now, she'd leave his ass for a nigga like me. I could skeet off just thinking about his chick bouncing that ass in the air, and he was over there moaning like a female while he got his pipe smoked by another dude. From what ol' dude across the hall told me, they get it in heavy, too. He said Cock Diesel drilled up in ol' dude ass so deep, it was like his asshole was a female's pussy!

Now I couldn't even look at that nigga the same, and he always wanted me to give him daps and play cards and shit. Shiit. Not me. Cock Diesel's hands had been all over another nigga's ass crack, and he wanted me to touch them? Hell to the muthafucking no. He'd better come again with that shit and stick to making love to his cellmate.

"You up?" Wolf, my cellmate, asked, breaking my train of thought.

"Hell yeah, I'm up. How I'ma not be up? I can't sleep with them bitch-ass niggas next door gettin' they *groove* on. Trust me. There is nothing I'd rather be than asleep, so I wouldn't have to hear that nasty-ass shit!"

Wolf laughed. "Man, I feel you. We might as well just talk until they finish, 'cause I'm fucking tired of listening to that shit myself."

I laughed. "Man, I hear that."

"So, you heard anything from your girl? The one who left?"

Now, out of all the shit to talk about, he had to bring up Trinity's raggedy ass, so not only could I not sleep, now I had to be pissed off too! Shit, I think I'd rather listen to them muthafuckas bump nuts than discuss that bitch.

"Hell naw. That broad ain't tryna see me. Bitches are scandalous. A nigga catch a case, and she gone before the feds even lock me up."

"That's fucked up. I feel you. My ex-old lady had the nerve to come up here and tell me face-to-face that she had to move on with her life. Talkin' about she was lonely and shit and the kids needed a role model and whatnot. I'm like, you weren't saying that shit when I was out there hustlin' to provide and shit. You didn't have no problems with me risking my life, but now that I caught a case tryna do just that, now you looking for a role model and you lonely."

"Man, I'm surprised you didn't catch a murder rap up in here. That bitch was bold!" I fussed, shaking my head.

"Yeah, she was. It's cool, though, 'cause I got her fucking number. The minute she told me that, I started writing her sister and talkin' real sweet on her. You know? Tellin' her about how my old lady hurt me. Her sister had just divorced at the time, so she was tellin' me her problems, too. We've been kickin' it ever since." He gave a sinister laugh.

"Oh, so *that's* the chick that be coming here?"

"Yep and writing me, too," he said with a chuckle. "She is straight up and honest, too. Anything I ask she'll do for me, and she's already making plans for us when I get out. Now, that's a down-ass chick. The funny part is that her sister don't even know about us. I told her to keep it between us until I get out. I just want to see the look on that bitch's face when she sees me with her sister!"

His revelation made me think, and I got quiet for a minute. If Chocolate Flava didn't come through and Lisa wouldn't come through, maybe I could get Wolf's girl to smuggle some shit on the inside for me. It would mean I'd have to bring Wolf in as a partner because I knew he was gonna want a cut. That might not be a bad idea considering he'd been in this joint for a minute, and because of that, niggas in here trusted him, so he had pull and contacts. But the question was could *I* trust him? Damn these other lame, fake, shit-packing muthafuckas. Could he be down with me and help me realign the Dope Boy Clique? Hmmm . . . a true hustla's wheels were always turning.

"You 'sleep?" Wolf asked.

"Oh, naw, man. My bad. I was thinking about some shit for a minute."

"Thinking maybe you'll do the same thing to your ol' lady?" Wolf asked.

I laughed even though I felt a pain in my heart. "Even if I could do that, I doubt it would even matter to her."

"Damn, bruh. That's cold," Wolf said.

"Tell me about it." I started to fume all over again about the situation. Tomorrow was Thursday. Chocolate had better have found out something, or I was gonna cuss her black ass out. "I'm going to bed. Them bumpin' buddies done finally nutted."

I stood in line, pacing like a muthafucka. This dude in front of me needed to hurry up. He was up there talking sweet nothings in this phone, and I had some shit to do. It was always best to catch Chocolate around six in the evening, right before she went to bed for a couple of hours to get ready for her night shows. It was 6:02 p.m. and counting.

"My dude, you gon' be long?" I asked him. I was trying to be nice about it.

He frowned at me. "Nigga, I'm on the phone with my lady," he said rudely and completely turned his back to me.

My temper flared. This nigga didn't want it with me. For real. I tapped him on the shoulder lightly. "My man. I understand that, but I got some important shit to find out, and I really need to get to that phone," I said, trying not to show my anger.

He held up two fingers. "Two minutes."

If I wasn't working on an appeal, I'd fuck him up while his bitch listened on the other end. I already had double life. Any more time after that didn't even fucking matter. Three minutes later, that nigga hung up then turned to look at me and laughed.

"You got it, bruh," he said to me.

It was 6:06 p.m. I got his ass. "A'ight, man." I grabbed the phone and made my collect call.

"Hello?" Chocolate Flava said sleepily after answering the phone.

"Did I wake you up?" I asked, knowing I did.

"Yes. You know I go to bed around this time," she responded with an attitude.

"I know, but some dumb nigga was holding up the line." Why was I explaining shit to her? Fuck that. "Forget all that. Did you find out anything?"

"Well, Attorney Stein is working on a deal—"

I interrupted. "We can talk about that next weekend or tomorrow. I'm talking about Trinity."

She huffed with irritation. "The only thing I can really say is Terrence is definitely not around, because I found out that he don't live in the same apartments no more. The landlord told me he put in his notice to leave like two months before you got arrested. I may be wrong, but I don't think Trinity ran off with him either. My cop friends told me that when they did the raid, the weirdest shit was that your house was left like someone was still staying there. Trinity's clothes and shoes were there, and the kids' furniture and clothes were still there. No furniture was moved, and there was still food in the refrigerator. Trinity's car was there, but it got confiscated with the rest of your cars. I think they gon' start auctioning all that shit off soon, too."

That was strange. If Trinity had left, wouldn't she take something with her? Now, a part of me was worried that someone had done something to her and my baby. If somebody had hurt Trinity, my unborn child, and Princess, I was straight gon' get another double life sentence because they was gettin' done the fuck in. Period.

"Wait a minute. So, nothing was gone? Absolutely nothing?"

"That's what it looks like, and we all know Trinity's high and mighty ass ain't going nowhere broke. Not the way you provided for her ass," Chocolate Flava sneered.

"Chill with that shit. She was my girl. That was my job."

"Well, I'm your girl now, and all you do is question me about Trinity," she snapped.

Ignoring her attitude, I said, "But this shit don't add up. Her mom and her little brother and sister are gone, too." My mind wandered. "Did you find out anything about them? Have any of her friends said something?"

"Them niggas pulled some Houdini shit. Her mom was just up and gone, and Ms. Tina, her neighbor, said the landlord was pissed about that. Like I said, Terrence's manager said he put in a notice like eight months ago, and he didn't know where he was at. I've seen Lucinda, and she said she ain't even talked to Trinity in months. LaMeka ain't talked to her neither, but them hoes might be lying. Charice is gone to New York with Ryan, so she probably knows less than all of them. I tried to catch up with Terrence's old friend Skeet, but I ain't been able to catch that nigga. I don't know, Pooch. I don't know what to make of all of it."

This shit just got stranger by the second. Something was definitely up with this shit. Somebody knew more than they were letting on. I knew Lucinda or LaMeka wouldn't talk regardless, and I knew those bitches knew something, even if it was nothing else but the reason why Trinity was gone. Shit, but who knows? If a muthafucka got to them, then they may be closed-lipped to protect themselves, too. Muthafuckas do know just how to lean to keep bitches quiet. Trinity's friends had kids too, so I knew they weren't risking they kids' lives to give up no info on Trinity. For now, I'd keep them in my back pocket. Even if that damn LaMeka wouldn't help, maybe I could lean on Lucinda. She and I went back, and I had leaned on her in the past. But for now, I'd take another route.

I couldn't help but sigh with frustration. "A'ight. You did all right. But look, catch up to that nigga Skeet. He may be the only hope right now."

"A'ight. I'm going to bed."

"I'll call you tomorrow about that appeal."

"A'ight, and call before six, or I ain't answering," she said and hung up in my face.

I stared at the phone for a second in disbelief. If I didn't need this bitch, I would cuss her the fuck out.

Now, I was stuck between being worried about Trinity and being pissed at her ass. My chest ached out of love for this bitch. Damn, why couldn't I just find out what's up? How the fuck could it be possible to hate and love someone at the same time? Part of me wanted to knock her block off, and the other half just wanted to hold her like I used to. That bitch fucked me all the way up. No surprise, because she'd had me fucked up since the fourth grade.

For now, it was back to my cell after a stop to the laundry room. This cool-ass cat named Pit, who worked in the laundry room with the disrespectful-ass phone dude, had a cousin in my Dope Boy Clique and told me to let him know if I ever needed anything. Now, I did.

"Strangle that bitch," was all I was gonna say, and by nighttime, phone dude's bitch was gon' get another phone call—from the administration for identification purposes only.

Chapter Three

Lucinda

"She's lying! She has to be!" Aldris ranted for the tenth time as he paced the floor. "People have seen her since we broke up. They never said shit to me about a baby except the one she was having with her husband!"

"Aldris, maybe you should go back to work so you can get this off of your mind," I pleaded with him again. In truth, I needed time to adjust to this news myself. I mean here we were, fine with our happy little family, and here comes another child the same age as Nadia out of left field.

"I can't, Lu!" he yelled. He stopped as soon as the words came out of his mouth, then walked over, and hugged me. "I'm sorry. I didn't mean to yell at you. It's just I'm so fucked up right now by all of this."

I hugged him back. "*Ay dios mío*. We both are." I walked him to the sofa, and we sat facing each other. "So, are you absolutely sure there couldn't be any possibility that this child is yours?"

He sighed and rubbed his face as he sank back into the couch. "I'm not saying that, Lucinda. I mean she *was* my fiancée. We had an active sex life, regardless of the fact that I was doing my thing on the side, and we didn't use protection all the time. So, I mean, there is a chance it could be, but *damn*. I'd think she would've said something before six years!"

"Well, when she left you, she was pissed off. What's the old adage? Hell hath no fury like a woman scorned. There's no telling what a woman's capable of if she gets hurt," I told him as I massaged his right shoulder.

"Ugh!" Aldris jumped up and hollered in frustration. "This is fucking bullshit. I have to make some phone calls," he said, walking to our bedroom.

I followed him. "Who are you calling?"

"First, my job to let them know I'm gonna be out a couple of days. Second, I'm calling my mother. And she had the nerve to name her after my momma! I can't believe that shit." He continued his rant while he put on some jeans and a polo shirt. "Third, I'm calling my fucking attorney so he can recommend a good family lawyer, and *immediately* after, I'm calling that lawyer for an appointment for today or tomorrow so I can take this paperwork to them to determine the best course of action."

I walked up behind him and planted reassuring kisses on his back. He leaned into my embrace. "I love you, papi. We'll get through this together."

He turned to face me and cradled my face. "I'm sorry, Lucinda. I know this must be hard for you, too. I know this affects both of us. I love you, baby, and I thank you so much for sticking by me and not blowing up. I swear to you that I knew nothing about this child that Jennifer is talking about. I hope you know that."

"Yes, of course I do, Aldris. You're a real man. You would never keep something like this a secret from me. You take too good of care of Nadia and me not to take care of your own child," I reassured, looking into his eyes with complete confidence.

He kissed me and smiled through his pain. "That's why you're my wifey."

"See, that's what I want to see—your smile. You're damn straight I'm wifey, and that ain't changing—baby or no baby. We'll just have to roll with the punches. Mrs. Lucinda Sharper can definitely handle it."

He kissed me again. "I love you," he said sweetly. "Now, I have some phone calls to make."

I knew he needed some space, so I went into my office with every intention to do some work, but I just couldn't get a thing done. It was at times like this that I could kick Trinity's ass for up and leaving me! I understood why she dipped, but I needed her so bad, and not only could I not see her, I didn't even have a direct line of contact. I was forced to talk with her on her terms, but I had no idea when she would call me. Being as such that I hadn't talked to her in a month already, you could see that our communication was rare.

With no one to vent to, I gave up hopes of getting any work done. It was obvious that my mind was stuck on Aldris and this child and probably would be until all of this got resolved. Why did all of my wedding bliss have to be tainted by this news? This should've been the happiest time of our lives, and now it was riddled with accusations from both ends of the spectrum. Call me selfish if you want, but I truly did not want to share Aldris' attention, time, or money with anybody else. Of course, if—and I do mean *if*—this child was his, I wouldn't stand in the way of him being a father to her. However, one thing was damn sure not about to happen; I wasn't sacrificing my happiness for Jennifer or Jessica. They were going to have to work around us because on June 8, which was in exactly four months, I was going to be married to Aldris. Period.

Chapter Four

LaMeka

I don't know why I was sitting there. I guess a part of me really couldn't believe that this fool actually recovered from being shot, but mostly, I guess I was there because I felt so sorry for him. After two emergency surgeries and three close encounters with death's door, Tony actually lived. After a full week in ICU, he was finally stable, but he was in a coma. I had contacted his parents, and despite the heartache and pain Tony had taken them through, they'd been up here day and night to look after and monitor him. Being a mother, I could relate. Nobody wanted to see their child knocking on Heaven's door, no matter what mistakes they'd made.

As suspected, Tony had been shot for trying to play stick-up kid to get rocks. No one confessed who the shooter was, but I already knew that was a no go. Nobody in the hood snitched, especially when a nigga didn't mind making an example of you, and Tony was exactly that, an example.

I didn't want Tony to die, but a small part of me was happy to see him suffer. I wanted him to suffer, just like I had suffered all those years I was with him. Yet, a part of me—the kinder and holier part—was hopeful for a full recovery. I wanted to see Tony get better and make a change for himself. He'd had his dreams snatched away at a young age, nearly lost his life while he was lost in a world of drugs, and now, he had to deal with being HIV positive. Yep, it was official. He had the "package," and I could bet a dime to a dollar he didn't even know it. The truly sad part about all this was that there was no telling how many women or *men*—hey, being on that shit does strange things to people, so you never know—he'd lain down with since he contracted this virus. These diseases were out there, man, so you had to be careful.

"I thought I'd find you in here," Gavin said as he entered the room, startling me.

I wiped my tears. "Gavin. You scared me."

"Sorry, I didn't mean to. I was just checking on you," he apologized. He sat down next to me and put his hand on my shoulder. "No change, huh?"

I shook my head. "Nope. He's still unconscious."

He rubbed my back and smiled at me. "He'll pull through. With you by his side, how could he not?"

I pushed him and giggled. "Your game is so weak."

"Girl, please. My game is tight. That wasn't real game anyway. That was just me comforting a friend."

"Thanks." I smiled at him.

He smiled back. "No problem."

Thinking about the possible gossip floating around, I released a dreadful sigh. "So, how bad is the rumor mill about the new student who knows the guy who is HIV positive?"

Gavin waved off my question. "Don't worry about that."

"So, it's that bad, huh?" I rolled my eyes, thinking about the water cooler gossipers.

"LaMeka—"

"Just be straight up with me," I interrupted.

He rubbed his face and released the same dreadful sigh. "On the real, it bothers some people. You know they got mad questions about how you really know his HIV status, and if I keep it one hundred with you, shawty, they want to know your status."

"I can't believe, with as much shit as we have to deal with, that these so-called *medical professionals* would worry about bullshit like that. This is what we do every day."

He nodded. "True. True. I feel you in a way, but they're human. That shit is scary, LaMeka. We deal with a lot of shit every day, but it doesn't mean we're immune to being scared of dealing with it."

"It's a manageable disease. Nobody is running to the other side of the building if a person finds out they have cancer or even herpes, which are incurable diseases as well."

"Come on now, LaMeka. I get your point, but those are totally different from the "package." For one, cancer, while incurable, is not contagious. Everybody in here can have cancer, but your body has to materialize cancer cells on its own for you to have it. Second of all, herpes may be incurable, but it's not life threatening. I mean, people on constant medication live perfectly normal—sexual activity inclusive—lives. Yet, I beg to differ on the running part. I don't know too many people voluntarily laying down with a person who has herpes."

"Right, and who wants something they can't cure regardless of what it is?" I argued. "Besides, with the new advancements in HIV treatment and with awareness, it's hardly the death sentence it used to be."

"True," he agreed, "but I guess the disease still has so many unknown factors that it's hard for people to be comfortable with it."

"So, I guess you're one of the ones who want to know the deal? Is that why you're defending their ignorant asses?" I asked with an attitude.

Pinching the bridge of his nose, he frowned. "Calm down, shawty, damn," he responded with a slight attitude of his own. "You asked me. I was only being straight up like you asked me to be. I haven't asked you a thing about your personal status or business. I figure if you want to tell me, you will."

Suddenly filled with remorse, I placed my head in my hands. "I know. I'm sorry. I shouldn't have snapped at you, but I'm just so frustrated with people looking at me as if I have a third eye in my forehead."

"Forget those people and what they think. It ain't nobody's business but yours. You don't owe nobody nothing, so it is what it is. Personally, I admire you. It takes a strong person to deal with someone who is HIV positive, and you handle yourself with grace and class. On the humble, I really respect you."

His words etched a blush on my face. "Now, that game was very tight."

He playfully pushed me. "Get the fuck outta here." He laughed. "Again, that wasn't my game, but I'll take that compliment."

Becoming aware of the time, I glanced at my watch. "Shit, my break was over ten minutes ago."

"Yeah, that's why I was looking for you."

"Well, aren't you going to chastise me for being late?"

He stood up and looked down at me with lust-filled eyes. "Do I get to spank you?" he asked seductively.

Giggles escaped me, and my cheeks instantly deepened in redness from blushing. "Oh my God."

He pointed at me. "Now, *that* was my game."

Standing up, I gazed into his smoldering brown eyes. "It sure as hell was." I winked at him and turned to leave.

He followed me out the door. "You didn't answer my question," he said once we were in the hallway.

Turning, I looked up at him. "I know. Maybe one day I'll answer it for you."

He laughed. "Maybe I'll get the answer I'm looking for."

"Maybe, Mr. Randall. Maybe," I said as we went to finish up our rounds.

Chapter Five

Charice

The atmosphere in the house had been extremely tense since our surprise visit from Lincoln. Come to find out, everything that he'd said was true to form. He had signed a contract with the Giants and was moving to New York. When Ryan verified that information, he cursed harder and louder than I'd ever heard. I knew he wanted to keep Lincoln far away from me, and I couldn't blame him. Not even a full year ago, I was about to marry that man. I guess I would be a little crazy about the idea, too, if I were in his shoes.

Hell, I had my own reasons to stay away from Lincoln. Yes, as you may have guessed, my baby girl, Lexi, was really fathered by Lincoln. I'd actually found out I was pregnant when Charity was first admitted into the hospital. At the time, I had every intention of telling Lincoln; however, my focus had to be on Charity. With the way our breakup went, I just couldn't stomach being around him while battling to keep myself together for my daughter.

When Lincoln left me, I felt like my world had ended, literally. I loved him with my heart, body, mind, and soul. I'd given him everything in me that only Ryan had once consumed, and my love for him had taken over every possibility of me falling for Ryan again. I loathed Lincoln for what he did to me. I was at my lowest point when he left me, and it was further compounded by the illness and subsequent death of my daughter. Even after Ryan and I got married, it took a minute for me to give my all to him because of my feelings for Lincoln. Now, with Lincoln being on the same team, it posed all kinds of problems. There was no doubt that he and Ryan hated each other, and personally, I didn't want him around me or our daughter.

The reason Ryan and I became as close as we did—besides the obvious reason of our daughter fighting for her life—was because he was the first person I told about my pregnancy. I expected him to go ballistic, but he was extremely calm and understanding. He stepped up as the protector that he is and really focused on me, so that I could be as healthy and as stress free as possible given the circumstances. That was what made me fall in love with him again. Ryan had proven to me that we were meant to be a family, and I decided to give our love another go.

I also decided that since Lincoln did not appreciate the family that I was willing to provide for him, then he didn't need to know about Lexi. I mean, really? Was I supposed to sit back and be like his other baby's mother, Lauren, and not get any physical, emotional, or financial support from him? Hell no. I'd played that part with Ryan for far too long, and I wasn't about to play it with Lincoln.

The only person that brought me joy and kept me grounded was Ryan. He made me feel like life was worth living again. He gave me the courage to continue being a great mother to our boys and to appreciate the blessing in my pregnancy. Therefore, Ryan and I agreed that we would raise Lexi as our daughter. I didn't need or want a thing from Lincoln Harper, and Ryan didn't want Lincoln involved in our lives, so it just worked.

Now, looking back on everything, I couldn't even believe I'd actually fallen for Lincoln and chosen him over Ryan. I'd always regret that moment. Always. It took a long time to get Lincoln Harper out of my system, and I'd be damned if he was going to bulldoze his way back into my life.

On my way home from clothes shopping for Lexi, I noticed a moving van parked in front of a house three doors down from mine, with movers unloading boxes. I drove down to the house.

"Excuse me, who is moving in here?" I asked a mover through the opened passenger-side window of my car after I pulled over.

One of the movers stopped and smiled at me. "The great Lincoln Harper. He's going to be on the greatest team on Earth now. I know those Cowboys are going to be upset! First, we got Ryan Westmore, and now Lincoln Harper."

My heart instantly plunged down to my toes. How the hell could he honestly move on the same street as Ryan and me? How heartless was this bastard? Why did he need a big-ass house like this anyway? He only had one daughter. Okay, well, two daughters—but only one that he knew of that would visit him. He wasn't married, and it was not like he needed the space for his family. They lived in New York. He could've purchased a two- or three-bedroom condo in the city.

"Looking for me?" Lincoln's voice resonated in my ear from my driver's side.

Startled, I jumped and clutched my chest. "You scared the shit out of me!" I gasped then removed my shades before turning off my car.

He kneeled down so that we were eye level. "I didn't mean to scare you. I just pulled up behind you and saw that you were in front of my house. It's good to see you again, Charice. I'm so glad that we get to be neighbors."

I rolled my eyes. “Why are you even here? You’re one man. You don’t need a house this big,” I fussed, ignoring his greeting.

“Is that any way to treat your neighbor? Geez, you’ve been in New Yitty too long. You’re already losing your Southern hospitality,” he joked.

“No, I haven’t lost my Southern hospitality. I just don’t feel like being hospitable to you,” I sneered, putting back on my shades.

He chuckled softly. “It really doesn’t have to be this way. Look, why don’t you come inside, have a drink with me, and take a tour of my house? We are neighbors. We should learn to get along with each other.”

Was he serious? Anger swelled inside of me, and I started my Mercedes McLaren to leave. “I would rather drink a bottle of ammonia and sit in the county hospital ER than to share anything—especially my time—with you.”

He put his head down and then looked back up at me with sadness. “I’m sorry that you feel that way, ma.”

No. The. Fuck. He. Didn’t. That one word triggered me. I glared at him. “Don’t call me *ma*. Don’t ever call me that again,” I warned.

“Charice, from the bottom of my heart, I swear I’m sorry—”

“Have a nice life, Lincoln. Enjoy your house but stay away from mine.” I drove off, leaving him standing in the middle of the street. *Bastard.*

Chapter Six

Lincoln

Watching Charice drive off was yet another dig in my heart. It was moments like those that really got to me. Why did I still have to love her after all this time? I'd put everything into my season with the Cowboys to make up for the agonizing pain I was feeling on the inside. Still, it could not take away the fact that my heart longed to be with the only woman I'd ever truly loved. Charice. I couldn't escape her. She invaded my thoughts and my dreams. At any given moment, my mind would drift off, just thinking about her. Every night I went to bed, I dreamt of her. At first it bothered me, but now it was just a part of my nightly slumber.

I remembered everything about her. *Everything*. I remembered how my fingers felt running through her long, thick, mahogany hair. I loved the way she used to caress my face after we made love. Her smile was innocent and infectious. I missed seeing her in my wifebeaters and jerseys and the way her luscious Georgia peach booty would bounce in short shorts. I missed how she would shyly play with her hair and bite on her bottom lip. I remembered how she'd close one eye and flutter the other while tilting her head back as she reached her climax from our lovemaking. I missed her dancing, her laughter, and the way she used to make me feel like there could be a hundred sexy men in the room and she'd only be focused on me. I missed the nutritious meals she'd made me, the advice she'd given me on my portfolio and my non-profits. I missed her intellect, her charisma, and her style. I missed the way she had a no-nonsense attitude while still allowing me to be a man. I missed—*her*. I more than missed her. I *loved* her.

Charice had been through so much, and I could've beaten myself for not being there for her the way I should've been. I felt like such a coward, and in a lot of ways, I was. When Charice really needed me to be there for her—the way I promised I would—I'd abandoned her and all the love she had to offer me.

As I grabbed my suitcase out of my SUV, I wished that Charice had come in and allowed me a chance to apologize to her. I needed to say it a lot more than she needed to hear it, but she had left me standing there, looking like the fool that I was.

"Excuse me, Mr. Harper," one of the movers called out to me, breaking my train of thought. I turned to face him.

"Yes?"

"You have a visitor on your back patio."

"Thanks." I wanted to be alone to sulk in peace, but now I had to entertain an unknown houseguest. "Why don't you fellas take about an hour break and come back?"

"You ain't said nothing but a word. Yo, fellas, break time," he called to the other four men. "Let's roll." They jumped in the truck and left.

I walked to the back. Ryan was sitting on my patio furniture, drinking a beer. He had a scowl on his face as he cleared his throat of the strong taste. He leaned forward and looked at me eye-to-eye.

"Stay away from my family," he ordered.

Look at this nigga, I thought. I couldn't help but to laugh. "You're over *here*. I'm not at your house. And just why are you on my property without my permission? That's called trespassing." I crossed my arms over my chest.

"If you don't stay away from Charice, you'll have more to worry about than trespassing."

"She chose you, right? So why should you feel threatened by me?"

He jumped up, angered. "I'm not threatened by you."

"Oh, really?" I asked, feigning shock.

Ryan walked up so that he was directly in my face. His jawline was tight. "If you even think of coming between Ricey and me, I will not hesitate to beat your muthafucking ass."

I laughed loudly, staring right back at him just as seriously. "Trust me, dawg. The Lincoln you ran up on the day you found out about *Ricey* and me is not the same Lincoln standing here now. Nawimean? You made damn sure of that. So, if you step this way, I *will* fuck you up, and that's a promise, *bitch*."

"No, *you* made damn sure of it, you trifling muthafucka! And ain't shit stopping me—"

"Get the fuck away from my house," I interrupted, getting angrier by the second. "I'd hate for the number one running back in the league to be out this season due to knee injuries."

Ryan stepped back and gave a derisive laugh. "I wish you would."

I walked up to him and pointed my finger into his chest. "In case you forgot, you're in my state now. Nawimean? This ain't Atlanta or Dallas, bruh. Please believe me when I say you don't want it with me. Now, I'm gonna tell you this one last time. Get the fuck off my property."

Ryan put his hands up to concede this round and began to walk off. "Just so we are clear that *this* is your property, and the house down the street is mine. The house, everything and *everyone* in it, are mine," he threw over his shoulder menacingly.

I laughed. "Okay, whatever you say to make you sleep better at night is cool. Just remember this, though. I was never a rebound fiancé, but you are definitely a fallback husband."

Ryan stopped dead in his tracks and turned around. "Like we say in football, a win is a win no matter what."

"And a bitch-ass nigga will always be a bitch-ass nigga no matter what."

"Bitch-ass niggas gotta learn it from somebody. I learned from the best."

"Have a good day, neighbor."

"You too. We should do this again real soon."

"Most definitely. Make sure you bring Charice with you next time. I'd love to show her all the rooms in my house. She can help me break them in . . . I mean decorate them."

Ryan looked at me as if he could spit fire, and his eyes were dancing with anger. "Last warning. Stay the fuck away from my wife."

I smiled devilishly. "Sure." I shrugged, throwing my hands up. "But you might want to tell your wife to stay away from me first. Seeing as how she just left here about two minutes before you showed up. Have a good one, bruh." I walked into my house without bothering to wait for a response.

I needed to take a nap to clear my mind. The last thing I wanted to do was take away my focus. That meant not exchanging in senseless arguments with Ryan. I knew coming into this that it would be hard to restrain my temper, but I had never in my life wanted to kill someone until the day I showed up at Ryan's house and actually saw him and Charice as a couple—a *married* couple. It was official. I hated him. More importantly, I hated what he'd managed to get away with. But in due time, he would understand that what goes around comes right back around again.

Karma, old friend, is a bitch, I thought as I stretched across my bed for a short but much needed nap.

Chapter Seven

Aldris

I was a good man. Sure, I'd made my fair share of mistakes in the past, but I was a good man. Yes, a great deal of my mistakes came by way of cheating on Jennifer, but still, I had made amends for my actions, even if not directly with her. I'd gone to church and leaned on Christ while becoming an active member. I may not have been doing everything right by fornicating with Lucinda and shacking up with her, but I only did that—well, the shacking up part—because I knew she'd be my wife. As for the premarital sex part, well, everybody has a vice. At least I was faithful to her and wanted to make her my wife. I never said I was a perfect Christian, and if you find one, please point them out to me so I can tell you in awe that you've met God.

After messing over Jennifer and meeting many wrong women, I was happy God sent Lucinda my way. I tried to get everything right after getting it wrong. I took care of her and Nadia. I loved them and treated them like the queen and princess they were, and I took care of all the household expenses. We went to church together, we prayed together, and we played together. We were a family.

Even when Lucinda and I got in disagreements, I'd walk away and let us both calm down. Even if I was right, I found a reason to apologize because I wanted Lucinda to understand that I truly loved her, and if I was wrong, I went above and beyond to make it up to her. They were my world, and I would give my life for them.

Like I said, I was a good man, so why, for heaven's sake, was I being slapped with a paternity suit? The possibility of being a father was something I looked forward to sharing with Lucinda. So why now? And why me? And why the hell didn't Jennifer tell me this sooner?

Wasn't there a loophole for karma, especially if you changed your life around? Perhaps some old college buddy clued her in to the fact that I was getting married and she wanted to get even, or maybe she just felt like fucking with me after all these years because she had a grudge. Maybe she was on some female liberation and revenge conquest. I just refused to freaking believe that I got her pregnant and she didn't tell me. I absolutely refused to believe that.

Even if it was true, how could this chick—yep, I said chick for lack of a more appropriate word—keep something as precious as a child away from me for all these years? I just couldn't believe she'd be that heartless and vindictive. Being hurt is one thing, but denying a parent their rightful relationship with their child is downright scandalous. I didn't want to believe that Jennifer could be that person, no matter how badly I had hurt her.

While at work, I impatiently waited for my attorney's phone call. So much was on my mind that by 5:00 p.m. I still hadn't finished my work, and it had taken me an extra hour just to submit my daily reports. When the call finally came, all I could think about as I listened to him feed me a bunch of shit I really didn't want to hear was, *this child is not mine.*

"What do you mean I *have* to take the paternity test?" I asked my attorney as I toyed with a pen on my desk.

"Aldris, I understand that you feel this child is not yours, and you have justifiable cause to feel this way. However, it doesn't dispute the fact that you've been court ordered to do so. She's paying for this herself, and the law requires that you comply," my attorney advised.

"So, I want to take my own test with people I trust."

"You're more than welcome to pay for any others that you want, but you still have to take this one."

"How will I know it's not rigged?"

"The courts are sending you to their facility, not one chosen by Jennifer. Therefore, no one has privileged information about the facility or its staff. Aldris, let me just shoot this to you straight. I can assure you no one there gives a damn about you or your situation. It's just their job."

I sighed, rubbing my forehead in frustration. "So, when do I have to do this, again?"

"Tomorrow at ten a.m. The results will be back in forty-eight hours, and we will go to court on that Friday at one p.m. That's where I shine. So far, she's asking for back child support, continued child support, a visitation schedule, and for you to provide health insurance. I'm flat out contesting back support unless she can provide proof that you either knew about the child, or that she's attempted to gain child support prior to the case. The health insurance is debatable depending on her employment. Visitation will be worked out, and I will try to get your child support reduced to as low as possible given the circumstances. Of course, all of this is based on the results of the paternity test," he explained.

Growing frustrated, I had to end this conversation. "All right, I'll be there at ten."

"Okay. Don't stress about this part, Aldris. We don't even know if this is your child yet. Like you said, you doubt that it is. Once we find out the truth, all this will possibly be a distant memory."

"Attorney Willingham, I understand, but it's not the *possibly* I'm worried about. It's the *probably*," I confessed.

"Even that can be resolved, Aldris. You can always opt to give up your parental rights if you do find that this is your child."

Nope. Not me. Regardless of the outcome, I was a man, not a coward, and definitely not a deadbeat. "No, that won't be necessary. It would just take a lot of getting used to, that's all."

"Well, let's just get past this first step, and on Friday, we'll worry about the rest."

After I hung up, I logged out of my computer and left the building, but I didn't feel like going straight home. I wanted to be alone and just clear my head. Ever since I found out about this possible child, I'd been so tense. I realized my tense behavior was unfair to Lucinda, but I was upset and worried because I just didn't know how having an outside child would affect our relationship. My baby wasn't a jealous woman, and I knew she'd expect me to take care of my own child, but living in that kind of scenario was harder than it sounds. This should've been the happiest time of my life. I was getting ready to marry the woman of my dreams, and suddenly, out of left field, there's a child. What the hell was Jennifer thinking, doing this to me?

After a while, I found myself at my mother's house. I knew I should've gone home to talk to Lucinda instead of my mother, but I needed an outside perspective for guidance. She didn't say much, but just her listening ear did more good than anything, and I was ready to get home to my lady and baby.

It was 9 p.m. by the time I got home, and I knew Lucinda was going to be mad as hell, especially since she'd called me ten times. When I walked in, I headed to Nadia's room to peek in on my sleeping beauty and smiled. Knowing that she had school tomorrow, I gently shut the door and made my way down the hall to our bedroom, eager to get out of my suit and get comfortable. I put on my basketball shorts and a T-shirt, then took a deep breath before I headed to our home office, where I was positive Lucinda was working. I could tell before I even opened the door that she was mad as hell from the way I heard her pounding on the keyboard.

I exhaled deeply and opened the door. "Hey, Lu," I said softly.

She stopped typing without facing me and said, "Hey."

Feeling a little safe that she didn't blow up right away, I continued inside and shut the door behind me before I sat down. "I know you're working, so I won't disturb you for long," I said, trying to give myself an easy out.

She finally turned to face me. Her anger was written all over her face. "Oh, so now you're concerned about my feelings? You waltz your ass up in here after nine o'clock at night without so much as a phone call, change clothes, and then tell me you won't disturb me for long? You have some nerve, Aldris! Where was this concern at five thirty? Where was this concern when I called your ass ten damn times?"

"I know I was wrong, but I had so much shit on my mind, Lu. This whole situation with Jennifer is really fucking with me right now."

"And you're fucking with me," she yelled angrily as she stood up and leaned against the wall. "So, just how is putting me on the back burner a requirement for you to deal with your issues?"

"I wasn't putting you on the back burner, Lu—"

"Bullshit and die, Aldris! Yes, you were."

"Nadia is asleep—"

"As if you care about that."

Now, that was a low blow. When I looked at Nadia, I didn't see my stepdaughter. I saw my daughter. For Lucinda to go there was just plain wrong. "Don't start *that* shit now. I *do* care about Nadia, and you know it."

"So, coming home any time of the night when she hasn't seen you all day and asked about you until she fell asleep is showing her that you care, right?"

Her point was valid, and I hated that because it made it seem as if my actions contradicted my words. I rubbed my head as I attempted to calm my tone. "I'm not saying I wasn't wrong, Lucinda. I'm just saying I needed some space to clear my head. That's it."

She ran her fingers through her hair. "Ay dios mío! Aldris, I understand that this shit with Jennifer has got you messed up right now, but I thought we were in this together. I want to be there for you and help you, but I can't do that if you're constantly pushing me away."

There it was: the reason for her brewing storm. Now I understood that her anger was based off sheer concern. She thought my actions were meant to push her away, when in actuality, they were meant so that I didn't find myself pulling away.

I stood, walked to her, and pulled her close to me. "I realize that now. Don't you know I'd never intentionally push you away? I'm just used to dealing with things in my own way. I was inconsiderate of your feelings and wellbeing, and I am sorry, Lucinda. I love you." Bending down, I kissed her on the neck. "Forgive me," I pleaded, breathing in scent. She smelled so fucking divine.

She giggled despite her anger. "You piss me off."

"I know." I tilted her head back and kissed the nape of her neck.

"I should give you my ass to kiss."

"I know." I kissed it again.

"I love you, Aldris."

"I know." I kissed it again.

"You're making me horny."

"I know." Mission accomplished.

She exhaled, wrapped her arms around my neck, and looked me in the eyes. "I forgive you," she said and planted a sensual kiss on my mouth.

I held her tighter and leaned my forehead against hers. "I know, and I thank you."

"Dinner is in the refrigerator—fried chicken, macaroni, chicken-flavored rice, and cornbread."

"That's what's up." I smiled at her. "I'm going to eat and then shower. If I'm asleep when you finish, wake me up. I've got some make-up work to put in."

"Yes, you certainly do." She sat down at the computer as I turned to leave. "And Aldris," she called out after me. "I know you don't plan on leaving out of this room without telling me exactly where you've been."

"I drove around for a while and then stopped at my mom's house for a while to talk about all this shit with her. I hope you don't mind," I explained, praying she didn't feel slighted that I'd chosen to talk to my mom about everything instead of coming home and talking to her.

She looked at me with a straight face. "No, babe," she said and began working. "I figured you were at your mom's. I gotta get back to work."

I walked out. *Liar*, I thought as I closed the door, but as much hot water as I had just gotten myself out of, I had no room to call her out. The moral of the story was: choose your battles—wisely.

Chapter Eight

LaMeka

Why did I still care so much? While a part of me hated what Tony did to me, it wasn't enough to keep me from overseeing his care. He was still in a coma, and while the doctors weren't optimistic, I tried to instill hope in his parents. It was a constant uphill battle with his condition, with some days being better than others, but I stayed by his side. Which brings me back to my original question: why did I still care so much?

Honestly, I still loved Tony. No, no, no. I was not, let me repeat, I was not in love with Tony. I simply loved him. I loved him because despite the hell he unleashed in my life, our relationship brought me my two greatest joys, Tony Jr. and LaMichael. I'd never known love like that before. My sons had been the center of my joy and the true loves of my life. If it weren't for all of the shit Tony put me through both mentally and physically, I wouldn't know that I was strong enough to stand on my own two feet, nor would I know exactly what I didn't want in my next man. My bad experiences had turned into life lessons, and my life lessons became my steppingstones, so in the end, I could thank Tony. If it weren't for him showing me what a bad man was like, I never would have learned to appreciate a good man.

"Still no change, huh?" Gavin's voice floated into Tony's room.

I jumped and turned to face him. "You scared me. Stop doing that."

"Sorry." He smiled and walked inside.

"But no, there's still no change," I confirmed, turning my focus back to Tony's motionless body.

"He'll pull through," Gavin encouraged.

"Hopefully you're right. From your lips to God's ears."

He looked at his watch. "It's time for us to get off. You wanna grab something to eat? There's a diner not too far from here that sells the best burgers and shakes."

"Are you asking me out on a date?" I asked with a grin.

"LaMeka, if this were a date, I'd be picking you up from your spot looking fresh, dressed like a million bucks, and I'd take you out somewhere nice, like Woodfire Grill or Chops Lobster Bar, and we'd get toasty on a bottle of Cabernet Sauvignon. Asking you to the local diner in our hospital scrubs hardly qualifies as a date. What kind of man do you take me for?" he asked seriously.

"I'm just playing with you. I know your game is tighter than that."

"Oh, you do?" he asked with mock excitement and a smirk.

"I'm just saying I would assume so." I tried to back-pedal.

"Ahh, it's too late. You've already admitted it."

"Okay, I admit it. You've got some game for a white boy."

"Girl, I'm Cablanasian. What you talking about? Ain't that what Tiger said? That man said he was a Cablanasian. We should've known he had issues right then." We both burst into laughter.

"You're a fool!"

"Hey, what can I say? I'm pretty fly for a white guy," he joked, referencing The Offspring song from back in the 90s, as we walked out of Tony's room.

After I clocked out, I called my mom and asked if she would watch my boys while I went to eat with Gavin. She agreed, so I followed him to the diner, where we were quickly seated, and we both ordered the new peach-flavored shakes and a cheeseburger.

I bit into my burger and closed my eyes. It was too damn good, so good that I moaned aloud.

"Didn't I tell you it was good?"

I nodded my head in agreement. "I really don't need this. I'ma have to walk the neighborhood an extra hour," I declared, then took a sip of my shake.

He waved off my comment. "Ain't nothing wrong with indulging every now and then. Besides, you're perfect the way you are."

"You're just saying that." I looked downward to try to hide my blushing.

"No, I mean it. You curve in all the right places. A real man likes a woman with a little meat on her bones. We like something to hold on to." He winked.

I nearly choked on my burger. "Boy, stop."

"Stop what? Telling the truth?"

"Kicking that bullshit," I joked. "I gained about thirty extra pounds after I had LaMichael, and it took a lot for me to get it off."

"So, what you're saying is that you got it off, but you still don't think you look good?" he asked inquisitively.

"No—"

"Oh, so I just make you uneasy when I notice," he countered, interrupting me.

"No, I mean, men these days are looking for those model types—the Beyoncés and the Selina Eubanks of the world. What kills me is that an average-looking man will have the audacity to expect his woman to be Beyoncé. I'm like, dude, until your ass can look like The Rock, miss me with that bullshit. If I had millions of dollars, I'd look like that too. Money can turn the worst ugly into the best pretty."

Gavin laughed. "Well, I don't look for model types. Like I said, I like something to grab and hold onto. I ain't looking for Beyoncé. For one, I don't have bank like Jay-Z, and I ain't signing no pre-nup if I do run up on her ass. Secondly, beauty is in the eye of the beholder. You beat Beyoncé and Selina every day of the week in my opinion."

"Yeah, and only to you."

"If it's only me and you talking, then mine is the only opinion that matters. You've got to learn self-confidence. Be proud of your curves, LaMeka. I'll bet there's a 300-pound woman out there wishing to God she had your body."

The pause I had to take jarred me. *Well, damn. Did he just put me in my rightful place?* He had. Had I been put down so much by Tony that I didn't even know how to take a compliment? Or worse yet, not think I was deserving of one?

"That's true. I can't argue with that," I conceded a bit embarrassed.

He bit into his burger and gazed at me. Once he swallowed, he pointed and stated, "Let me ask you a question, if you don't mind. Why are you so damn hard on yourself?"

Leave it to him to ask a loaded question. "Well, I've been through so much and had so many let downs and negativity in my life that I just learned to expect the worst. I guess I expect it so much until I don't know how to recognize the positive."

"Yeah, but you're confident with nursing and school. You're confident in your abilities as a mother, especially a young mother with a special needs child. It only shows when you're talking about your self-image and relationships. So, what's that all about?" he quizzed.

"Damn, who are you supposed to be, Dr. Phil?" I laughed.

"Whatever," he said with a chuckle. "I'm just making an observation."

"You white people are just fucking nosy," I joked. "That's why y'all be getting fucked up and shit."

He burst out laughing so hard it brought him to tears. "You may have a point about that! From fights to natural disasters, it's always the white people getting fucked up or needing rescuing on the news," he admitted, causing me to erupt in hysterics.

After the moment of laughter, I took a deep breath and decided to answer his question. Regardless of the fact that he was interested in more, Gavin had become a friend, and I didn't mind being honest with him about my ordeal. "Well, since your nosy ass must know, I was in a very abusive relationship with my kids' father. He beat me down mentally and then physically until I didn't know which way was up or out. But I'm thankful to be out of that situation."

Gavin gave me a knowing look and then broke it down. "Yet you still let his twisted actions affect you. You may be out of the situation, but you need to work on being out of that abusive state of mind."

Maybe Gavin was Dr. Phil in disguise because once again, he was positively correct. What was funny was that up until that very moment, I didn't realize that was exactly what I was doing. It was a shame the bad experiences and negativity had become so much a part of my life that I'd begun to accept that as my lifestyle and my way of thinking. I was so stung by his revelation that I just sat there and stared at him.

"What?" he asked nervously. "You're not mad at me, are you?"

I shook my head. “No, nothing like that. It’s just that I never thought of it that way, and I guess I really needed to hear that.”

He reached across the table and gently grabbed my hand. “I’m not trying to be mean to you, but we all need someone to give us the diehard truth. That’s what’s wrong with the world today. You are a strong, intelligent, and *sexy* woman, and I need for you to know that,” he said, gazing into my eyes.

I didn’t know what fire Gavin lit up under my ass, but I was definitely feeling it, and I was feeling him too. Just the touch of his hand was sending me over the edge, and I was fighting to stay in control. As Gavin and I began twirling and interlocking our fingers, the fire growing in my hotbox made me want to put one of his damn fingers between my legs until he found that gushy spot. I crossed my legs and tried to fight my growing desires. Something about this man was doing something to me!

“I swear you know just what to say sometimes.”

“So, why don’t you let me take you on a real date so you can see how I would treat you all the time? Or did ol’ boy ruin any man’s chances of showing you that not every man is bad?”

A blush rose on my face. I palmed my cheek to cover it as I nodded my agreement. “Okay, Gavin, I’ll let you take me out as long as I get to choose where we go.”

An excited grin spread across his face. “That’s what’s up! I can do that. So, where do you want to go and when?”

I stood up and pulled out my wallet to pay my bill, but Gavin put his hand up to stop me. “Next Saturday the Hawks have a home game against the Lakers. Get us some tickets and let’s check it out.”

He looked at me sideways. “I was kind of hoping for something a little more—”

I interrupted. “I like basketball, and if you make it past this date, we’ll see where the next one takes us.”

“Playing your cards right, huh?”

I winked at him. “Always, Mr. Randall, always,” I said and walked off.

Chapter Nine

Aldris

"Do you want me to drive?" Lucinda asked as we walked down the driveway toward my BMW 745i.

"No, driving will keep my mind off of it," I answered as we got in the car.

She turned to me and grabbed my hand. "No matter what, I'm there for you. Everything is going to be all right because I've got your back, baby."

Her sentiments meant so much to me. I was grateful to have her in my life, and I leaned over to kiss her. "I love you so much, Lu. I really do."

"I love you too, papi."

"Please don't say *papi* right now. Right now, that takes on a whole new meaning." I groaned in frustration.

My grumblings meant one thing: it was paternity test time. It would also be the first time that I'd seen Jennifer since we broke up, and the first time I'd lay eyes on the child she claimed was mine. Part of me was hoping that when I saw the child, I would be able to say I know for a fact this ain't my baby because she'd be biracial or some shit. I just wanted this nightmare to be over with.

I was happy that Lucinda was coming with me. I was thankful that despite my actions the night before, she'd forgiven me. I was so thankful, in fact, that as soon as she logged off from work, I made sweet love to her. Usually our lovemaking relaxed me, but afterward, the only one sound asleep was Lucinda. I faded in and out all night, having nightmares of every woman I used to date pop up with paternity suits. Then, like gremlins, they just kept multiplying! It all climaxed on my wedding day. Just as Lucinda was about to say "I do" the entire wedding party and guests turned into females—some I knew and some I didn't—all claiming to have a baby by me. Lucinda ran out of the church in tears, and like zombies, the women all crowded me as if they were going to eat me alive. The point of the dream, I gathered, was that I was truly worried about how everything was going to affect my relationship with Lucinda. So far, she was by my side and I was eternally grateful, but we were facing so many unknowns that I would rather have faced as a married couple. That way, she couldn't just up and leave me. It was a selfish thought, I know, but who wouldn't be selfish when it comes to the person they love?

When we arrived at the lab, I got out of the car and stretched to shake off my nerves. As Lucinda came around the back side of the car, I couldn't help but to ogle her as she walked around to the driver's side. Damn! I was already there for a paternity test, so sex should've been the furthest thing from my mind. But she looked damn good. Not that she didn't on a regular day, but today it seemed she put a little extra effort into it. It was probably more to show off to Jennifer than for me, but I didn't mind. I was just proud to have her by my side and helping me through this ordeal. So, if she wanted to show out a bit, she could. Either way, I would enjoy the show.

Reaching up, she smoothed out my striped Polo shirt, then I straightened the leg of my jeans and fixed my baseball cap.

"You're fidgeting. I know you're nervous, but I'm here for you. We're gonna be all right," Lucinda encouraged.

With those words, I exhaled the nervousness. She always knew exactly what to say. Grabbing her hand, I held it tightly as we walked into the lab together.

Once inside, I checked in with the receptionist, and before we could take a seat in the lobby, the nurse called us back. Good. I was glad to get it over with quickly because I didn't want to sit in a waiting area while this situation ate at me.

"You're here for a paternity test with Jessica Brooks, correct?" the nurse asked.

"Yes."

"Okay, just follow me," she instructed. I gripped Lucinda's hand tighter.

We entered the room, and I gasped when I saw Jennifer sitting there. She looked amazing. She'd even lost a few pounds since the last time I saw her. She was never overweight, but I could tell she was leaner, more fit. Her milk chocolate complexion and Taraji P. Henson inspired hairstyle coupled with her mid-thigh-length dress exuded a certain sex appeal. Her smile lit up her face, and her big brown eyes looked warm and inviting as she looked at her daughter, Jessica, who, upon first glance, looked just like a female version of me when I was six.

"You're Jennifer Brooks, right?" the nurse asked, bringing Jennifer's attention to me and Lucinda.

She looked at me and rolled her eyes. "Yes, and this is my daughter, Jessica."

"Hello, Jennifer," I said through uneasy feelings.

"Aldris." She nodded at Lucinda. "Who is your company?"

"This is my fiancée, Lucinda Rojas."

Lucinda smiled and waved. "Hello."

Jennifer snickered. "Ookayy. Hello," she said as if something came across her mind that she didn't want to say out loud. "This is Jessica. Jessica, this is Aldris and Lucinda."

Jessica smiled shyly at us. "Hi." She turned to Jennifer and asked, "Mommy, is this my *real* daddy?"

She sighed and looked directly at me. "Yes, he is."

"Then why do we have to take this test?" she inquired.

"Well, honey, so that *no one* can dispute the fact that you are his child," Jennifer said with finality in her tone.

"What does dispute mean?" she asked.

"It means to argue. No one can argue that you are not his daughter," Jennifer answered.

"Do you really think we should be discussing all of this right now?" I asked Jennifer, growing uncomfortable with the direction of the Q&A session.

"I have nothing to hide, and I'm honest with my daughter. If she asks me a question, I'm going to answer her truthfully the best way I can," she said with a blasé attitude.

Lucinda turned me to face her. "Just let it go, baby."

I gently pulled her close and kissed her forehead. "You're right. I'm just a little uptight," I whispered before I sat down to fill out my portion of the paperwork.

Once I finished the paperwork, within five minutes we were both done. The technician bagged and tagged our samples and told us the results would be back in forty-eight hours. I didn't need the results to know that Jessica was my daughter. The moment I laid eyes on her, I felt an instant connection, not to mention she reminded me of myself at that age. In my gut, I knew she was my child, and that meant there was about to be trouble in the city.

"Well, I guess I'll see you *two* in court on Friday," Jennifer declared condescendingly after we all reached the parking lot.

"Why are you doing this, Jennifer? You could've come to me—oh, say six years ago—and told me about Jessica. Why do you want to disrupt everyone's lives now?" I asked angrily.

She was clearly taken aback by my comments. "Excuse me? I'm not even going to dignify that with a response."

"Oh, you're going to tell me—"

"Aldris, don't do this now. Jessica is looking at you," Lucinda interjected.

I looked over at a scared and nervous Jessica. "I'm so sorry, Jessica. I wasn't trying to be mean to your mother. I just—"

"Mommy, can we go?" she asked hurriedly, interrupting me.

"Get in the car," Jennifer ordered, unlocking the doors with the key fob remote. Jessica jumped in the back of an Infiniti SUV and shut the door. "Nice going, Aldris. You've scared my child with your attitude. But you so have a habit of fucking shit up."

"I didn't mean to, but I have a right to know, Jennifer. You owe me that much, and you know it."

"I don't owe you shit," she snapped.

"*Please,* you two. Let's not do this here." Lucinda stepped in. "We'll be in court on Friday, and everything will be answered then."

"As much as you are pissing me off by trying to check my behavior, *Lucinda*, you do have a point. Come Friday, every question will be answered. But that is just a formality. All three of us know that the little girl in this SUV is Aldris'. Now, you both can blow that out of your ass," she shot back before getting inside her SUV.

Jennifer sped off, leaving Lucinda and me flabbergasted by her verbal assault. After a few moments, we made our way back to my car.

Once in the car, Lucinda looked at me. "I'm trying to be calm with her, but her attitude is going to piss me off, Aldris. Now, I wasn't trying to step out of line, but if Jessica is your child, her mama is gonna have to check her attitude or she's gonna get chin checked," she fumed, her Spanish accent growing thicker by the word.

"I know, baby. It's gonna be all right. Don't you worry about anything. Just concentrate on planning this wedding." With that, I leaned over and kissed her.

"How can I with this mess with Jennifer and this foolishness with Raul hanging over us?" she asked, rubbing her forehead. "I've still got to talk to my dad about Raul and go back to court about Nadia's child support. My head is spinning from all the issues."

I put my arm around her shoulder and pulled her close to me. "Let me stress for the both of us. You just focus on becoming Mrs. Sharper."

Looking up at me, she smiled. "I love the sound of that."

Friday morning—the day of reckoning—was full of gloom. With Nadia off at school, the house was quiet. Usually, Lucinda would cook breakfast, but this morning our nerves were getting the best of us, so we settled on our morning smoothies to tie us over and continued on with our normal morning routine.

We showered together—something we always did to keep us connected. There was something about bonding together through bathing and massage that seemed to link our souls together and release all our stress. But *today*, it was only a temporary fix. No sooner than we both dressed for court, the nerves were back again. You could almost sense the impending news in the air hanging like a thick fog. Lucinda and I had already discussed the fact that there was a strong probability that Jessica was mine; the resemblance was uncanny. I could see the pain and discomfort in Lucinda's eyes as the reality set in. I wanted nothing more than to shield her from it and let her know that no matter what, she and Nadia were my life. But we couldn't bring ourselves to delve any further into that conversation.

Now was the time to find out if my life would be forever changed, or if I could breathe a sigh of relief. As we sat in the courtroom waiting on the judge to review the paternity results, I looked over at Jennifer, who was toying with some Dolce & Gabbana shades in her lap. She appeared to have done well for herself just by appearance alone. It was there in court that I noticed that she didn't have a wedding band on her finger, and her husband had not been present at the lab nor in court today. Had she not married? Or was she now divorced? It was weird because Jennifer's maiden name was Crawford, but both her and her daughter's last name was Brooks.

"Mr. Smith and Ms. Brooks, I have reviewed the results of the paternity test, and I find them to be in order. Therefore, without further ado, according to the results by 99.985%, Mr. Smith, you are the father of Jessica Brooks," the judge said.

It happened so fast that it took a minute to catch up with me. "Say . . . what?" I asked, looking at my attorney.

"You are the father, Aldris," he repeated to me.

I loosened my tie and looked over at Jennifer, who was smiling with delight yet smirking at the same time. The look on her face said, "take that." Lucinda held her head down, and I grabbed her hand.

"I'm so sorry, Lu," I whispered. She mustered a slight smile and squeezed my hand as a show of support.

"Judge Chambers, in light of these results, my client is asking the courts for back child support for the past six years in the amount of $28,800, which averages out to four hundred dollars a month. We also seek continued child support at the legal limits of eighteen percent of Mr.

Smith's base pay. We ask that Mr. Smith provide health care coverage for Jessica and that a visitation schedule be set up by the courts," her attorney stated.

"Going for the gusto today, Attorney Philips?" Judge Chambers asked.

My attorney looked at me, smiled, and then interjected. "Your Honor, my client has been more than willing to cooperate with Ms. Brooks. Please understand that he was blindsided by this suit. Mr. Smith and Ms. Brooks have not been in contact in over six years. He had no knowledge of a pregnancy or even the possibility that he might be a father. If he had, he has stated that he would've gladly been a part of the child's life. Currently, he's engaged and is fully supportive of his fiancée, Ms. Lucinda Rojas, and her daughter, Nadia Garcia, who both live with him. He is also a Big Brother mentor and has been for the past four years. Asking for back support for a child he was unaware of is unfair to my client and would impose a financial hardship on him," Attorney Willingham countered.

"Is this true, Attorney Philips, that Mr. Smith was unaware of the child or the possibility that your client was pregnant?" the judge asked.

He looked nervous. "Yes, Your Honor. However, there were circumstances—"

The judge put his hand up. "I don't care about the circumstances. This child is six years old. If your client had made Mr. Smith aware, I believe based on his apparent character and their proven information that he would've been involved. I am dismissing back child support altogether," Judge Chambers ruled.

I wanted to smile, but I felt bad about being happy at the ruling.

The attorneys went back and forth over paychecks and dragged our home lives through the mud. Come to find out, Jennifer got married a year after Jessica was born, and she and her husband had Jessica's name changed to Brooks. They got divorced a year ago, citing the all-time favorite: *irreconcilable differences*. Jennifer had moved back to Atlanta, where she was a marketing director for Coke, making only a grand less than me. Once the judge heard all the evidence, he rendered his decision.

"Taking everything into account, here is my ruling. I am ordering that Mr. Smith pay child support at sixteen percent of his current base pay for a monthly payment of $453.33. The first payment will be due April first. Each subsequent payment will be due by the fifteenth of the month. Back child support is not allowed. Ms. Brooks currently carries medical and dental insurance on the said minor child, and she will continue to do so. I am ordering Mr. Smith to add Jessica Brooks on to his current insurance as a secondary carrier and maintain a life insurance policy. It is also so ordered that the last name of the minor child be changed from Brooks to Smith within ninety days at the cost of Ms. Brooks, since it is without question that the fees are solely her responsibility. I am ordering visitation for Mr. Smith every third weekend of the month. Major holidays will be split between the parents. Mr. Smith, I am granting you Thanksgiving and New Year's Day, and Ms. Brooks, I am granting you Christmas and New Year's Eve. Summer vacation will be split, with the second half of summer custody being awarded to Mr. Smith. Are there any other issues that I am not aware of?"

Both attorneys shook their heads and simultaneously answered, "No, Your Honor."

"So be it. It is so ordered. Paternity results will be given to your attorneys before the end of the business day. Court is adjourned." Judge Chambers banged his gavel.

After we left the courtroom, I caught up with Jennifer in the parking lot. "Hey," I called out to her as Lucinda and I approached.

She put on her shades. "Well, hello to the Smith family. I see you got your day in court today. I'm sure you're happy," she sneered.

"Jennifer, do we have to act this way? I just found out that I have a beautiful little daughter, and all I want to do is try to figure out a way for us to be involved with her."

"News flash, Aldris, I am already involved. You're the one who has to get with the program," she said harshly.

Lucinda sidestepped me with anger in her eyes. "Look, *chica*, this is new to the both of us. You just ran to Georgia and slapped a paternity suit on my fiancé without so much as a word, and then tell him he's playing catch up. *You've* disrupted our lives, when you could've told him this news six years ago. I think you owe us a lot more respect than what you're giving us."

Jennifer cocked her head to the side and removed her shades. "Look-a-here, little *mamacita*. First of all, you need to chill because I wasn't talking to you. Secondly, you have absolutely nothing to do with this. This is between Aldris, me, and Jessica."

"Let's get one thing straight right now, *chick*. *Your* business is officially *my* business because he is my fiancé. Hate it or love it, you have to deal with me." Lucinda popped off with a finger point and a neck roll, steadily decreasing the space between them.

"Ladies! Ladies!" I stepped between them to deescalate the situation. "Calm down. Jennifer, you have to accept the fact that I have a fiancée, and that makes her every bit as involved as me. Lucinda is going to be Jessica's stepmother."

"*Stepmother*? Hell, she barely has a damn father! And up until the paternity test, I didn't know a thing about no damn Lucinda, so both of you can jump on whatever banana boat it was that you rode over here on," Jennifer shouted angrily.

"Oh, bitch, no you didn't," Lucinda spat back, throwing her hands on her hips.

I knew it was on and popping at this point, so I pulled Lucinda to the side, with her cursing in Spanish the whole way.

"Why the fuck are you grabbing on me, Aldris? You need to get that bitch straight!"

"Lucinda, for one, this is a courthouse, remember? For two, I want you to get in the car. It's enough already, and I don't need any more drama," I tried to explain to her.

Lucinda put her hands up. "Wait a minute, Aldris. So, *I'm* the one bringing the drama?"

"No, no. I didn't say that. I know you've got my back, and I have yours too, but at the end of the day, we all have to deal with each other. I'm asking you not to get on her level, and I'm begging you to get in the car," I pleaded. "Please."

She threw her hands up and groaned in frustration. "Fine. I'll get in the car." Obviously unpleased, she snatched the keys from my hand and stalked to my BMW.

I took a deep breath and walked back to Jennifer. "You know, it's one thing to hate me, but it's a completely different thing to disrespect my woman. Now, because we have a child together, I'm going to be calm about this, but I'm only going to say this once. Do not disrespect my fiancée again."

She scoffed. "Wow. Look who grew some balls."

"No, I just grew up, Jennifer. Try it," I spewed at her.

"Go straight to hell, Aldris!" she yelled as she turned to leave.

"Please. Stop," I asked, realizing someone had to be the peacemaker. "Look, I just want to see my daughter. Isn't this all for Jessica anyway? I've missed out on six years already. Please."

After a brief pause, she slowly turned around. "You're right. I was out of line, and I apologize. It is all about her, and since it was my decision to tell you about Jessica, I shouldn't be upset about it. When would you like to see her?"

"I'd love to see her today. She could meet Lucinda's daughter, Nadia—well, our daughter. Not mine biologically, but she's like mine biologically—"

She laughed and put her hand up to stop my stammering. "I understand."

I pulled a business card out of my wallet and wrote my address. "Here," I said, handing her the card. "My address is on the back, and my cell phone number is on the front."

She reached in her purse, pulled out a business card, and did the same. "Address is on the back and cell on the front. I will bring her by at say six o'clock?"

I put her card in my wallet. "Yes, that will be fine. Please show up."

"I give you my word that I will be there with Jessica," she told me. "Can you please tell Lucinda that I apologize?"

"Sure," I said to her. "So, I will see you and Jessica at six."

"Yes."

"See you then."

When I got in the car, Lucinda gawked at me, attitude on go. "So, I guess you two are kosher now."

"I told her about disrespecting you, and she apologized because she agreed this should be about Jessica. In fact, she specifically asked me to tell you that she was sorry."

Lucinda rolled her eyes. "She had no problem disrespecting me to my face, but she wants to send an apology via courier. How genuine."

"Baby, please. This day has been trying enough. I understand that it doesn't seem genuine, but I can assure you that it was. She's even going to bring Jessica over to the house tonight at six." I looked at her with pleading eyes.

Massaging her forehead, she looked at me and relented. "For you, I'm going to be the bigger person in this situation."

I leaned over and kissed her, happy to dodge one more bullet. I cradled her face in the palm of my hand. "Thank you, baby. Thank you."

There was a hint of a smile on her face. "I guess you're welcome. You better call your mother and tell her the news."

"I was going to make that call as soon as we pulled off."

Giving her a reassuring smile, I started the car and silently thanked God for the reprieve. This was why I loved her so much. Lucinda always put bullshit aside for the bigger picture. She was mature beyond her years, far more than I was at her age. I wasn't naïve enough not to know that the biggest reason she didn't mind was simply because she loved me. She wasn't stupid in love with me—you know, that kind of love where a person will do anything to keep another at all cost—but simply truly in love. The kind of love that is selfless and honest. She was truly amazing, and I couldn't wait to make her my wife.

Chapter Ten

Aldris

"Come with me," I told Lucinda once we returned home.

"Aldris, I'm going to change clothes—"

Ignoring her comment, I grabbed her hand and led her to the bathroom with me. "I need you right now, Lu," I said huskily in her ear as I began undressing her.

After removing her suit jacket and blouse, Lucinda leaned against the vanity with her head down. My concern for her immediately set in, and I pulled her into my embrace.

"What's on your mind, mami?"

"Everything."

"What is everything?" I kissed her forehead.

She gazed into my eyes and bit her lip. "You have a child, Aldris. That is a lot to swallow for one day. I keep saying to myself nothing will change, but I can't lie to myself because I know it will."

"I have two daughters instead of one. That's the only change. I'm going to take care of all three of my ladies. I understand that Jennifer, you, and me will definitely have to come to a place where we are respectful of each other, and that will come. Everything is just so fresh right now. I'm not trying to discount what you're saying, though. I'm simply reassuring you. In fact, I am worried, too, because I have a child who I don't have a bond with nor know anything about. Trying to build a relationship with her after all these years scares the hell out of me."

When Lucinda didn't respond, I continued undressing myself and preparing the shower, allowing her a few moments of peace as her private thoughts roamed through her mind. Without a word, I held out my hand for her to join me in the shower, and she did. We held each other for a moment and let the hot water cascade down our entwined bodies.

"Aldris, you will be a good father to Jessica. That will come just as natural to you as it does with Nadia."

"I hope you're right. It just feels surreal, you know? I have a daughter."

She picked up the shampoo. "Well, let's do something to take our minds off of it for a little while."

I took the shampoo from her hands. "Turn around and lean back." At my request, she did, and I began lathering her silky hair. As I massaged her scalp, I stroked my Mandingo gently across her luscious backside. My baby may have been Latina, but she had a donk like she was a sista. As a matter of fact, her donk rivaled many sistas'. Now, that was a blessing for me because I loved a fat ass, and I never grew tired of spreading those butterfly wings.

Soon, our breathing grew ragged as I began rinsing the shampoo out of her hair. Sensing my need, Lucinda reached behind her and made long strokes up and down my shaft. I was so hard I could split bricks. I was ready to devour her. I turned her around and saw that her creamy nipples were as hard as gumdrops, just the way I liked them. I bent down and captured one in my mouth, stimulating it with my rolling tongue. She gripped the back of my head as pleasure took over her, and her sexy moans sent my need into overdrive. I couldn't stand it any longer. Picking her up, I met her lustful gaze as I leaned her against the wall, entering her painfully slowly. I reveled in the feeling as I pushed inch by inch inside of her.

She wrapped her arms around me. "Oh dios, Aldris," she moaned.

Bracing my palm against the wall, I pulled out just as slowly and then, not able to contain my desire any longer, began to pump faster. Our eyes locked on each other as I made love to her mind, body, and soul.

"Lucinda," I moaned, struggling not to succumb to the impending climax.

"Ay, papi. No one can do me like you do. I love you so much," she wailed, slamming her pussy against Mandingo.

At that point, I knew I was gonna fucking blow. The mixture of her juicy womanhood and her beautiful fat ass taking all ten inches of this thick Mandingo curve was enough to draw all my soldiers together to blast off.

"Baby, please come with me," I groaned.

I pushed to the cushioned center and tapped her G-spot, making her ejaculate instantly. Even in the shower, I could feel the spray of her essence running down my shaft like rain. She held me tight as I brought my middle finger to the front and stroked her engorged clit to take her over the edge again.

"Aldrisss!" she screamed as her body convulsed, and that did it.

I held her against the shower wall as my throbbing Mandingo exploded like a volcano. "Fuck, Lucinda! I love you, damn it. Oh, shit!" I released, placing her down.

Lucinda dropped to her knees and licked Mandingo like an ice cream cone, and I knew I was about to release another load. She held the base of my shaft in her hand, squeezing every few seconds, and continued to suck and lick the sensitive area around the tip. I was losing my mind, and my legs began to tremble.

"Mami! Oh God, what are you doing to me?"

Suddenly, she released me. I shot off hard and fierce like a geyser all over her chest. Then I collapsed to my knees in front of Lucinda, unable to stand up any longer.

"I love you, Aldris."

Once I found my voice, I replied, "Baby, I will always love you. You are certified hell."

She giggled. "I like to please my man as much as he pleases me." She kissed my lips.

"That you do, baby. That you do."

After we actually showered, I cleaned up the house with the little energy I had left, while Lucinda cooked dinner. Once it was time, I picked Nadia up from school, since I wanted some time to explain as best I could who Jessica was and to reassure Nadia of my love for her as my daughter as well. I felt it was my responsibility and my place to do that.

The moment Nadia and I got home, she ran to Lucinda with sheer excitement about the news that Jessica was her sister. She asked if they could do about a million things all in that one night. Lucinda was amused by it, and it warmed my heart. It reminded me just how resilient kids were, seeing how accepting Nadia was.

By the time we finished eating and helping Nadia complete her homework, our doorbell rang. It was time.

All of us walked to the family room together, and I proceeded toward the foyer. Just before I crossed the threshold, I looked back at Lucinda, and she nodded with encouragement. It gave me the strength I needed, and I opened the door for Jennifer and Jessica, who stood outside looking just as nervous as we were.

"Hello, Jennifer and Jessica," I greeted them nervously.

Each of them offered an equally nervous, "Hi."

"Come inside. Welcome to our home." I ushered them inside and took them through the foyer into the family room.

"Hello." Lucinda waved. "It's good to see you again, Jessica."

Jessica waved back. "Hi, Ms. Lucinda."

"Jennifer, Jessica, this is my daughter, Nadia," Lucinda introduced. "She's six, too."

Jessica smiled at Nadia. "Hi, Nadia!"

"Hi, Jessica! Do you want to see my room?" Nadia asked, barely able to contain her excitement.

Jessica turned to her mother. "Mom, can I? Can I, please?"

Jennifer smiled. "Yes, Jessica. It's okay."

Nadia grabbed Jessica by the hand. "Come on! We're going to have sooo much fun. I have a sister!"

"Who?" Jessica asked as they walked to the back.

"Well, you! Duh, silly!" Nadia shrieked, both of them erupting into laughter.

Jennifer, Lucinda, and I all looked at each other after the girls disappeared to the back. There was an uneasy tension in the room amongst us. The more I looked at Jennifer, the angrier I became. I had missed out on so much with Jessica—the joy of seeing her being born, her first words, her first steps. Hell, her first day of school. I tried to calm myself long enough to enjoy this visit, but I wouldn't make it through the evening without making her give me the answers I so deserved.

"Umm, we can all sit down, I guess," Lucinda said, cutting the silence.

"Oh, thank you," Jennifer said and sat on the loveseat. Lucinda and I sat on the sofa. "You all really do have a beautiful home."

"Thank you," Lucinda said. I just sat there with my hand propped against my face, deep in contemplation.

"Oh, and Lucinda, I'm sorry about earlier. I was way out of line, and it was completely uncalled for," Jennifer apologized.

Lucinda shrugged. “It’s okay. It was a stressful time.”

They got quiet again, not really knowing what to say or how to address the elephant in the room.

“Would you like anything to drink or eat?” Lucinda offered.

Jennifer shook her head. “No, thanks. We ate already.”

At this point, I couldn’t take it anymore. I was trying to avoid drama, but the more I listened to Nadia play with Jessica, the more it reminded me that I suddenly had a daughter—a *six*-year-old daughter—that I knew absolutely *nothing* about.

“So, why the hell did you keep your pregnancy from me?” I blurted.

“Excuse me?” Jennifer asked, clearly taken aback.

“You heard me,” I seethed. “You made me miss out on some of the best moments of her life, and you sat in court like we did something to you. You had the audacity to give my child another man’s last name and then treat me like I was the deadbeat father. I want my answers, Jennifer, and I want them . . . *right now*,” I said angrily as I hopped up, pacing the floor.

“Oh, please. I didn’t come here to be harassed. You claimed you wanted to get to know your daughter, but if this is an attempt to get me on home turf so you can go off on me, we will leave right now.”

“*Go off on you?* Go off is the easiest thing for me to do to you at this moment. I’m mad as hell, and I have a right to know!”

Lucinda jumped up to calm me. “Baby, the girls are in the back. Please.”

“Oh, you don’t have to ask him to calm down. We can leave,” Jennifer stood up and said with a hellacious attitude.

“Over my dead body,” I spewed.

"Whoa!" Lucinda stood between us. "Listen. Aldris, calm down. Jessica doesn't need to see you attacking her mother like this. I know that you're upset, and you have every reason to be, but we have to show the girls that we can act like adults regardless of the situation," she preached, then turned to Jennifer. "And *you*, be fair. You do owe him an explanation. It's been six years, and you've not mentioned anything to him about his daughter. Regardless of whatever was going on in your life, he deserved to be given the opportunity to be a dad to Jessica. Imagine if you had not known about her. For that reason alone, you should talk to him," Lucinda bravely spoke up.

Jennifer and I looked at each other and both relented. Lucinda was right on both points. I didn't need to disrespect Jennifer, and she did owe me an explanation.

"Fine. I will tell you anything you want to know," Jennifer said before sitting back down.

"And I am sorry for attacking you. I'm frustrated, and I was wrong," I said, sitting down also.

"How about I take the girls out for ice cream? Dairy Queen is not too far away, and it will give you two time and space to talk as adults," Lucinda volunteered.

"That's fine by me," Jennifer answered.

"Baby, I think that's a great idea. Thank you."

Lucinda give me a soft peck on the lips, then went to Nadia's bedroom and gathered the girls. Once they were out the door, I looked at Jennifer to begin.

"So, I guess you're wondering why I did it," Jennifer said when they left.

"Yes. I think I deserve that much."

She leaned back, pointing her finger at me. "Aldris, you act as if I deserved what you did to me. We were engaged and you slept around on me, God only knows how many times, but at least twice with the same bitch!

You disrespected me, our love, and our home! Now you have the nerve—the fucking nerve—to talk about what you deserve," she shouted.

"And I apologize for what I did to you. I'm sorry about that, and had you even allowed me talk to you, I would've told you so a long time ago. But that still gave you no right to keep Jessica away from me. She's my blood!"

"It gave me no right? You treat me like shit, the scum of the Earth, and you have the audacity to talk about rights. You are the most self-centered, self-serving son of a bitch I know."

As if she could talk. "And you're not? What kind of woman are you to keep a child away from her father? How can you even look at yourself and call yourself a woman?"

"I can call myself a woman the same way you could have called yourself a man even though you were screwing me over!"

"So, we're back to this again," I quipped, sighing in disgust.

"Why not this again? I put all that I was into our relationship, Aldris, and you took my heart, ripped it in half, and stomped on it!"

"So that gave you the right to determine whether or not I had a relationship with our daughter? Is that really what you're saying to me?"

She was trembling when she finally stopped ranting and looked up at me. "No, it didn't. That's not why I did it." She struggled through a teary voice.

"Then why the fuck did you do it?"

"I thought you wouldn't care. You didn't even realize that I was four weeks pregnant the day I caught you in our bed with that nasty heifer. How could I tell you about our child and think you'd be a good father when you didn't even care about me as a future wife?" Tears streamed down her face. "I never wanted to keep her away from you. I just didn't think I mattered enough to you for you to care."

Instantly, I felt horrible. I could see how she would think that. Here I was hoeing around when she was at the house, pregnant with my seed, and I was too busy chasing ass to notice. I guess I wouldn't have trusted me either. Standing, I went to her. The way she broke down shredded me, and I could think of nothing else to do but hug her. I just wanted to hug our sordid past away and do it over, back to a time when she respected me and I would've been in my daughter's life. A time when she wouldn't have felt she had to protect my child from me because of my misdeeds against her.

"Don't cry. Please don't. I'm so sorry, Jennifer. So sorry," I apologized as she held me and cried in my chest.

"Why couldn't I be enough for you, Aldris? Why?"

Her pained declaration shot through me, and I held her tighter. "You were enough. I was just young and dumb."

Realizing her words, she pulled back and tried to wipe the endless tears. "I'm sorry. I see you with Lucinda and Nadia, and even though we've both moved on, I still feel like it's a slap in the face. All the things I wanted and needed from you, you are giving to someone else," she admitted, continuing to cry.

That was a gut punch. As much as I hated to admit it, she was right. I knew in that moment that my irresponsible actions had set off a chain of events that weren't easily fixed with "I'm sorry."

I tipped her face up with my fingers to look at me. "Jennifer, I can't apologize enough. I realize seeing the man that I've become now is hard because I couldn't appreciate the woman you were back then, and it's compounded because we have a child together. I wish I could change things, but I can't. The only thing we can do is move forward. I hope that you can and will forgive me so that we can do that."

Her eyes held my gaze for a beat before she looked away. Her shoulders relaxed as she whispered, "For so long I've wanted to hear that." Her eyes found mine again before she continued, "It really means a lot to me, Aldris. It really, truly does."

Reaching on the nearby table, I pulled a Kleenex and handed it to her to dry her eyes. "So, do you forgive me?"

She smiled warily. "Yes, I do. I have to apologize as well. Initially, I felt justified in keeping the news of my pregnancy away from you, but I never should have kept it from you for six years. For that, I will always be sorry."

Motioning to the sofa, I said, "Sit down with me and let's talk for real." She nodded in agreement and we sat side-by-side on the sofa. "So, why did you keep it from me for so long, and what happened to your husband?"

With a deep breath, she exhaled and explained, "After I graduated, I got a marketing job with an ice cream company, which is where I met Donnie. He worked in public relations. Jessica was six months old at the time, and we fell in love fast and hard. I told him all about what happened, and he told me not to worry, that he would do the best he could by us. He had a son from a previous relationship, and we became an instant family. Six months later, we were married, and I was the proud mother of Jessica and my three-year-old stepson, Brendon." She wiped tears from her eyes. I patted her on the leg for support, and she continued.

"After a couple of months in our marriage, I expressed to Donnie that I felt I should tell you about Jessica. He was livid. He said that he was Jessica's father, and that he wouldn't have another man coming into his house or his marriage trying to run things. Even though I knew it was wrong, I was trying to be the good wife and did as my husband said. We were all good, I thought, but last year, he started doing some really shady shit. I won't go into details, but long story short, he was messing around with Brendon's mother again. I tried to make it work, but he asked me for a divorce, so I gave it to him. Why stick around for a man who doesn't want you?

"A month later, our divorce was final, and the next week, he was married to Brendon's mom. I didn't think he'd just abandon Jessica. She loved him—I mean *absolutely* loved him. After a month of him not coming to visit Jessica, I drove to his home to confront him about it, and do you know what that heartless bastard told me? He said that *now* I could find you to be a father to Jessica because his wife wasn't going to allow him to take care of a child that wasn't his. With me standing there still in shock, he shut the door in my face, as if the last five years of our marriage had been nonexistent and that he wasn't the only father Jessica knew." She broke down again, as if it had just happened.

"So, I did what I should've done from the beginning, I told Jessica about you. Ever since then, she's wanted to meet you and be around you, but I was so bitter after you and Donnie that I refused. Once I got the job offer to move back to Atlanta, I did what I thought was best and located an attorney about paternity. I know I should've just talked to you, but my anger overshadowed my rationality. I was wrong for what I did, Aldris, and I can't apologize enough for it," she said as tears began to fall again.

Part of me wanted to be upset that she'd let another man dictate her life and keep her from doing what was right. However, I vowed to move forward, so I swallowed that pill and did just that. I reached for her and hugged her again.

"I'm sorry you went through so much with your ex. He is a damn fool, and neither Jessica nor you needed a coward like him in your lives. As for me, don't get me wrong, it hurts because I missed so much. But I know now, and I can make the best of the time I have now. I'm not going to hold that against you. Jessica needs both of her parents, and she doesn't need us constantly bickering, so all is forgiven. We just need to be about the business of raising our little girl."

She smiled, still enfolded in my arms. "Feels strange, doesn't it? Saying your little girl."

I chuckled. "Yeah, it really does."

"Thank you for making this process easy for us."

"Thank you for giving me the opportunity."

"I never should have taken it away."

"But you gave it back, and that's all that matters," I said as we stood up. "I guess I should call Lucinda and tell her to come back."

"Yeah, and Aldris, I really thank you again. Friends?"

"Of course," I said as we embraced each other in agreement.

Just as we embraced, Lucinda and the girls walked in the family room. Lucinda's mouth dropped as I hopped backward away from Jennifer, who just stared back and forth between Lucinda and me.

"Okay. Awkward," Jennifer said.

"So, I see that you two have certainly settled your differences." Lucinda's tone was even, but the look on her face could've burned a hole straight through my heart. I rubbed my forehead because I already knew it was going to be a battle in the Smith residence that night.

Chapter Eleven

Terrence

Victory never felt so good, I thought and smiled to myself as I watched my wife and our kids play in our indoor pool. I finally had the woman of my dreams back, and I prayed that fuck-ass nigga Pooch rotted in that fucking hellhole. I'd never been happier in my life than sitting there holding my baby son while watching my family having fun. This was the shit I'd dreamed of all my life. My chest swelled with pride that I could finally provide the life that Trinity deserved. When she looked over at me and smiled, my heart melted. I lived to see that smile, and now that she was back where she belonged, I'd make sure we always remained a family, or I'd die trying.

Part of making sure we remained a family was making sure I would never be taken away from them again. I'd wised up and gotten out of the dope game. What niggas didn't realize was that the real money was in corporate America, and if you could get a slice of that pie, you were in. Investments, real estate, stocks, and bonds—that was the shit that made real dough; the shit that had real power. I wanted to be legit because I didn't need any more fuck niggas trying to set me up for some real prison time, nor did I need to worry about thug niggas chasing my lady. I didn't want to be worried about losing my family ever again.

That was the thing that pissed me off about Pooch. That nigga was mad as if Trinity had been his woman first. That bitch-ass nigga set me up because that was the only way he could get next to Trinity, and he had the nerve to want to get at me? Turnabout is fair play, and that grimy muthafucka got exactly what he deserved courtesy of me. In fact, he was lucky he was even still breathing to be able to go to prison. Niggas had been killed for lesser offenses. What really put a smile on my face, though, was knowing that that nigga was scratching his head, wondering what the fuck happened to his family. He was a smart cat, so I knew he probably already assumed that Trinity and I ran off together, but I also knew that if he found out how abruptly Trinity and her moms had left, he would doubt that theory, too. Right about now, he was probably stuck between wondering if she ran off with me or if some dope boys got next to Princess and her. I wished him luck figuring that one out, and if he did figure it out, I didn't give a fuck. He could choke off the same cup of karma he brewed for me, muthafucka.

"What are you smiling about?" Trinity asked as she changed Princess out of her wet clothes and sat her in the gated play area. She wrapped a towel around her waist and sat on the lounge chair beside me, smiling all the while.

I locked Tyson in the bouncer. "Nothing. Just admiring my family."

She leaned over and kissed me. "I love you."

I cupped her face and stroked her hair. "I love you too, li'l mama."

I heard a simultaneous, "Ooohh," followed by a fit of giggles from Brittany and Terry.

I looked over and laughed at them. "Oh, I got y'all's *ooohh*!" I sprang from my chair and ran to the deep end of the pool. “Cannonball!” I yelled and jumped in to splash them.

I sprayed them with water as they laughed and tried to splash me back. Trinity cracked up as they took their water guns and forced me to retreat back to the deep end.

Trinity walked over and sat on the edge of the pool beside me. “Looks like you lost, soldier.”

“You gonna lick my war wounds later?” I asked seductively.

Her gaze was intense. “Absolutely.”

I was just about to kiss her when Consuela interrupted us. “Mr. Kincaid, you have some visitors,” she called out as she walked out poolside.

“Visitors?” Trinity asked, looking at me.

“I had a realtor stopping by about some property, but he wasn’t due until later,” I explained to her. “Let me go check it out.” I climbed out of the pool.

“Terry, work on that backstroke. If you want to join the swim team, you have to practice,” I told my son. He could swim like a fish and desperately wanted to compete on a championship level.

I dried off and threw on some shorts and a tank top before following Consuela inside. “They are in your office,” Consuela said as I walked into the main part of the house.

“They? You mean there really is more than one?”

“Yes. They said they were members of the Kincaid family.”

I furrowed my brow. “I’ll check it out. Thanks, Consuela.”

I headed to my office and grabbed my gun from the secret compartment beside my office door. I didn’t know who the fuck was showing up unannounced, but if they came for trouble, they’d just found it. Nobody was breaking up this family again, and I meant that. Fully loaded with one in the chamber, I opened my office door with the safety off and trigger ready.

"Nigga, put that gun down!" Tot yelled as he and Big Cal hit the floor.

"Thomas? Aaron? Y'all muthafuckas better call next time. I was 'bout to put y'all niggas to sleep." I put the safety back on and placed the gun on my desk.

"Shit, man. What the fuck you so antsy about?" Big Cal asked.

"Two unknown muthafuckas roll up to your house unannounced and you ain't asking no questions first either, nigga. I may not live in the hood no more, but you can't take the hood outta me," I said, giving each of my cousins a one-armed hug.

"Shit, we see." Tot laughed. "We just came by 'cause we need to talk to you."

"Man, I ain't getting back in the game, Thomas—"

Tot cut me off. "Naw, man, it ain't that. Pipe down."

We all sat down.

"So, what's up, fam?"

Big Cal shook his head. "Word on the street is that Pooch trying to get his lawyer to strike a deal. He wants to rat out Thomas and the Crown brothers for a lesser sentence or even parole."

Sounded about like that bitch-made nigga. "Who is his lawyer again?"

"Jacob Stein," Big Cal said.

"Stein *is* good." I contemplated.

"No, Stein is great," Big Cal corrected. "A judge would gladly look into Pooch's deal if it meant bringing down more hustlas."

"So, Aaron, why he ain't after you?" I asked Big Cal.

"He thinks I'm locked up upstate," he answered.

"And he believes I went into hiding because of his arrest," Tot added.

I rubbed my forehead. "So, what else is going on?"

"Some of my detective friends are telling me that stripper, Chocolate Flava, has been asking a lot of questions about your whereabouts and Trinity's. So far, you know she's been coming up short," Big Cal informed me.

"Good."

"So, what we gon' do about this whole deal Pooch tryna make?" Tot asked.

I leaned back in my chair. "Thomas, you shoulda got yo' ass up outta da business like I told you," I fussed.

He frowned. "So what? You just gon' let my ass hang out to dry? After all the shit I did for you? I told you to do that fuck nigga in from the start. That nigga ain't gon' sit idly by and ride out until death behind bars."

"Do you know what kinda fucking heat woulda immediately come down on me for some shit like that? I got a family to protect!" I yelled.

"Nigga, we family, too!" Tot yelled.

Big Cal stood up. "Y'all niggas pipe down. Damn!"

"Yo, you a pig. What the fuck can the old black and blue do to help out your brother?" I asked Big Cal.

He rubbed the back of his neck. "Nigga, if I knew that, we wouldn't be sitting here. Unfortunately, if I step in, I run the risk of blowing my cover, and Thomas gon' get an informant tag on his ass. If that happens, fuck going to prison. He gon' get got in the streets before his docket ever hits trial. And shit, me too. You forget that Pooch ain't the only drug lord I've brought down."

"So, what the fuck you gon' do, T? 'Cause me and my brother done had your back for a long time because we family. You don't turn your back on family," Tot said sternly.

I hated this shit. As much as I wanted to do Pooch in, the mere fact that my arresting officer, trial judge, and Pooch were closely related to me was enough for anybody to know I had something to do with anything that happened to him. I wanted to help my cousins because they rode hard for me and Trinity through all this, but I just wanted to get to a place in my life where I didn't have to worry about this shit; a place where all my family was good.

"Let me sleep on this shit. How long you in town, Thomas?"

"Just tomorrow," Tot answered. "I'm staying at Aaron's house."

Suddenly, Trinity opened the door to my office. "I'm sorry, baby, but—" She stopped in mid-sentence when she saw Big Cal and Tot. "Aaron? Thomas?" she asked in confusion as she walked in and hugged each of them. "What's up, family? What brings y'all by?"

"Oh, ain't nothing, cuz-in-law. Just checking in on my big cousin," Tot responded.

Big Cal smiled at Trinity. He rubbed his hands together and licked his lips. "It sure is a shame you ain't got no sisters your age." He shook his head and looked her up and down, taking in her extremely short shorts and bikini top. "T, you got one fine-ass woman."

She blushed. "Aaron, you're a mess." She playfully nudged him as he chuckled.

"Yeah, well, stop looking," I demanded with a warning look. "What's up, baby?" I directed my attention back to my wife.

"Princess and Tyson are asleep, so I was about to go fire up the grill. I'm seasoning the hamburgers now, and Consuela put on the potatoes and made the salad. I just wanted to know if you wanted to throw some steaks on."

"Yeah, you got the Omahas, right?"

She nodded. "Yeah, baby, just what you asked for."

Big Cal and Tot looked at each other and smiled.

"A'ight. Bet that. Go ahead and season 'em up for me then. I'll be down in a minute to throw 'em on the grill."

"A'ight. It was good to see you two again." She hugged Big Cal and Tot before turning to leave. "Y'all staying for dinner? We've got plenty."

"She is so hospitable," Tot turned to me and said sarcastically. "You're a real member of the family."

I rolled my eyes at his slick comment. "So, y'all staying or what?"

"Naw. We gon' roll and let y'all do your family thang. We'll be back tomorrow," Big Cal said.

"How long you in town for?" Trinity asked Tot.

"Just until tomorrow," he replied.

She nodded. "A'ight. Well, you at least have to let us treat you to lunch or something tomorrow. I was gonna do some barbeque chicken and dirty rice."

"I'm down with that," Big Cal said happily, and Tot agreed.

"Yeah, and you a Georgia girl, so I know you can burn." Tot laughed.

"I do a little somethin' somethin'," she said with a slight chuckle. "Well, look, you guys, I have to get back downstairs, but I'm so glad you stopped by, and I'm serious about tomorrow."

"We wouldn't miss it for the world." Big Cal winked at her.

"And ain't no bullshit with Pooch, is it?" she threw over her shoulder at Big Cal.

He shook his head. "Naw, Trin, ain't nothin'. You know we always got you covered, though. You ain't got to never worry about Pooch getting next to you."

She let out a sigh of relief. "All right then. See you cats tomorrow," she said and walked out.

As she glided out the door, I couldn't help but notice her long, silky hair and phat ass. Her Coke-bottle figure and luscious melon-sized breasts were enough to drive any man crazy. Her almond-shaped brown eyes, naturally long lashes, and pretty white teeth were just as infectious, and she had the cutest little feet I'd ever laid eyes on. Her smooth milk chocolate skin wrapped around all those features showed why black and white men alike always wanted a sista. Yeah, one thing was for certain. I had one fine-ass woman.

I shook myself out of my trance so that I could bid my cousins goodbye and walk them to the front door. "See y'all tomorrow. I'ma think of something." I hugged each of them with one arm.

"I need you, man. Real talk," Tot said as he walked out the front door and headed for the truck.

Big Cal turned to look at me. "Thomas is worried."

"We gon' think of something. Tell him not to worry, and you don't either," I reassured him.

He nodded. "A'ight. Bet that." We touched knuckles.

"Blood before bitches and bands," I said with a head nod.

"Always." With that, he and Tot got in his truck.

Now I have to deal with this shit, I thought, as I locked away my gun and headed toward the barbeque pit. Trinity stood there drinking a beer and watching Terry and Brittany play on the playground equipment. I walked past her to the grill.

"What's on your mind?" she asked, walking up beside me.

"Nothing," I said plainly.

"I know you."

"Give me a sip."

She turned the bottle up to my lips.

"Thanks," I said after I swallowed the beer. "But it's nothing."

She shrugged. "Suit yourself. I'm going to go play volleyball with the kids."

"A'ight. Dinner will be ready in a minute. Hey, Trin!" I called out before she walked off.

"Yeah, babe."

"Tomorrow, cover yourself. Ya know, with clothes."

"Huh?"

"Don't be out like that around my cousins is all I'm saying."

"It's just Thomas and Aaron—"

I raised my voice and cut her off. "And I'm just saying. Just . . . wear some clothes."

She shook her head in disbelief. "A'ight," she conceded and walked off to play with the kids.

I would kill *any* muthafucka for Trinity—*any muthafucka.*

Chapter Twelve

Ryan

I never confronted Charice about Lincoln's accusation. See, I was a better man than that. I knew Lincoln had only said that to get a rise out of me. He wanted me to go insane with jealousy so that it would cause a rift between Charice and me. I wasn't stupid. He wasn't about to use me so that I would leave my wife and he could slip his trifling ass back in to help mend her broken heart. Not me, and not on my watch.

Likewise, I knew Charice would never betray me by hanging around Lincoln. She was extremely loyal, and besides that, Lincoln had broken her heart, so he could miss me with that bullshit lie. I had home field advantage. I hadn't been with Charice since I was sixteen and not learned something. I knew Charice had a big heart, but once she gave it away, she wouldn't easily be swayed away, even if that person happened to be her ex-fiancé.

I did, however, express several times that I wanted her to stay as far away from Lincoln as possible. That nigga wasn't doing shit but lurking, and I wanted Charice to be on her p's and q's at all times. It wasn't that I was afraid to lose her, but I knew that grimy-ass nigga wasn't going to leave well enough alone. I got my wife back fair and square, simple as that. So far, all things had been kosher, and I intended to make sure it stayed just that way.

Charice had finally begun feeling at ease with our life in New York, especially since she felt comfortable leaving Lexi at home with our nanny, Johanna. Her extensive background check had come up as straight as an arrow, and we even met her seven-year-old son, who became easy friends with our boys. We also had our maid there during the day for extra precaution. You could never be too safe. After the death of our daughter, she barely wanted to let the boys out of her sight, let alone Lexi. Moving to a different state with people she didn't know only heightened her discomfort level for a while. So, I was happy when she began to settle into our new normal.

Together, we were making major moves, both personally and professionally. Prior to moving to New York, I joined efforts with three of my teammates to open an afterschool center for inner city kids. They could do their homework with the help of tutors, read, play basketball, or take recreational hip-hop dance. Once Charice and I married and moved, she jumped immediately at the chance to volunteer as a dance instructor at the center, being that dance is another true love of hers. I was against it at first because of the loss of Charity and because she was pregnant, but Charice wouldn't hear of it. She loved both the kids and dancing, and I could tell that being involved at the center helped heal her pain.

At the center, we converted one of the larger rooms into a dance studio, complete with a mirrored wall and large picture window for our viewing pleasure. Charice taught the kids until she was six months pregnant, but after that, I demanded she bring in help to actually do the dance moves. She oversaw everything, but it made me more comfortable to know my pregnant wife wasn't out there putting her and our unborn child at risk. Nearly all the girls and a lot of boys loved her class, and she'd even managed to put on an exhibition and arrange a competition with other local dance teams. Her devotion to the kids and the program just made my heart swell even more with love for her. When she wasn't teaching dance, she was providing financial advice as an online consultant at home. I was extremely proud of her for stepping up and following all her ambitions.

What she didn't know was that I was engaged in talks to try to get her her own dance studio and was close to finalizing those plans. She'd have a full staff, could set up her age limits and requirements, and offer dance lessons how she saw fit. I loved Charice, and I'd spend every day of the rest of my life proving that to her.

Today was one of the rare occasions that I was at home because I didn't have to make an appearance, be a part of some charity event or awards presentation, shoot commercials for any of my endorsement deals, or be a model in some designer's show. My off season was just as busy as being in season at times, so I enjoyed sitting back and shooting the breeze. Johanna was there with her son, and so was our maid, Ms. Pauline, so I decided to take my boys along with Johanna's son, Clarke, to the center to shoot some hoops. Not to mention, I never got tired of watching my wifey shake her ass on the dance floor. Oh, the memories I have of that both in the center and after hours in the bedroom!

As we walked in, her class was in full swing. She had about fifteen kids rehearsing a new routine that was hot to death. She glanced out the window and winked at me, and I blew a kiss back at her. She was so sexy in her workout pants, fitted tank top, and tennis shoes. Yes, that was my baby and my heart; one out of only four reasons I had to live. Yes, that included Lexi. I loved Charice so much that it made me love Lexi despite who her biological father was. To me, she was *my* daughter and I was her father, and that's how I vowed to keep it.

The boys and I admired the dancing for a few minutes before we went to see if we could join in with the game that was already going on one of the courts with a few of the regular members and one of my teammates.

"'Sup fellas!"

"What's up, Ryan?"

"Your wife got it on fire today, boy," my teammate, Rico, said.

"Yeah, well, stomp your fire out." We both laughed at my comment. "This is my nanny's son, Clarke."

"Hey, my man," Rico said, giving him and my boys a pound. "How are you enjoying yourself with the Westmore clique?"

"It's so awesome! I can't believe I get to meet you and Mr. Westmore! I love my mom's job!" Clarke exclaimed.

Ryan Jr. laughed. "Our dad is super cool and down to Earth."

"How can you all live in the house knowing your dad is Ryan Westmore?" Clarke asked, clearly starstruck.

The boys laughed. "To us, he's just dad," Ray answered.

"That's right. I'm always going to be dad first," I confirmed.

"I'll tell you what, though. I'm sure Ryan and I can get you some autographs and pictures so that your friends will know you have pro ball players for friends," Rico offered.

"Cool! So totally cool," Clarke exclaimed excitedly. "Oh my God, and there's Lincoln Harper. Three in one day," he yelled, looking toward the door.

"What the hell is he doing here?" I abruptly turned around to see Lincoln walking in the door. Wasn't this fantastic? And where did this Casanova-acting nigga think he was going? Gliding in the building with his jeans, tight T-shirt, and shades, he thought gorgeous was just falling off his ass. This nigga really thought he was cooler than a breeze. Clown.

"I invited him. Lincoln does a lot for the community in Texas and in New York, and I figured his presence and expertise would be beneficial," Rico said.

"We don't need him," I sulked.

Rico laughed. "Listen, my man, we're a team. Whatever this thing is between you and Lincoln, you two gon' have to chop that shit up and grill it. Besides, Lincoln is my man from back in the day. We used to play against each other at rival high schools," he explained before he ran to catch up with Lincoln. "Yo, Linc!" Rico called out.

"Mr. Westmore, why don't you like Lincoln Harper? I mean, he's Lincoln Harper," Clarke asked.

Ryan Jr. put his hand up to stop him. "Now is a good time for us to go play basketball. Trust me on that one."

As Lincoln came in, all the kids and teenagers crowded him for autographs and photos, which he happily gave out. The bastard did love the kids. Soon, he and Rico made their way over to me.

"We meet again," Lincoln said.

I looked at him plainly. "So we do."

"Okay, so Rob and Dean also thought it would be a good idea to get Lincoln's feedback and input about the center. You cool with that?"

I shrugged. "I'm outnumbered, so the majority wins," I said tensely as I eyed Lincoln. At the least, my teammates and business partners could've consulted me first.

Rico shook his head. "Well, anyway, Lincoln, these are the basketball courts, obviously. I can show you the tutoring side once they are done—"

Suddenly, Beyoncé's song "Work It Out" floated out of the speakers of the dance studio. Lincoln turned toward the music. "I'm sorry. What's over there?" he inquired.

"Nothing," I blurted.

Rico looked at me as if I'd bumped my head. "Actually, it's the free dance class. Ryan's lovely wife graciously stepped in to be our volunteer hip-hop dance instructor," Rico explained.

Lincoln smiled at us. "Really? Do you mind if I go and watch?" He headed in that direction before the question barely left his lips.

"Yes—" I began.

"This is for feedback and input, right?" Lincoln cut me off.

"Yes," I said through clenched teeth as I followed him and Rico toward the dance studio.

"Fine then. I'd like to check out all of the activities," Lincoln said as we all came up to the dance studio.

"Okay, this time we're going to combine steps three and four into the cross sequence—" Charice was saying as Lincoln opened the door.

"Word, son! It's Lincoln Harper," one of the guys from the class yelled. Several of the kids—boys and girls—ran over to meet him.

"Hey, hey people—" Charice called out to the kids, but it was no use. She walked over to Rico and me. "I really appreciate how you all disrupted my class," she fussed, folding her arms across her chest.

"My bad, ma. It was my fault," Lincoln apologized. "I just wanted to check out all of the activities in the facility."

Charice looked at me with confusion.

"Apparently, Rico and the crew think Lincoln's experience with other programs similar to this one could be useful to us," I explained.

Charice laughed and looked at Lincoln. "Oh, really now? Word on the street is that you had help reinventing and structuring the programs that you sponsor, Lincoln," she said matter-of-factly.

Sucking in a sharp breath, Lincoln chewed on his bottom lip and then nodded. "That is true. I did. My program director was the best of the best, and I really valued her opinion. I learned a lot from her."

Charice put her head down and looked away.

Knowing that he was referring to Charice, I'd had enough. "Look, kids, you all really need to get back to class."

"Mr. Westmore, can we please get an autograph or photo with Mr. Harper?" Marvin, one of the younger students, asked.

"I'll tell you what," Lincoln said, facing the kids. "If you all and Mrs. Charice show me the routine you were about to work on, I'll give everyone in here an autograph and a photo."

"No way," Charice said, shaking her head as I agreed.

"Oh, please, Mrs. Charice, please? Lincoln Harper is my absolute favorite ball player," Marvin whined.

Charice rubbed her forehead. "I don't know."

"Are you chicken?" he asked her. "Just pick one."

I gritted my teeth. "If it wasn't for these kids," I mumbled.

Charice laughed. "Okay, sure. Liza, put on 'Irreplaceable' by Beyoncé. I love the lyrics to that song," she said, staring directly into Lincoln's eyes. That definitely wiped the smirk off his face, and I couldn't help but laugh at that.

Lincoln stood fixed in place as Charice danced, acting out a scene as if she were kicking him out to the left, to the left. At the hook, I nearly cried in laughter as Charice and some of the girls began singing: *"So, since I'm not your everything, how about I'll be nothing, nothing at all to you. Baby, I won't shed a tear for you, I won't lose a wink of sleep, 'cause the truth of the matter is, replacing you is so easy."* The clincher was when my Ricey grabbed me as the supposed "new" guy that was replacing Lincoln then kissed me as we pretended to walk away. All the kids stood up and clapped for that one. Hell, even Rico clapped.

Charice laughed. "This is dance craze week, where we are paying homage to current artists who have changed the game through entertaining performances. Today, we are paying tribute to Beyoncé. So, if Mr. Harper is finished clowning around, we can show him what the program is really about," she said matter-of-factly.

He nodded. "By all means, do your thing," he said, sounding crushed. He took his place beside Rico and me, and "Upgrade U" filled the room as Liza hit a button on the stereo system. Charice motioned for me to join her as the boys paired off with the girls.

"Just let me use you," she whispered.

Pecking her on the lips, I quipped, "I'm your muse, baby." Just as the intro was coming to a close, I mouthed along with Jay-Z, "What's higher than number one?"

Charice had choreographed an amazing, clean-cut routine pairing the boys and girls with each other. I loved how they easily worked one-on-one and then could fall into a group routine on the chorus. She was really working me just like Beyoncé had done Jay-Z during the rap breakdown, as a couple of B-boys breakdanced behind us and the others stood to the side. Then, they all finished it with group choreography. I felt like I was in a video. Afterward, Rico and Lincoln cheered, and the kids went wild.

"Yeah, C! Talk yo' shhh!" I yelled out, laughing as I hugged her.

"Very nice." Lincoln nodded, even though we could both sense that his feelings were hurt. No one cared about his hurt feelings; not me, and *definitely* not my Ricey.

"So, can we get those autographs and photos now?" Marvin asked.

"Of course," Lincoln agreed as the kids surrounded him. Rico went to grab the office camera and some paper, and Charice and I walked out of the studio.

"So, you think he gets the point now?" I asked Charice, holding her in my arms.

She looked up at me and giggled. "Oh, I think he definitely gets it. I'm so wicked."

"And I love your wicked ways," I joked with her.

"And I love you, Ryan." She gazed into my eyes intently.

How could I even think I could live a lifetime without this woman in my life? I was glad that I had gotten my act together and that Charice had given me another chance. She was the glue that held my life together, and I loved her with every fiber of my soul. There was no doubt in my mind that she was supposed to be my wifey. I kissed her passionately.

"I love you, Ricey. I love you so much," I professed, leaning my forehead against hers.

With our foreheads pressed gently together, we gazed into each other's eyes, and at that moment, nothing else mattered, not even Lincoln being in New York. As I held her in my arms, I thought about how grateful I was that she'd given me the chance to be her husband, and my spirit felt secure that this was meant to be. We basked in our private moment for a few moments longer before one of the kids came to get Charice.

"You may have had the last laugh today, but sooner or later, your web is going to unravel. When it does, you won't have anyone to blame but yourself, and I will be standing on the other end, patiently waiting," Lincoln seethed from behind me. I turned to face him. "Trust me. What goes around comes right back around again," he warned. With that, he put on his shades and turned to catch up with Rico.

I just stood there glaring at Lincoln from a distance. When I turned back around, Charice winked at me through the window. I smiled at her. This was *my* wife, and if Lincoln thought he was going to make me lose her, he'd lost his mind. I was playing for keeps this time, no matter what I had to do to keep her. *No matter what.*

Chapter Thirteen

Charice

So far, it had been calm around the house. Ryan had been really tense at first, demanding that I stay far away from Lincoln. Hell, he was preaching to the choir. If I could physically move him myself, I would. Fortunately, since the famous afterschool center visit, there had been no more surprise visits from Lincoln, and outside of the occasional drive-by in the neighborhood, we hadn't seen him. That was wonderful. Maybe we could all coexist without drama.

Who the hell was I kidding? Both my husband and Lincoln were locked into five-year contracts with the Giants. The pay was too good and the team was too awesome for either of them to walk away or risk being traded. Another four years of being forced to interact with Lincoln was going to bring about the inevitable. He'd find out about Lexi sooner or later, and I prayed that it would be at the end of Ryan's contract, so we could move to another team and get the hell away from Lincoln, at least for another year.

What I couldn't understand was why he was acting like I was stolen from him instead of him leaving me. I was ready to give him all of me—hell, I had—and he said he didn't want it. Even after I begged him like a fool, he denied me. It was him, not me. He'd given up his chance, and I wasn't giving him another one. It was no use crying over spilled milk now, so whatever residual feelings he had, he could light it up and smoke it. Fuck him and anything he had to say about it.

As I turned off my alarm clock to get ready for my early morning workout, I could've kicked myself in the butt. I was pissed that I'd spent my last ten minutes of good sleep thinking about Lincoln's raggedy ass. I had a long day, and I knew this was the last few minutes of good rest I'd have.

Since it was finally warming up, I decided to jog in the neighborhood instead of driving all the way to the gym. After putting on my nylon pants and sport tank top, I grabbed my iPhone and water bottle then headed out the front door.

A good fifteen minutes into my awesome jog, I heard a faint noise behind me, so I pulled out my earbuds and turned only to see none other than Lincoln Harper jogging. *Great.* And of course, as soon as he spotted me looking over my shoulder, he called out to me. The absolute last thing I needed in my life was to be bothered by him, so I put my earbuds back in and increased my pace. Now, why did I do that knowing he was in the NFL? He could've run circles around me, and sure enough, within a few seconds, he was next to me.

"Why you make me run for you?" Lincoln asked, a little winded from his mini sprint.

I pulled out my earbuds and laughed. "Somebody needs to condition a little more. You sound like you're going to huff and puff and blow my house down," I joked.

"Maybe I'll sign up for your dance class," he laughed cynically. "Why are you out here by yourself?"

I rolled my eyes but made sure to keep them looking forward. I wasn't even going to address the comment about my dance class. "Not that it's any of your business, but this is my 'me' time," I answered. Just for shits and giggles, I asked. "And you?"

He looked over at me, which I refused to acknowledge. "This is my workout time."

Note to self: go to the gym all the time.

We jogged side-by-side in silence for a few seconds more, and I began to feel really uncomfortable. I refused to give Lincoln the satisfaction of thinking we were even remotely cool with each other, and I damn sure didn't want him to feel as though I had any lingering feelings for him. That chapter in my life was closed, and never again . . . no more was I reopening it.

"Well, nice chat. Have a good one." And with that, I placed my earbuds back in my ears and jogged ahead.

I felt a hand on my arm. "Can't we just jog together?" Lincoln asked with desperation.

"No." I pulled away without breaking my stride.

"Why not?" he yelled.

My blood pressure was beginning to boil. Unbeknownst to him, he'd already ruined my last ten minutes of good sleep, and I refused to let him ruin the first thirty minutes of my day. I turned and jogged backward. "Look, man, this is my 'me' time. That means me and me alone. *Nawimean*?" I said sternly, mocking his New York accent.

He laughed. "Look at who is picking up the New Yitty accent and slang. It's kinda cute to hear you speak. You sound like a born and bred New Yorker."

I shook my head in frustration. "And you sound like you're getting on my nerves. Be gone, Lincoln." I turned around and began to jog forward again.

"Charice, I just want to talk to you."

Now I was pissed. Pissed. What part of being left alone didn't this fool understand? It was the same way he had asked me to leave him alone, so why in the fuck couldn't he do the same?

I stopped jogging and turned to face him with my hands on my hips. "I wish you'd respect my wishes the same as you requested of me. Ten months ago, you asked me to leave you alone, so please abide by your own request. Leave me alone."

He put his head down as if I'd taken the wind out of his lungs. He took a deep breath and looked up with eyes full of sorrow and regret. "Charice, there's so much I should've told you that night. So much I regret—"

I didn't need or want to hear this shit. We'd crossed this bridge long ago, and I wasn't taking any trips down memory fucking lane just to relive that heartache.

I threw my hands up. "Why does it matter now, Lincoln? What could you possibly have to say to me?" I asked with an attitude.

He jogged up to me and stood right in front of me. His overbearing presence was too much. I bit my lip, unable to move. I knew I should've run for the hills, but it was as if my legs were cemented to the ground, and my heart was racing a mile a minute knowing he was about to say something that I both dreaded yet longed to hear. He stood so close to me that the sweat that dripped off the tip of his nose landed on my T-shirt. My God, Lincoln was still as fine as ever. Even in the early morning before the sun rose, I could see the chiseled jaw line I'd caressed many a night, that masculine chest I'd lain on more times than I could count, and those powerful arms I'd been held in. Those massive thighs had locked around my legs during lovemaking too many times to remember. And those lips. Those kissable . . . LL Cool J lickable . . . lips. Those lips had been on *every* inch of my body.

The intensity in his eyes was so real it was as if he'd waited for this moment for a lifetime. "I need to tell you that I am so sorry, and I . . . I still love you. I love you so much." He struggled to get his thought out, and his voice was filled with emotion.

Before I knew what happened, I was in his arms, being kissed with wild passion. My knees buckled, and I swooned from the pleasure he unleashed. Instantly, I thought of Ryan and pushed him back.

"Bastard!" I gasped for breath and wiped my mouth. "How dare you kiss me? Have you lost your fucking mind? I'm married."

He put his hand to his chest apologetically. "I'm sorry, Charice, but I've waited so long to apologize to you. I just couldn't help myself. I never stopped loving you," he confessed hurriedly.

Tears threatened to fall from my eyes as I shook my head. "Why are you doing this to me? Was it not enough for you to ruin my life one time, so you have to try to do it again? Please stop this. What did I ever do to you besides love you? I have a life that I'm happy with and a husband who loves me as much as I love him. Stop interfering in that and leave us alone. Leave me the fuck alone, Lincoln."

He shook his head as if he couldn't, nor wouldn't, do that. His eyes pleaded for me to just listen to him. "Charice, there's something you need—"

"No!" I shouted, interrupting him with a finger point. "Nothing. I don't want to hear nothing else. Leave me alone, Lincoln, and if you ever force yourself on me again, I will hurt you."

He threw his hands up. "Charice, I'm so sorry—"

"Save it," I said angrily and jogged off.

I was so distraught that I couldn't finish my workout and went straight home to shower. I had to wash Lincoln's scent off my skin. I couldn't believe he had tried to push up on me. I washed everything from my hair to my toes and let the warm water from the multiple showerheads rain in a fury down my body. I touched my lips with my fingertips; I could still feel his kiss burning there. His scent was etched in my nostrils, even after scrubbing my skin. I closed my eyes, and a vision of Lincoln came over me. All the memories I'd fought so hard to suppress started to invade my thoughts. I remembered the first time we made love and how he slept, so peaceful and naked, in my bed. I remembered how we made love on the terrace in Paradise Island. I could almost feel him standing behind me in the shower like he used to, slowly making love to me through the back door. Still to this day, he was the only man that was able to make me enjoy anal penetration. I was so lost in the thought that I moaned.

"Thinking about me already?" Ryan whispered in my ear from behind me.

I jumped. "I was . . . I was . . . umm . . . you scared me." I trembled, refusing to turn around out of fear that he'd sense something was wrong.

He snickered softly then kissed my neck. "I just wanted to give you something to think about today," he sibilated in my ear as he stroked his manhood up and down my ass. "Let me try the back door," he urged, breathing huskily.

Lost in my erotic thoughts about Lincoln and our anal moments, I consented. He grabbed the KY Jelly and smeared it on both of us, and my back hole twitched with excited anticipation. Once I felt the head of his erection making its entrance, I directed his path and moved to show him the direction to wind. He followed suit and slowly penetrated me, going deeper until he reached the destination. I stroked my clit as he glided lovingly in and out of my back door.

"Oh, shit. Ricey, you feel so fucking *good*," Ryan moaned.

"I'm about to come," I mumbled, flicking my finger back and forth over my throbbing bud.

Ryan held my waist tight as he buried his dick deep in my ass. I flattened the palms of my hands on the shower wall. "I'm 'bout to explode," Ryan said, winded. He couldn't hold off his climax any longer, and he shouted my name as he came.

With my eyes closed tight, my climax erupted as the last time Lincoln and I made love like this invaded my thoughts. "Oh gawd. Oh gawd. Oh, Lincolnnn," I yelled, quivering uncontrollably.

"What!" Ryan screamed.

Chapter Fourteen

Lucinda

Yes, I was still mad. Mad as hell. What if Aldris had walked in our house and saw me hugged up with Raul? Exactly. He thought I should let it go just because he explained that there was nothing going on between them. He was such a genius. I knew that much. I was not stupid, but I damn sure wasn't blind either. Jennifer still loved Aldris, and even though he hurt her, knowing how good of a man he was, she'd take him back in a New York minute. Especially since she had so-called first dibs on him, and her ex-husband left her for his ex. What loyalty did she owe to me? None. Like she so eloquently put it before the paternity test, she didn't know I existed.

But I can't get Aldris to see that. I swear men have tunnel vision. Well, damn it, I saw the big picture, and the writing was on the wall in big, bold letters. Jennifer wasn't going to play me for the okey-doke, and neither was Aldris. If I let that shit slide one time, it was going to keep sliding until Jennifer managed to slide my man right out the door with her. I might have been younger than both of them, but I wasn't born at night, and it damn sure wasn't last night. Life had made me wise, and I wasn't going to let anybody make a fool of me.

Sitting at home, chilling with my cup of hot cocoa and studying up for my test, I'd opted not to go to Sunday morning service with Aldris since we still weren't gellin'.

Sure, it had been three days since that little incident, but Aldris just didn't seem all too sincere with his *apologies,* if I could call them that. It was more like he was apologizing because it was the right thing to do and not because he truly meant it or saw something wrong with what he did. I wasn't the one to accept half-ass apologies, especially not from men.

I'd put up with way too much bullshit from Emilio Rojas and Raul Garcia to allow room for anybody else's half-ass anything. And I didn't feel like sitting up in church, trying to praise the Lord, while I was full of nothing but pure hell. I mean really, how could I sing, "He Saw the Best in Me" while the worst in me was ready to kick some ass? Exactly.

"Hey," Aldris said quietly as he came in the house from church.

"Hey," I replied and drank my hot cocoa.

Aldris walked over to the breakfast table where I was studying and just looked at me for a moment as he jiggled his car keys in his hand. Then, he bent down to kiss me, and I turned my face, only giving him access to my cheek. He pulled off his suit jacket and sat down across from me.

"So, are you studying for a test?" he asked, sitting back and staring at me as if that was supposed to make me stop.

"I'm trying to." I flipped a page aggressively, showcasing my irritation.

Aldris pointed to himself. "So, I guess I'm disturbing you, huh?"

I continued to look in my book.

He sat back, releasing a slow and deliberate breath. Then, he tapped on the table, looking at me as if he was contemplating what to say to me next. "Church service was good. The pastor and a few members asked about you."

"Uh-huh." Was he not going to get the hint that I had nothing to say to him?

"The message was great. Do you want to know what the sermon title was?"

My harsh expression flashed as I tossed a heated glare his direction. "What, Aldris?"

"Pardon my past."

He honestly looked at me as if I was supposed to take what he had just said to heart. Not so subtle of a hint now, was it? He was on my nerves, and if he thought this was in his past, he was sadly mistaken.

"Sometimes you can't just pardon the past," I said snidely.

He threw his hands up. "Are we still on this?"

"When did we get off of it?"

Aldris stood up and paced. "Lu, I've apologized for my actions. What more do you want? My blood?"

That was it. I jumped up and threw my hands on my hips. Attitude on go. "Your way of apologizing was saying, 'Lu, it wasn't like that. It was nothing, just a friendly gesture. Come on. You know me.' I don't remember an honest 'I'm sorry' coming out of your mouth."

Aldris shook his head in disbelief. "I can't believe you are acting like this. I mean really, Lucinda."

Now I was offended. Was he trying to say I was being childish? "Okay, so *now* I'm being petty. Is that what you're saying?"

Exasperated, he threw his hands up. "Well, if the shoe fits."

I wished I had on some shoes right then. I would've fit them right up his ass. "Okay, so if you ever in your life walk up on Raul and I being all hugged up close and personal, I don't wanna hear a damn word about it. Just remember that, Aldris! Turnabout is *always* fair play, papi."

"So what, you're going to do some intentional shit?" he asked, his expression getting angrier by the second.

I shrugged. "Why should it matter to you?" I asked just to be a bitch about it.

He looked at me as if I were crazy. "It fucking matters because you're *my* fiancée."

"Exactly! And you're *mine*! So why the fuck should I just '*be cool*' with what happened? Why must I brush it off and let it ride as if it was nothing? It may have been nothing, but damn, it hurt my feelings, Aldris, and that should mean something to you," I yelled, my voice quivering, full of emotion.

I hated the fact that he'd gotten me this upset. When it came to my emotions, I was an introvert. I never wanted anyone to see me sweat, and I damn sure didn't like for them to see me cry. Showing that I was upset or angry didn't bother me, but showing my vulnerability bothered the shit out of me. Even though I loved and trusted Aldris, he'd only seen me vulnerable once, when his boys popped up at his mom's house and told her about Spanish Fly, my on-stage stripper persona when I used to dance in Pooch's strip club, Moet. I didn't even shed a tear when he proposed—well, at least not in front of him, and that was definitely a hard feat. Seeing as how he was the source of my emotions now ensured I didn't want to showcase them, especially not in front of him. I cursed myself for being so damn weak for this man.

Aldris knew immediately that I was extremely upset, and he instantly walked up and reached for me. "Come here, baby," he said, attempting to hug me.

I waved him off. "No, just give me a minute." I turned my face, trying to suppress the tears that threatened to fall.

He turned me to face him and hugged me anyway. "It's okay to be vulnerable in front of me, Lu. We're getting married, so we're entitled to share those emotions that we'd rather not show anyone else."

With that, I hugged him back and let a few tears fall. The truth of the matter was I didn't want to lose Aldris. For the first time in my life, I was truly in love. The thought of that love being threatened was enough to break me down. Damn, I never knew love like this before.

He held me tight. "I'm so sorry, Lucinda. You're right. I was wrong for what I did, but I promise you I wasn't trying to do you dirty. I would never do that to you. I love you, mami."

"I just don't want to lose you, Aldris," I confessed.

"Baby, you've got me. I'm not going anywhere." He kissed my forehead.

He tilted my chin upward, and the sincerity in his eyes shone just brightly as his love for me, and we began to kiss passionately. There was nothing that ended an argument better than make-up sex, and I was prepared to give him some of this Spanish Fly booty until my cell phone rang.

"It's my phone, Aldris," I said between kisses.

"Fuck that phone," he said, kissing me on my neck.

"What if it's my mom about Nadia?"

He eased up. "Ugh. You're right." He relented as I answered.

"Yeah, Mama."

"Lucinda? Can you come over here, please?" she asked, panicked.

"What's wrong, Mama?" I asked fearfully. "Nothing is wrong with Nadia, is it?"

"No, no, not Nadia. She's fine. Your father is over here . . . and *Raul*. Raul stopped by to see Nadia, and Emilio was here, and it's a mess," she yelled frantically.

"Dios mío," I exclaimed. "I'm on the way!" I hung up.

"What's wrong?" Aldris asked me for the millionth time.

"My dad and Raul are over my mama's house," I said hurriedly.

"Oh, damn," he said as he grabbed his keys.

I stuck my feet in my tennis shoes, and then we headed out of the house.

"What the fuck is your dad and Raul doing at your mom's house?" he asked.

"All I know is Raul stopped by to visit Nadia, and my papa was there. Why? I do not know," I said to Aldris as we hauled ass to my mama's house.

With all the shit going on with Jennifer and Aldris, I had completely dismissed the whole fiasco brewing between Raul, Maria, and my papa. Of course, when Raul claimed Rosemary and Emilio Jr. as his kids, the paternity test papers went straight to my papa's house. You wanna talk about furious? Try listening to your "wife" explain that she had been sleeping with your daughter's baby's daddy behind your back, and that he was possibly the father of not only your stepdaughter but the baby she just had. My papa was so damn livid he kicked Maria and all the kids out of the house—even Eva, whose paternity wasn't in question, but with a ho for a housewife, you never knew. As of now, they were staying with Maria's sister in her three-bedroom apartment.

Now, why the fuck my papa was at my mama's house—or even Raul, for that matter—was beyond me, but I was about to find out. I wasn't letting nobody put my child's life in any type of danger. I didn't give a damn who they were.

"Papa! Calm down." I heard my brother, Jose, yelling as Aldris and I ran inside.

I had to take a step back. Jose had Papa pinned down on the sofa, while my sister, Lucy, and my mama struggled to hold Raul. My mama's living room looked like hurricane season in the tropics. Furniture was overturned, glass was everywhere, and there were scuff marks and holes in the walls.

"Lucinda, thank God," my mama yelled when she saw us.

Immediately, Aldris ran over and pinned Raul up against the wall.

"Get your fucking hands off of me," Raul yelled. "I'ma beat your ass first and then that muthafucka over there," he screamed, nodding his head toward my papa.

"Don't even set yourself up for failure," Aldris hissed at him.

"I'm gonna kill his fucking ass. You fucking *puto*," my dad screamed.

"Where are the kids?" I asked frantically.

"In the back, in the twins' room," my mama answered.

I ran to the back and opened the door. My siblings and Nadia were all back there, crying their eyes out.

"*Mama*," Nadia exclaimed and ran up and hugged me tight. "Daddy and Papa are fighting. Why?"

I held her tight. "It's going to be fine. You're all gonna be fine. I'm going to get you guys away from here for a little bit, okay?" I said to all of them as they nodded. "Stay right here and do not move, none of you," I ordered and ran back out.

I grabbed my mama's van keys. "Lucy!" I yelled out my sister's name as she ran into the kitchen where I was.

"Yes, Lu," she said nervously.

"Are you okay to drive?" I asked, looking at her intently.

She nodded and swallowed the lump in her throat. "Yeah, I think . . . I mean . . . yeah."

"I need for you to get it together, please," I said calmly, placing my hands on her shoulders to soothe her.

She nodded and sighed. "Okay, yes, I'm good."

"Good. Take the kids to the park up the road. Make sure you take your cell phone with you. Go now," I instructed, and she gathered the kids up and left out the back door.

When I walked back in the living room, Aldris had taken Raul to the laundry room, and my papa was still screaming at Jose to let him get to Raul.

"What the fuck is wrong with you?" I screamed at my papa. "You coming over here, tearing up Mama's house and scaring your kids and grandchild. Act like you have some muthafucking sense before I call the police."

"Lucinda, that's not even necessary—" my mama began.

Confusion etched across my face. "What the hell is wrong with you? What is not necessary is for you to be standing up here trying to downplay this situation. They are in here endangering everyone around and traumatizing the kids."

"Don't talk to your mother like that," my papa yelled at me.

"You don't talk to me like that," I yelled. "We need to talk outside." I grabbed him by the arm and yanked him out of the door.

"What the hell is wrong with you?" I laid into him as soon as we were outside.

"I was fine until your bastard-ass baby daddy showed up. How dare he show his face around this family with all he's done to you and me?" my papa exclaimed angrily.

Wait a minute. Was this the same man who had refused to have my back when it came to Raul when I needed it? The same man who left my mama to fend for eight children while giving the world to Maria and her stepdaughter? The same man who worshipped the water my half-sister, Eva, toddled on and the poopie Pampers Emilio Jr. shitted in, yet treated his eight children by Mama—me, included—like crap? Yep, this was the same man.

"You are not even concerned about what Raul did to me or Nadia. Nor are you concerned about him being around this family. Don't even play those damn cards with me. You're pissed because the joke's on you. The ho you were hoeing around with on my mama hoed around on you. That's why she didn't want you to bother Raul for me. You got made a fool of, and you know what, Dad? You deserve every fucking bit of it. So, spare me the 'we are family' routine. I'm allergic to bullshit."

"I don't have to listen to this. You're always in somebody's face as if you're perfect."

"I never said I was perfect, but don't get mad because I'm right. That's your problem. You can't take the heat. Every time something gets a little difficult, you run. I may have gotten my temper from you, but I'm so glad I took Mama's everything else because God only knows what type of situation Nadia would be in with two good-for-nothing parents. You made your bed, Papa. Sleep in it. Don't come around here scaring my brothers and sisters, and hell will freeze over before I let you traumatize Nadia any further," I said sternly.

He just glared at me and paced back and forth. I knew a part of him wanted to argue, but how could he? I was right.

"Just stay here until I can get Raul away," I instructed him, and I walked back in the house.

By this time, Aldris had brought Raul back into the living room. "We've been having a nice talk about how he's going to help your mother pay for the damages, which will not interfere with his child support payments," Aldris said as my mama and Jose glared at Raul.

"Yeah, whatever. I promised your mom I'd help pay. I ain't worried about child support because as soon as I can add on Rosemary and Emilio, I know it's getting reduced," Raul said snidely.

"You are such an asshole. My dad's wife? How fucking lowdown and nasty are you?" I asked, shaking my head.

"I had Maria first. When you broke up with me, Maria and I started kicking it. She thought this dope dude was gonna marry her, so she left me for him, and he tossed her to the side. She started dating your dad later after that," Raul confessed. "I just came by to see my fucking daughter—"

"Bullshit, Raul!" I yelled, interrupting him.

"*Ay chico, por favor*. I have had enough fighting and cussing in my house to last for an eternity. I don't care what your reason is for coming, Raul, but I need for you to leave," my mama commanded.

He shrugged. "Fine." He straightened his clothes and left.

Once Raul was gone, my papa came back in the house, and Aldris, Jose, and he began trying to straighten up what they could of the living room. I wanted to help, but I needed to speak to my mama, so I asked her to talk to me in private.

She walked with me to the kitchen. "Really, can you believe that damn Raul?" she asked as we sat the table, looking at each other.

"Yes, I can. That's his M.O." I eyed her closely. "Okay, spill it, Mama. Why is Papa here?"

She exhaled nervously. "I'm helping your father get through this. He's facing a lot on him—"

I cut her off. "Wait a minute. Are you telling me that Papa is staying . . . *here* . . . with you?"

"You make it seem so—"

"*Madre*."

"Yes," she confessed with an attitude. "Yes, he is. Your papa needs me, and I'm going to be there for him," she admitted.

"By letting him stay here? He has a house. Why isn't he there? He kicked Maria out," I questioned my mama with a scowl.

"He says the house reminds him of Maria, and he can't handle that right now. He's just trying to find his way, Lucinda. He needs someone he can trust and depend on. I know you and your siblings don't like it, and you all refuse to be there for him so right now, I'm all he's got," she said with a sense of finality to the discussion.

It didn't matter, though, because I couldn't say a word. Not one single word. I was too shocked and appalled to say anything. I may have loved Aldris, but I wasn't stupid. If he ever treated me how my papa treated my mama, he had better not ever ask me to help him with nothing. I knew that my mama still loved my papa, but was there that much love in the world? I guess so . . . for her.

Chapter Fifteen

LaMeka

"I can't believe I have to sit beside you the entire game," Gavin said, shaking his head as we sat down in Philips Arena to watch the Hawks play the Lakers.

He was fresh to death in his Polo jean shorts, all black Nikes, and his T-shirt and throwback Al Horford jersey. He was just pissed that I had on my mid-thigh jean shorts with my purple-and-gold Lakers Legends jersey, complete with my LA Lakers baseball cap.

I was actually impressed when Gavin popped up with tickets. That game had been sold out for about a week. Gavin said he had some good friends he was able to get some tickets from at the last minute, which proved that he would go the extra mile to please me. I really did want to go to the game, and I felt like it would be the perfect outing for a first date. The only thing was that I was a die-hard Lakers fan, and he was a die-hard Hawks fan. I probably should have told him that first, but I honestly didn't know he was a true Hawks fan. He said he thought I was too, since I asked to go to the game, but that was because I wanted to see my Lakers play, since I may never get to California to see them. It was pretty hilarious to me. He'd been fussing about it since he picked me up.

"Oh, be quiet, Gavin. You just mad because my Lakers are the truth, and by end of the second quarter, they gonna be spankin' that ass!" I laughed.

"Whatever, man. If it wasn't for—"

I started pretending to rub my ear. "I'm sorry. Were you saying something? I couldn't understand you. It sounded a lot like wonk-wa-wonk-wonk," I giggled, interrupting him.

"I got a question. How can you be from Georgia and be going against your home team? That's so *disloyal.* I'm appalled," he joked.

"I am loyal to my home team. The Falcons don't play until football season starts again."

He laughed at me then we settled down. After a few minutes, the music came over the arena, signifying they were announcing the starting lineups. It's just something about hearing that music that comes over the arena. It makes you feel like you can go out there and knock down a couple of 3-pointers yourself. I nearly lost it when I saw my favorite Lakers players strut across the floor. Gavin thought it was hilarious to see me screaming my head off while everyone around us just looked at me foolishly. I didn't give a good damn. It was my first time going to a Lakers game, and I was going to enjoy every minute of it.

Gavin and I talked crap to each other the entire first half, and just like I predicted, the Lakers were in the lead at the halftime buzzer. During halftime, we managed to grab some drinks and a couple of T-shirts. Of course, I wanted all Lakers stuff, so Gavin snagged me two T-shirts—one with the Lakers logo, and another one with a picture of the entire team. For good measure, I also agreed to get a Hawks T-shirt. He also got Tony Jr. a Lakers basketball and LaMichael a T-shirt. By the time we got back to our seats, the third quarter was under way, and Gavin was out of more than a hundred bucks between shirts, the ball, and the drinks, but we were having a ball, made better by the Lakers beating the Hawks, 103 to 89!

"I don't want to hear a word about your Lakers," Gavin fumed as we got in his car.

"Why are you even acting shocked? You already knew what time it was. Boy, please."

"Okay. You got that one." He laughed. "Well, did you have a good time?" he asked, looking over at me.

"Yes, I did. I want to thank you for a great time," I answered, beaming from ear to ear.

"You don't have to thank me. It was my pleasure, Meka. I really enjoyed myself with you too. Do we have to end it now, though?"

His request left me intrigued. "No, my mom is cool with keeping the kids for me. What do you have in mind?"

"I want to go grab a bite to eat and get to know each other a little better."

Impressed, I slowly nodded. "We can do that."

I felt amazingly comfortable with Gavin. It wasn't like I hadn't been approached while I was with or even after Tony, but I wasn't interested in the men that asked. I felt that I had to take some time getting LaMeka together first. Coming out of such a hellacious relationship with Tony was not an easy feat to overcome. I felt men would be a distraction from my goals in life, and I also needed time to find out what I really needed in a man so that I could ask God to bless me with that.

I had two boys to look out for, so not only did I need a stand-up gent for myself, but I needed someone who was going to step in and be a father to my boys. It was too many damn pedophiles and shiftless niggas out there just to date any and everybody. Nowadays, you had to do a damn background check, medical history check, credit check, interview, and reference check before you could agree to go on a date. It was sad but true, and if I had to do all of that to ensure my safety and the safety of my boys, then that was what I'd do. Tony had proved that it doesn't matter how long you've known a person; you can still end up not knowing them at all.

So far, I'd been doing rather well for myself. Just like I said, I made the money for me. I ended up not paying Pooch. It had nothing to do with me dipping and dodging him, and everything to do with him getting locked up. Before I could cash the check good, the feds had brought him and the entire organization down. I wasn't crazy. I knew that Dreads had something to do with that, but I kept my mouth closed. All I knew was that Trinity ran off with his ass, and that's all I *needed* to know.

Hell, even that was way too much information. The less I knew, the better for me. That bitch, Sonja, or rather Chocolate Flava, had cornered me in the grocery store once, questioning me about Trinity, talking 'bout she was just asking. Yeah, right. Everybody who knew Pooch knew that bitch was riding for him. Hell, it was a known fact that she had wanted to get at Pooch ever since she started stripping at Moet like three years ago. Now, she wanted me to believe she was just "*asking*" like I didn't know she was going back and feeding Pooch any piece of information she could find.

But anyway, the point was I ended up not having to pay for the truck, which was a blessing. My mom and Misha moved in with me, and my mom took care of the monthly expenses so that Misha and I could concentrate on our studies. So, I just continued to deposit Tony Jr.'s monthly disability checks in my interest-bearing checking account and savings account. The only bill I paid was out-of-pocket expenses for health insurance so that Misha and Tony Jr. could get the best care. At any rate, I only had a month left in the transitional house, and I had found a nice four-bedroom, three and a half–bathroom home in a nice middle-class neighborhood. This was the dream of a lifetime; my dream deferred. I was praying it was going to become my reality. I had accrued so much money due to the lump sum disability payment and the investments made from that money that I could pay cash for it, so I made an offer on it and hoped that the owners took it.

It was the perfect place for us. The absolute first thing I noticed about the home was the back yard. I'd never had a back yard growing up in the hood. It was one of those things I always wanted growing up: you know, a swing set, a treehouse, and maybe even a pool in my back yard. With this yard, I could do all three if I wanted to for my boys. There were so many other pluses to this home, like a bonus room and my master bedroom was to die for. I was going to use the bonus room as a playroom for the boys, and my master bedroom had a little sitting area and my own stand-up shower and Jacuzzi tub. Lastly, there was no more gawd damn Laundromats for me. I not only would have my own washer and dryer, but my own room for it, too. Hell, I was just in love with everything about this home.

Some people might not see that as being special, but what may seem small to others means the world to someone else, especially someone who has never had it. Like me. So, right now, life was good. Real good. Perhaps Gavin could be the icing to top it all off.

"Enjoying your food?" Gavin asked.

"I'm stuffed. It was great."

"Yeah, me too," he said, patting his stomach. "I'm just glad I'm off tomorrow. I just wanna chill out, watch some sports, and listen to some old school. Put on a little Al, a little Teddy. Shit, *all the drawls fall*," he joked.

"You're so crazy, Gavin. I can't with you. I swear you're a black man trapped in a white man's body," I howled, throwing my hand over my face at his antics.

"Well, I guess what's on the inside of me matters more, since they say the blacker the berry, the sweeter the juice." He winked at me, and instantly, there was a fire between my thighs.

My blush could not be contained. "Boy, what is your obsession with black women?"

He looked at me as if I were foolish. "Are you kidding me? I admire your strength. I see black women hold down the kids, the house, and the job as if it ain't shit. Even the ones that are married hold it down and still make their man feel like a man. Don't get me wrong, it's some strong women in every culture. It's just that I grew up around a lot of black kids coming from single mothers, and ever since I was little, I've always admired that. I guess more so because my mom was in the same boat with me. Not to mention, black women are the finest things on this Earth. Every shade of you. That sway in those hips and those round backsides . . . man, please. I don't mean no disrespect, but I feel sorry for any man who hasn't had the pleasure of getting with a black woman, especially from the back, if you know what I mean," he explained in awe.

"You started out so beautifully and ended up on ass. Yep, there is definitely a black man trapped inside of there," I joked.

"Well, I've got news for you, Miss LaMeka—that's *any* man. Hell, black, white, or Cablanasian, we all like to get ass," he kidded. "You can't point out one man who don't like it. Even gay men like ass. That's what they do. Hell, they're probably getting more ass than any straight man."

My stomach was cramping up from laughing at him. Gavin was a certified fool. "Something is wrong with you." Tears rolled out of my eyes at this foolery.

"It feels good to see you enjoying yourself, though. I'm glad I could make that happen."

There it was again, the blush. "Yes, you really have."

He gently rubbed the top of my hand. "Meka, I really like you, and I know you're trying to do your school thing, but I just wanna get to know you," he said sweetly, staring me in the eyes and licking his lips.

"You're serious, aren't you?"

He gave a crooked smile. "Hell yeah. Man, you already know what you do to me. I ain't got to tell you that, and I ain't gon' front about it either. I've told you more of my business than I tell my homeboys. What you see is what you get with me, Meka. I'm a white boy who has one brother. I came from a single parent home. My mother died and left me some grip. I loved science and took an interest in nursing. My best friends are black men. I love R&B, hip-hop, and gospel. I've never been married and don't have any kids. There ain't much left to tell you."

"Well, you gotta love kids to be with me. I'm a package deal."

"I didn't say I didn't want kids. I just don't have none of my own. Of course, if you give me a chance, I realize your boys are a part of that deal, which is what I signed up for. Knowing you have two sons doesn't bother me, LaMeka. My mother was a single parent with two sons. How could I judge you? I would never judge you about that. In fact, I admire you the same way I admired my mom. You put it in every day for you and your boys, and I would love the opportunity to be a part of their lives as well as yours," he said seriously. "I want to be a part of your entire life, LaMeka, not just your ass."

My heart melted right then. It had been so long since a man showed me this kind of intimate attention. I had been so bogged down with Tony and his nonsense that I forgot how good it felt to be cherished and appreciated. Even so, I was still going to force myself to take things slow with Gavin. There was a lot I had to tell him about my life, namely Tony. However, for the most part, I was definitely throwing caution to the wind and giving Gavin Randall a chance because he indeed was pretty fly for a white guy. Who would've thought this shit would happen? But when I looked at Gavin, I didn't see white or black or, as he would say it, Cablanasian. I saw a man who was willing to be down for me, and that was all I wanted.

"That is the sweetest thing."

Gavin lifted my chin up, and our lips met for our first kiss. On the real, I'd never been with a man of another race before, but Gavin could kiss. I mean a helluva lot better than Tony, too. Shit, he lifted up first, but I could've kissed him forever.

"I better get you home because it's some shit running through my mind right now, for real," Gavin said sexily as he rubbed his hands together.

I glanced at my watch. "We . . . we have time. You want me to come and chill with you?" I asked, not wanting to leave him or those lips.

"Hooked already, huh?" He chuckled.

"See, there you go."

Pulling me close, he hugged me. "It's cool. It's whatever you want to do. I just want you to be ready for it. There's no pressure here."

"I'm ready," I declared, staring him in the eyes. "I'm ready for you."

The smile that spread across his face was priceless. Without another word, he paid our tab, and we walked out, holding hands and cheesing at each other. I was so gonna give him *some* when we got to his house. Shit, there was no need to keep fighting it. I wanted Gavin, and it had been a long time since I'd had enjoyable sex, so I was more than ready to take my time and enjoy the experience. In fact, it was well overdue.

When we got in the car, we kissed again passionately. He was sending me on a high that I'd never experienced before. He was gonna have to double strap up because the way I felt, I knew we'd be going half on a baby if he didn't.

"I love the feel of you in my arms."

"Wait until you feel all of me." Just then, my cell phone rang. "Hello," I sang into my phone.

"Meka, it's Mrs. Light. Tony's awake!" she said excitedly.

"Huh?" I asked, trying to regroup.

"Come to the hospital quickly. Please. *Tony is awake.*"

"Oh my God," I exclaimed happily. "I'm on my way."

"What's wrong?" Gavin asked, concerned.

"Nothing. Everything is perfect. Take me to the hospital," I said excitedly.

"Huh? What?"

"Tony's awake."

"The patient?" he asked, confused.

It was confession time. "Yes, the patient."

"I get that you know him and all, but this is a little extreme. Don't you think?" he asked. "I mean, we had some plans."

"I know, but this is important," I said, facing him. Swallowing the lump in my throat, I found the courage to the release my secret before I could change my mind. "Gavin, there's something you have to know now. Tony, the patient, he is my sons' father."

Instantly, all the color drained from his face.

Chapter Sixteen

Pooch

If I had one more person to put me off or give me some bad news, I was straight gon' start knockin' niggas off. For real. If it wasn't for bad luck, I wouldn't have none, and I did *not* take too kindly to bad luck or bad news. Hell, I didn't take too kindly to anything bad. I was a nigga who was used to getting his way, and I'd be damned if I was gon' let any nigga, bitch, or prison sentence stop that, so I considered all of the shit that was going on right now minor setbacks. If somebody didn't start getting these setbacks set right, it was gonna be some hurt-up-ass individuals around here. Patience may be a virtue, but I was not a virtuous man, so I simply didn't give a fuck about being patient. Men of power only had patience with two things—making money and making love. Anything else was unacceptable.

I had spoken to my attorney, and I was pissed about how slow he was being on the particulars of this deal I was trying to strike with the DA, but at the same time, I knew eventually that would come through. It was all about finding the right way to lean to make shit happen. Being straight up with shit never got no nigga far, but I was gonna try it. If not, I knew I would have to lean to the root of all evil. Money. Wasn't no sense in me being the only hustla locked up. It was hilarious to me how I got locked up for making money by pushing dope, but the legal system was flooded with the biggest and best dope dealers, scammers, schemers, pimps, and hustlas around. Muthafuckas got paid to arrest and lock niggas like me up, but them same muthafuckas was either on drugs, selling drugs, or in cahoots with somebody who was selling drugs. These bitches settin' up rules and regulations about human rights when it came to murder and other heinous crimes, but they were the ones running prostitution rings, pimping little girls, running pornography, settin' up hits, and stealing money left to the fuckin' right. The worst muthafucka to fuck wit' was a muthafucka in the legal system. Them bitches could lock you up, take over your operation, set up new laws to keep your black ass locked up, and still make it home to dinner on time with their wives or husbands. Those were some bad muthafuckas.

On top of that, I still hadn't got no more information about Trinity. Ugh. If I was out, I woulda known that shit in an hour. That was the thing about depending on people and not being able to oversee what they were doing. Nothing got done right, or in this case, not the fuck at all. Chocolate said she'd been searching high and low for information, but I wasn't stupid. That bitch was just glad Trinity was out of the picture. She was glad to be called my girl now, and the only thing she wanted was for me to get out so we could be together and she could be the new bottom bitch. I wasn't completely heartless. I knew Chocolate wanted to be down wit' me since before forever, and I couldn't knock that she'd been working her ass off to keep my books lined up and my appeals intact. She held it down for me like a real bottom bitch should, but I'd only given my heart to one woman, and I was not fucking up and doing that again.

She could ask my first real girlfriend, Kaman, about that. While I loved Trinity since elementary school,

Kaman was the one showing me love in junior high. She was a petite, fair-skinned chick with long hair and a cute little round booty bump and nicely spread hips. I knew even then that she would definitely be a diva to be reckoned with when she got older. Yet, I had never truly paid her any attention because my heart belonged to Trinity. My raging hormones and Kaman's fast-developing body were enough to make my eyes wander, even if my feelings didn't. So, it did. I was good to Kaman, and though she was my first, I still couldn't love her. I'd hurt her so much that she cheated with my childhood best friend, a cool-ass white boy named Ethan. Still, it only turned what little loyalty I had for her cold and my focus back on Trinity.

But who was I kidding? Trinity had always been the focus. Even now. She always would. So, while I appreciated all that Chocolate did, I wasn't gon' never feel for her like I felt for Trinity, no matter what she did.

Matter of fact, if she didn't find out about Trinity, her ass was getting dropped as soon as my feet stepped outside this barbed wire hellhole. Real talk. That was, unless we found Trinity and she agreed to get down with Chocolate Flava. Then I could get some girl-on-girl action at the house and a ménage à trois going any time I wanted.

Yeahhhh, my thoughts drifted. Random thoughts of a better time crept in my mind. That's what being locked in cage did to a nigga. I hated not getting pussy when and how I wanted it. Granted, it had only been from Trinity over the past few years, but shit, I swear that bitch had pure gold between those thighs. I was missing that shit like a summa bitch, so my fantasies about what I wished I could do with it were running rampant on me.

Shifting my focus off Trinity, I turned to getting that paper. I spoke with Wolf and Chocolate about his girl being a carrier. Chocolate was down wit' it like I knew she would be, because that would help her out with not being responsible for my books. Besides, she lived life on the dangerous side like that. Man, why didn't I fall for her first?

But anyway, I had also talked to Lisa about it, but she was all on some losing her job bullshit. She explained if she got caught sneaking money and food, she could lie about that and just get reprimanded, but she couldn't risk her job, license, and yada fucking yada. She talked all that yin-yang-ass talk, but the next thing she had was my dick deep in her pussy. Now, how the fuck could she explain *that* if she got caught? *Oh, his dick accidently fell inside of me, and I was just moaning because it hurt, not because it was the best dick I ever had in my life like I told this nigga plenty of times before,* I thought as I laughed to myself and imagined her trying to lie her way out of it. How the hell you not gonna wanna risk your job to make some real grip, but you'd risk it for some good dick? At least if you lost your job, you'd still have bankroll. So, I took it as she felt the dick was worth the risk. Ha! Well, I couldn't argue wit' that. That was why it didn't bother me that she was out of the operation. For one, I didn't need no scary bitches on my team when it came down to that. Scary bitches made for stupid snitches. Ya feel me? And secondly, if she kept her nose clean, then I didn't have to worry about losing out on my "fringe benefits" up in this camp. She had a way of making a nigga feel like a king around this bitch, knowing I had the magic stick.

Damn, I really need some, and I have to wait until Monday. Fuckin' no weekend workin'-ass bitch. My side thoughts took over again.

It was times like that when I really missed Trinity. For real. Watching that big-booty bitch slide down a pole . . . I can't even describe the shit. It made me feel closer to God or some shit. It was like heaven on Earth. And niggas wondered why I never fucked with any of my strippers. Shit, I didn't need to. I had the best shows from my lady in the privacy of my own home.

Frustration grew in me because of the random-ass thoughts, but it was how I cleared my head. It also gave me space to wrap my mind around how this system shit really worked and the true understanding of incarceration. You know they said being locked up was for the rehabilitation of criminals. Now, being that the majority of the world's criminals were men, I think that was a bunch of bullshit. They know the only two things men love and cannot live without are money and sex, and in the cage, you were cut off from both, so I figured it out: They were tryna kill us, slow and deliberate. Kill us all. Give us the blue balls and charge us a dollar for a stick of gum when they knew we only make fifteen cents a day on duty detail. Summa bitches.

Anyway, random thoughts aside and back to the business. Wolf's girl had been up in the air about being a carrier. I told him if she didn't come through, his percent would drop from thirty to ten. Why give him that big of a cut when the only thing he did was pretty much help set up alliances? It ain't like he had to recruit customers. And a lot of these niggas were like me—locked up for life and then some—so they were on drugs anyway, just killing themselves slowly, making that life sentence shorter and shorter. I couldn't see it for myself because this wasn't the end for Pooch Smalls.

At any rate, Wolf had better do some fast talking over there with his bitch. This operation was on a roll, and it was moving with or without her. Still, I didn't want Chocolate being responsible for all the weight coming through because if she got caught, I didn't need her with an amount that would land her doing hard time. She only needed just enough to get slapped on the wrist so she could lay low for a while and then continue making it do what it do.

"What are you so antsy about?" Chocolate asked, breaking my thoughts.

"Umm, just hoping Wolf's girl comes through."

"I don't know why you worried about that bitch. You got me. That's all you need."

I couldn't help but laugh. I swear I wish I hadn't fallen for Trinity's ass. I took her hand in mine. "I know, baby, but what kind of man would I be to you if I didn't look out for you first? I just don't want you to get caught up on some serious bullshit. Let that bitch take some of the wrap. I don't know her, so I don't care. That's Wolf's problem."

"You really do care about me, don't you, Pooch?" she cooed.

"You know I do, baby. I have to look out for my number one." That wasn't no lie. I did care about her because I needed her for this operation and my appeals, and in that respect, she was my number one—at the moment—and Lisa was my number two.

That tidbit caused a bright smile to spread across her face. "I put some money on your books, and Stein is trying to meet with the DA this week."

"That's my girl." I rubbed her chin.

"So, you think that's gon' be enough to get you started?" she asked, referring to the weight I already had.

"Yeah, for now," I said, rubbing my hands together.

"Just let me know. My dude Skrilla said he's definitely all in. He remembers how you used to do on the streets."

"Tell Skrilla it's a bet." I beamed, feeling good about the news I was getting. It seemed some things were lining up. I just wished this Trinity situation would line up.

"What?" she asked, looking at me, puzzled.

I shook my head. "Nothing. Why?"

"You looked like something was on your mind."

"Well, I do have a lot of shit to think about, don't you think?"

I didn't want to admit that I had been thinking about Trinity. I wanted to ask Chocolate about her, but she was just starting to do shit right, so I fell back on it for now. I didn't need this bitch gettin' all blowed the fuck up, especially since I just laid it on thick about her being my girl and looking out for her. I guess I was learning patience. This situation was definitely giving me no choice with that. Right now, I needed this bitch, so I had to play my cards right.

"Yeah, I know that, baby. I'm just saying it looked like a little extra was on your mind." She shrugged.

Shit, a little *extra* was on my mind, and to be honest, she unknowingly gave me a great idea. I looked around. I always had her pick this corner because with my back turned, the guards couldn't see Chocolate or what she was doing. Originally, I chose it so we could discuss our dope dealings without eyes and ears, but being as such I was hurting for some loving, it was about to get used for other purposes.

I unzipped my fly. "I do have something *extra* on me, but it ain't on my mind. You could release some pressure for me."

A devilish grin graced the corners of her lips. "What if I get caught?"

"You won't."

"You do realize this would be our first actual time together, ya know, outside of masturbating off pictures."

Now she wanna get all sentimental. Fuck that. I needed to bust a nut, not get romantic. "Yeah, I know, but it ain't gon' happen if we keep talkin' about it."

She nodded and acted like she dropped her purse. She crawled under the table, and the next thing I knew, my dick was in heaven. My eyes rolled back as I imagined Trinity's lips wrapped around this pipe, and I swear fo' the good Lawd, in a record thirty seconds, I blew like a volcano. *Fuck.* I missed Trinity. I zipped up as she got up and wiped her mouth with her Kleenex.

"Man, I wish you could do me. You taste good, baby."

"You know how I do it." It was all that damn fruit Lisa gave me. She said I had to taste right for her to be swallowing. *Damn, thanks, Lisa.* "You could just play wit' yourself in front of me."

She jumped at the chance. "You know I never wear undies anyway."

"On second thought, never mind. As much as I'd love to see that, I can't bust no more. It took all my energy not to holler on that last one." I stopped her.

She pouted. "I gotta hurry up and get you out."

You ain't lying, I thought. I looked up and saw Wolf walking toward me. As he walked past, he gave me a head nod. I nodded back and turned to face Chocolate.

"That's Wolf, and his girl is down." I slid her telephone number to Chocolate. "Her name is Adrienne. Call her and get her straight."

"Is that his girl leaving?" she asked, looking directly at me.

Damn, this bitch was learning quickly. I might have to keep this ho after all. "Yep."

She licked her lips. "She looks real good."

"Then make it do what it do. Put a little Flava in her life."

"I'm already on that shit, Pooch." She stood up. "I'ma hook it up and hook myself up, too. It's been a while since I fell in between some good kitty."

I swear I coulda nutted right then. "Well, you get at her, baby. Make her do some thangs for you." I winked at her, and then we kissed.

"Don't worry. I got it covered." With that, she slipped her shades on and left.

Seemed like old Pooch's luck was taking a turn for the good. That's the way I liked shit. I was so happy, I decided that when I got outta there, I was gon' keep old Flava around for a little while, especially if she was able to get up with Adrienne. I liked Wolf, but I didn't owe him shit, and the only thing I could think of, besides my money, was having both of them in a room with me, celebrating my release. Then, I'd find Trinity.

Chapter Seventeen

Terrence

Man, oh man. I had a lot to think about in a short amount of time. If niggas would just stick to the fucking plan, then it wouldn't be no problems. I got in this hustle shit to make a way for me and my family, and my objective the entire time was to be in and out. Make the money then let the money make itself. *Boom.* End of discussion. Leave it to Tot to get caught up in the lifestyle. Our only plans were to make this money, bring Pooch down, and be out like the wind, but he had to go and keep on being a damn D-boy. I had set this nigga straight. He was sitting on five hundred grand that I helped him make, plus whatever he made on his own from our dope dealings. *Damn.* What more did he want? I told this nigga. I. *Told.* Him. Now, *he* was 'bout to get caught up for being hardheaded, and *we* gotta get him out.

I was not ungrateful for the things Aaron and Thomas did for me. Aaron risked his life and even took a punch off of Pooch to help me. Granted, he got one hell of a collar on his job for assisting, but the point was the whole reason he asked to be on the assignment was because of me, and his brother, Thomas, stepped up from local hustlin' to the big leagues to make sure all aspects were covered. Therefore, we knew between the information Trinity was unknowingly feeding us, Big Cal being able to obtain personal records, and Tot's dealing with

Pooch, we was gon' hit that nigga hard in them pockets and put his ass away. Without them, I may not have had an opportunity to have Trinity back. At least not the way I wanted—as my wife—so, for that I was more than grateful to them. We'd always been the closest three in my family, but my obligation had to be to Trinity and my kids. I just couldn't keep getting tied up in this street life bullshit. So, here I was, torn between helping out the nigga who helped me get my life back, or staying out of the shit so that the life he helped me get back wouldn't be jeopardized. Ugh.

"What's on your mind, baby?" Trinity whispered in my ear and kissed it as we lay in bed together. I loved when she woke up in the morning and kissed on me.

"How'd you know I was up?" I asked, turning to face her.

"I could feel you—thinking."

What the hell? Did she have some kinda sixth sense no one knew about? That shit was eerie.

"Just running over some things in my mind. Nothing major."

"Liar."

"Now, why you think I'm lying?" I asked, looking at her, puzzled.

She pursed her lips. "Baby, nothing gets you riled up even when it should. You are the most laid back and even-tempered person I know, so when you're up thinking about shit early in the morning, it most definitely has to be major. So, you wanna tell me what the hell is really going on? You've been acting weird since Aaron and Thomas left yesterday."

My baby knew me so well. Too well. Losing her and my kids again was the only thing that could get up under my skin. Trinity had been in my life since I was just nineteen years old. Even while I was doing my bid, she was all I thought about. I kept her picture on the wall in my cell and a picture of her and our kids under my pillow. So, every night I went to sleep with my family beside me, and her face was the first and the last I saw every morning and night. Sure, I'd been with plenty of other chicks before I hooked up with Trinity, but none of them were real or down for me like she was, nor had I ever known love—real love—until I met Trinity.

I loved her like I had never and would never love another woman. She held me down and gave me my kids. I knew then that nothing and no one would ever come between us. Shit, even the couple of broads that I was with after I got out of jail were only to release the pressure and frustration from being locked up and to keep me at ease enough not to kill Pooch. Muthafucka got me locked up and then gon' go after my lady. I shoulda shot that bitch between the eyes the moment my feet hit free land, but the purpose of getting out was to stay out. So, I kept my eyes on my prize: getting my li'l mama back. Now that I had her back officially as my wife, I was determined not to have to live a life without her.

I pulled her toward me. "It ain't nothing for you to worry over. Trust me."

She looked at me strangely. "It's about Pooch, isn't it?"

"No, Trinity, come on. That's under control. Don't worry."

"Your lips are saying one thing, but your actions are saying I should worry," Trinity said. "Dreads, be straight up with me. I'm not one of the kids, and you don't have to shield me from everything."

I rubbed the back of my neck in frustration. "It's my job to shield you. Li'l mama, please let me deal with it. I got it," I said with frustration.

"Do I need to call Aaron myself?" she asked, turning to pick up her iPhone.

I pulled the phone from her hands. "No. Let it go," I said seriously. "Wait a minute. What the hell are you doing with Aaron's number?"

"He gave it to me when we first got to Chi town," she explained, taking her phone back and putting it on the nightstand. "It was just to keep in contact or if I had any questions about Pooch. Get back to the subject at hand, damn Aaron's number."

I got up, walked to her nightstand, and picked up her iPhone. "There ain't no subject to discuss," I said, scrolling through her contact list. Damn, it was right there: Aaron "Big Cal" Marsh's cell phone number and email address.

"Why do you have Aaron's email address?"

"Terrence, you need to focus on telling me what's going on." She crossed her arms defiantly.

"*Again*, why do you have Aaron's email address?" I asked, glaring at her with the phone in my hand.

"Did you just '*Pooch*' me?" She laughed. "Boy, stop." She fanned me off.

My nose flared. Now I was about to get pissed. "Trinity, I ain't playing."

She rolled her eyes and snatched her phone. "We exchange funny jokes over email. You know, email forwards and shit. The things people do with *modern technology*. Why are you so twisted about it?"

"I'm not. I'm just curious."

"Why?"

"'Cause I mean—Trin, you know I'm just jealous like that." I sat down beside her.

"Over Aaron?" she asked, staring at me as if I was crazy.

"*Over any nigga*," I corrected, rubbing my forehead.

This Pooch shit and this Tot shit was really fucking with me.

She got up and straddled my lap and wrapped her arms around my neck. "You know damn well that I am Mrs. Kincaid. There is no other nigga who can come between that," she reassured me, and we began to kiss.

"Fuck, li'l mama. I just get so crazy over you. It scares me," I admitted, shaking my head as I rubbed my hands across her ass. "I've had to live without you too long. I can't do that shit no more."

She kissed me all about my face and then lips. "You don't have to. I'm your wife, and I'm not going anywhere. I love you, Terrence."

That did it for me. I looked into my wife's big, beautiful, almond-shaped eyes and fell in love harder than I was just seconds before. Trinity was my entire reason for existing. I swear I didn't realize I could love a woman more than I loved myself, but it was definitely possible.

With love in my heart and lust in my eyes, I stood up and laid her on her back so I could take in the contours of her body and the curve of her backside in the sexiest pink teddy I'd ever seen held together by two pieces of string. I prided myself for giving her the bodacious booty courtesy of Terry and Brit.

I licked my lips, thinking of things I wanted to do to her. "I love you too, li'l mama." I bent down and kissed her on the neck. "Let me make love to you, baby," I whispered in her ear.

She nodded in agreement. "Anything you want, baby."

Kneeling down, I eased down her thong. As I slid the fabric down her creamy milk chocolate thighs, I got excited as if it were my first time with her. Every time I made love to my wife felt like a new experience. I lifted her foot and began sucking on her toes. I loved the color of her polish—jasmine, of course. I gave each toe special attention as she blessed me with a show, using her two fingers to strum her womanhood. Her moans were intoxicating as I slid my tongue up her leg to her thigh and lightly blew on her clit before I slipped the bud into my mouth.

She grabbed my dreadlocks. "Oh damn, Dreads!" she moaned.

I wanted her to save all of her climax for me, so I rose and licked the few trickles of her sweet nectar that lingered on my lips. I was about to pull down my pajama pants when Trinity sat up and did it for me. Before I knew it, my manhood was inside of her warm and inviting mouth.

Damn it, man. Her head game was out of this fucking world. She was the only woman I'd ever been with who knew just what to do and who could swallow me whole. Trust me when I say both were a big feat to accomplish, if you get what I'm saying. I struggled to hold on to the back of her head as my eyes rolled back in mine. I couldn't take it. She was making me weak in the knees, and I buckled.

She giggled. "You already weak? I haven't even brought you to a climax yet, baby."

I put my finger up. "Just give me . . . whoa . . . damn. Give me a sec," I fumbled, trying to gain my composure as she continued to giggle.

I stood up weakly, then Trinity pushed me down on the bed and straddled me. She placed my manhood inside of her, and I gripped that juicy backside. She was putting her back into it as she glided up and down with ease. I had to admit that Trinity had definitely picked up some hella skills since she was fifteen. I was used to putting it down, but my baby had me whipped. Yep, I was whipped, and I was not ashamed to say it.

"Baby, I love you," I moaned. "I love you so fucking much."

"I love you too," she moaned as she dove deeper on my nature.

My eyes rolled back, and my toes curled.

Trinity leaned close to me and whispered in my ear, "Come for me, baby."

"Ah, shit," I hollered as I gripped her by her shoulders and exploded. "Say you'll never leave me," I belted as she came to her climax too.

"I. Won't. Ever. Leave," she panted, struggling to catch her breath.

Before she could move, I pulled her down on top of me and held her in my arms. There was no way I could ever risk losing any more time with this woman. I just wanted to raise our kids and grow old together. I was entitled to this. More importantly, Trinity deserved a man who was going to be around for her forever.

"Baby, what is really going on?" Trinity whispered in my ear. "I'm all for affection, but something ain't right."

Like I said, she knew me. There was no use hiding it, so I decided to be honest. "Pooch is offering info on Tot so he can be released."

She sat up and looked at me. "*What?*"

"Calm down, baby—"

"No. See, I knew something was gonna happen." She jumped up and paced the floor.

Following suit, I jumped up, pulled her to me, and held her close. "Stop. It's not gonna happen. I'ma take care of everything."

Suddenly, she pulled away from me. "*How?* What does that mean, Terrence, to *take care of everything*? No, I don't want you risking your life—"

"No, I'm not risking my life. I'm just not losing you or the kids again. I put that on everything I love and that's you all."

Clearly upset, she huffed, shaking her head. "Promise me you'll stay out of this and let Aaron handle it."

"Trinity, I—"

She threw her hands on her hips. "*Promise me.*"

"I promise that nothing will happen to me—"

"*Terrence Reginald Kincaid,*" she cut me off, giving me the evil eye.

"Baby, you know I can't leave Thomas and Aaron out there alone with this. I have to do something to protect our future," I confessed.

She shook her head angrily and walked off toward our bathroom. "Fine. Get your ass locked up or killed. I guess me and the kids will just deal with it when it comes."

"*Trinity*!" I yelled as she kept walking. "*Trinity Krystal Kincaid.*"

She turned around in the doorway of the bathroom. "What do you want me to say, Terrence? Huh? Go out there and be Geronimo? You're my *husband.* I need you around. The kids need you around. This is a dangerous game you're playing, and I'm tired of it. Pooch doesn't know where we are, and I seriously doubt he'd get out. Just stay away from the situation. Aaron and Thomas are just gonna have to understand. Now, you told me not to worry about Pooch. I'm asking you to do the same."

I felt the same way she did, but how could I risk the unknown? I was ready to give Tot and Aaron my high mighty speech, but the thoughts of losing Trinity that invaded my mind during our lovemaking changed me, and I knew I had to do something. The key was doing a little but not getting too drastic with it.

"Trinity, everything I do is for you and the kids. I just have to do something to take care of this situation. Say you understand, please, li'l mama."

She turned around, walked inside our bathroom, and slammed the door. I just plopped down on the bed. I was damned if I did and damned if I didn't.

***

All morning Trinity had ignored me, ever since I told her I was planning on doing something to keep the monkey better known as Pooch Smalls off our back. I decided to stay in my office most of the day until it was time for this little get together. Besides, I had to figure out what exactly I was gonna do that would be enough to deter Pooch's plans and keep me a married man.

When I finally came out to check out the situation, everything was turned off in the kitchen. "Where's your mom?" I asked Brit.

"Getting dressed. Can we eat under the tent outside and play volleyball afterwards?"

I smiled at her. "Sure. Okay, you and Terry set the table for me and Mommy."

As soon as I walked back inside the house, the doorbell rang. I ran to the door to find Aaron and Thomas at the door.

"Cuzzo!" Thomas and Aaron greeted me.

"It smells good up in here," Thomas said, rubbing his stomach.

"Yeah, y'all come to the back yard. We're eating out there."

Aaron hit Thomas. "Our cuz has really been hanging out with them white boys. This nigga got on linen shorts."

I laughed at him, looking down at my khaki linen shorts, V-neck fitted white T-shirt, and brown slides. What could I say? Being legit made you dress and act different.

"Shit, T has always been the pretty muthafucka of the group." Thomas chuckled. "If he ain't supa fly, he ain't right."

"Y'all niggas got jokes. I should send you on the road hungry."

"Man, please. There is a Mickey D's on every major intersection in America." Thomas laughed.

"But I bet it won't taste as good as Trinity's cooking," Aaron said.

"When have you tasted Trinity's cooking?" I asked, puzzled by his statement.

He playfully hit me in the chest. "Pooch gave me some chicken wings once that she'd fried up. *Ohhh weeee.* That's when I knew I had to get me a Southern girl. I ain't never tasted chicken that good," he said as we walked outside to the covered patio.

Thomas laughed. "Yeah, man, he talked about that chicken for at least two weeks. Had me going to Roscoe's and every Popeyes for at least a week straight."

I chuckled as I walked over to the cooler and grabbed a beer. I was about to ask if either of them wanted one when Aaron came up behind me.

"Can I get one of those?" he asked.

"Sure." I handed him one. "Cal, let me ask you a question."

"Shoot," he agreed, taking a swig of his beer.

"How come you gave Trinity your cell phone and email address?" I asked, drinking another swig of beer.

Finessing his beard, he shrugged. "She was a little worried about Pooch, and since I am in law enforcement and I was his right hand man, I told her if she had any questions or concerns, she could call me, and I'd handle them."

"I'd prefer it if all the info about Pooch comes through me."

Facing me, he frowned with look of slight confusion. "And it does. When I came here yesterday, what did I tell Trinity? Nothing. I came to see you first. Damn, T, give me some credit. I just gave her the number to put her at ease. I witnessed firsthand the hell that Pooch put her through, so all I was doing was trying to appease her."

For a moment, I contemplated his reason, then decided it wasn't worth the argument. "All right. You're right."

"So, my dude, have you thought of something?" Thomas asked, interrupting our conversation.

Choosing to let that tidbit go with Aaron, I focused on the subject at hand. "Yeah, I believe so," I answered, looking at both of them. "Stein is appealing to Judge Watson, right?"

"Yeah," Aaron confirmed.

"We all know Watson is crooked as hell. He's been crooked since we were in high school, getting niggas locked up on trumped-up charges," I said as they nodded in agreement. "So, we kill it at the source. We go after Watson. At the end of the day, money talks and bullshit walks." Since Judge Watson was a crook, maybe I could get away with bribery instead of doing anything extreme, which would hopefully please Trinity.

Aaron laughed. "Boy, T, you came out the box on that one." He pounded it up with me. "If it's one thing we know is that Watson bleeds green."

"That's why I'm the brains of this operation. Look, Aaron, get some anonymous nigga to tell Watson to decline any plea bargain for Pooch, and tell him to name his price."

"Name his price?" Aaron said as he and Thomas looked at each other. "You may wanna put a cap on that, cuz."

Realizing they were right, I looked back and forth at them as I thought of a good round figure. "Start off at one hundred grand. Get that offer on the table ASAP."

Thomas reached out and hugged me. "Thank you, man."

"Don't thank me yet, because you paying me back. I'm just doing this to keep Aaron's nose clean and so it won't be traced to you, but I do expect my little duffle bag to be full within two weeks after this little transaction goes through."

Thomas shrugged. "That's cool. I'm just thanking you for looking out for me."

"Yeah, well, after this shit, your D-boy days best be over," I warned him. "I mean that shit, Tot. I'm not doing this shit again."

He nodded. "All right. Bet that," he agreed.

Aaron patted my shoulder. "'Preciate that, cuz. I'll make sure he flies straight."

"All right. I'ma hold you to that too, Aaron. Call me next week with the particulars so we can get this shit on a roll. I need it over and done with quick."

Aaron, Thomas, and I sat there for about ten minutes more, shooting the breeze as we watched the kids play. I decided to get up and check on Trinity to see what was taking her so long. At this point, everybody was hungry and ready to eat.

"Looking for me?" she asked, and we all turned toward the doorway.

My eyes nearly popped out of my head. She had on some kind of halter top sundress that stopped barely mid-thigh with some wedge sandals. The front of it revealed just a little more cleavage than she needed to be showing. To make it worse, she had her hair pinned up, so there was a clear visual from the neck down. Now, I'm not gonna lie. She was rockin' the hell out of this getup, but I was uncomfortable with her rockin' it in front of my cousins.

"Yeah, babe, we . . . uh . . . we all are ready to eat," I stammered.

She fanned me off. "A lady always makes an entrance. Besides, you ain't starving. Let me speak to our guests first." She dismissed me, walking over to Thomas.

"Hey, Trin, what's up?" Thomas hugged her.

When I saw the back of that dress, I could've tore some shit up. It was backless, not just at the shoulders as I would've suspected, but midway down her back. Not to mention, she had on a sexy-ass scent that lingered long after she'd walked away. What the fuck was she doing?

"Hey, Aaron," she greeted him.

"Girl, you get more beautiful every day," he said.

"Big Cal, I can always depend on you for a beautiful compliment." She blushed and hugged him. "You hungry? I know you love my cooking."

"Shit, yeah. I didn't think nobody could fry chicken better than my grandma, but you do have her beat," Aaron said.

"See what I mean? You're a sweetheart, Big Cal."

"I'll help you bring out the food," I said to Trinity as I grabbed her by the hand, walking behind her into the kitchen. "What the fuck do you have on?" I asked no sooner than we were safe inside the house.

She shrugged nonchalantly. "A sundress."

"*Half of one*," I seethed. "You know I'm pissed off, right?"

"Join the club," she said smartly.

"Okay, I'm trying to protect us, and you're trying to piss me off." I paced angrily. "I don't want you in that dress. Take it off."

Her eye roll caught my attention as she fanned me off before crossing her arms. "I'm grown. Boy, please."

"So, you just gon' disrespect me like this?" I asked her, getting angrier.

Trinity turned to me with a sinister look on her face. "Big Cal likes it," she said snidely and turned around.

Before I knew what came over me, I snatched her and turned her around while gripping her arms. "What the fuck did you just say to me? Be clear. You will not disrespect me in my own house."

Trinity's eyes filled with tears, then she snatched away and slapped me. "Don't you ever put your hands on me. I put up with that shit from Pooch. I will not go through it again. Do you hear me?"

Her words stung me, and I shook my head as I snapped back into reality. "Trinity, baby, I'm so sorry—"

She backed up, and her scared reaction stopped me in midsentence. "Grab the trays, take the food outside, and leave me alone," she ordered while taking a paper towel and drying her teary eyes.

"Li'l mama, I was just—"

She cut me off. "Not now, Terrence. Take the food out to our guests and leave me alone."

As far as I was concerned, this food could wait, but I knew she didn't want to see me right now, so I relented. "I'm so sorry, baby," I apologized as she turned her back to me. Walking up behind her, I kissed her cheek, but she tensed up, so I grabbed the trays of food and left out so I could tell everyone to get prepared to eat.

I decided to go ahead and bless the food, and I made the kids' plates, and then I told Aaron and Thomas to go ahead and eat. I was just about to go check on Trinity when she walked out with Tyson in her arms and Princess walking beside her. When Princess spotted Aaron, she smiled and tried to run for him. He got up and picked her up before she could fall down.

"Hi, Cal." Princess grinned.

"What's up, little Princess?" Aaron said. "Man, Trinity, she is getting so big. I miss seeing my little buddy," he said, tickling her. "I'll tell you what. You're gonna have to beat the men off with a stick because she looks just like you, so I know she's gonna be one beautiful woman," Aaron complimented before hugging Princess and putting her down.

Trinity smiled demurely. “She’ll have you to watch her back, though.”

Now, I sat there holding my son and observed the scene and conversation. Trinity and Aaron. How close had these two really gotten during his stint as Pooch’s right-hand man? I felt like an outsider in my own house. And trust me; I didn’t forget that fucking comment Trinity said in the kitchen. *Big Cal likes it.* Big Cal liked a lot of things that I was noticing lately.

The funniest shit to me was that Aaron kept complimenting the food and even volunteered to feed Princess for Trinity so she could eat. Now, this nigga didn’t volunteer to feed Tyson for me so I could eat, and I was this nigga’s cousin. Uh-huh.

“Man, Trinity, my brother was right. You damn sure can burn girl. *Wooo.* I am stuffed. We may have to take a nap before we get on the road.” Thomas laughed.

“You just make sure you take a plate to go,” Trinity said.

“You already know it’s going down,” Aaron added.

“I’m glad everyone enjoyed the meal. I’m going to lay Tyson down for a nap then start washing up,” she said as she picked up Tyson. Princess followed her inside.

“Yo, Terrence, can I talk you in private for a moment?” Thomas asked.

“Yeah,” I agreed reluctantly as we walked off the patio toward the play area. I kept an eye on Aaron, who was on the patio, drinking a beer.

“Look, man, I really appreciate you having my back with this. I think it’s gonna work. On the humble, thank you,” he said, bringing my attention back to him.

Unable to fully focus on what he was saying, I returned my gaze to Aaron. He was still drinking his beer. “Don’t mention it. We’re family,” I said. “On the real, though, Tot, you need to let that street shit go. You can’t still be out there with this foolishness. All I want you to do is keep your nose clean," I lectured as we gave each other a one-arm hug.

"You right. Bet that."

"Dad, will you and Thomas play basketball with us?" Terry asked.

"Yeah, man," I said as Thomas and I ran onto the court. "Me and Brit against you and Thomas."

"All right. We're gonna win, Daddy." Brit laughed.

"You know it," I told her.

"Man, please. We got this," Thomas said, high-fiving Terry.

"Whatever, my dude. Don't take this ass whipping personally." I laughed, snatching the ball from Thomas.

We started playing, and soon we were engrossed in the game. In fact, Brit and I were up eight to six when I glanced at the patio and noticed Aaron wasn't there.

"This old man has to take a restroom break," I said.

"Ahh, Dad," Brit whined.

"Seriously, Thomas, will you stay here and watch them?"

"Of course. Go take a leak, old man," he joked.

I hit him in the shoulder playfully and ran off. I eased my way into the house and stood in the entry of the kitchen, where Aaron was standing beside Trinity while she washed dishes. Good. Their backs were turned to me, so they had no clue I was there.

"Thanks for bringing the dishes in for me," Trinity told him.

"Ain't no thang. You know I don't mind," he replied. "You know this is why you have a dishwasher. You don't need to be messing up your nails doing no damn dishes."

"Spoken like a true bachelor. I always wash my dishes before putting them in the dishwasher. If not, you'll have dried-up crud on them."

"Umph. I didn't know that. You can tell that I only eat out or visit someone else's table. I ain't like T. I don't have a dime at the house that can cook, clean, and look good while doing it."

She giggled. "You're a mess. Don't worry. You'll have all of that one day, Detective Marsh."

He licked his lips and grinned. "Oh, so it's Detective Marsh now?"

"Well, I was trying to get you to change hats for a minute."

He sighed, rubbing his beard. "Oh. Let me guess. Pooch."

She nodded. "Why you didn't tell me what was going on?"

He put his hands on the counter and leaned over to her. "I didn't want to worry you. You know I'm not gon' let nothing come up that would hurt you."

Trinity rubbed her forehead. "Big Cal, I just want this shit to be over."

Aaron turned toward her and placed his hands on her shoulders. "It will be. I'ma make sure of it. Don't you worry about nothing, a'ight?" he said, gently massaging her shoulders.

That was my cue. I'd seen enough and walked in. "Yep, everything is gonna be all right because *I'm* taking care of it," I announced as Aaron pulled back from Trinity. They both turned around to see me standing there.

"Jesus, Terrence, we didn't even see you," Trinity said in shock.

"I know." I looked back and forth between the two of them.

"Yeah, man. I was just reassuring her that we got that Pooch shit under control," Aaron said.

"So I see." I eyed him. "What time are you all leaving?"

He looked at his watch. "I guess now. I made Thomas and me some to-go plates."

Everybody said their goodbyes, and then I walked Thomas and Aaron to their truck.

"All right. Time to handle business," I said.

"Consider it handled," Aaron said.

"Yeah, I know you have mine and Trinity's back."

"Always, cuz," Aaron said.

"All right, cuz. Again, I appreciate you," Thomas said, one-arm hugging me.

"Ain't nothing. Just do as I said in the future," I told him. Then, I turned to face Aaron. "I trust you to do your thang. I *can* trust you, right?"

Aaron looked at me as if I were crazy. "Of course you can, man. Always."

"I'm holding you to that."

When I walked in the house, Trinity was sitting in the family room, watching television. "Are they gone?" she asked.

"Yep. We need to talk."

"We can talk later. Right now, I just wanna rest." She yawned.

"Whatever, but we *will* talk," I said to her as I left out and sprinted up to the room to take a nap of my own. I don't know what the fuck the deal was with Aaron and Trinity, but I knew I'd come too far with this to be disrespected by the two people in the world I trusted the most. Yeah, I was a jealous muthafucka, but this wasn't about that. I didn't like this fucking friendship between them, so something was gonna have to give. That I meant.

Chapter Eighteen

Trinity

Terrence and I still weren't on good terms. To be honest, ever since our blowup over Big Cal, I'd been avoiding him. I left for my art gallery before he awakened, and most nights, I'd stay awake until he fell asleep. Hell, I was close to moving into one of the guest bedrooms altogether. He'd rescued me from the entrapment of Pooch only to turn around and get entangled in the same foolishness. What the fuck was the point in changing our names and moving if we were going to be tracked down because he refused to let sleeping thugs lie? He knew firsthand the power that Pooch had. He'd touched him. Just because he was a free man now didn't mean that Pooch couldn't touch him again. Moreover, this time, Pooch would touch me too. What would happen to our children if Pooch killed us?

Then, to add insult to injury, he'd put his hands on me. Out of all the people in the world, Terrence was the last person that I thought would do something like that to me. Pooch, yes. I really wasn't even surprised when his jealous ass turned physical. Hell, I'd expected it to happen a lot sooner. But Terrence? Never in a million years. Regardless of what we went through, he'd never been the type. I didn't know if it was the bid he had done or the chickenhead bitches he fucked around with before we got back together, but the mere fact that he'd reached that point with me bothered me. If he thought he could start trying to control me through physical abuse, then he had another thing coming. The first and last man to do that to me was Pooch. No other man would get that chance again. Not even Terrence. Until he could properly apologize for what he did and leave this Pooch vendetta alone, then he could prepare himself for many more lonely days.

As I rode to the art gallery, I connected my phone to my car's internal speaker and dialed a number.

"Charice Westmore speaking," Charice answered her private line.

"Hey, Charice."

She gasped, and I heard her moving about before everything went quiet and she spoke again. "Trinity?" she whispered. "How are you calling me? I thought you all were disconnecting from everyone until the coast was clear."

"We are," I said around a sigh. "But I needed to talk to someone, and I knew you were the safest since Ryan has y'all's shit secured like Fort Knox because of his celebrity status."

"Yeah, that helps me, but how does that help you?"

I scoffed at my friend's naiveté. "Girl, this is a burner that I just picked up for cash at the corner store. You think I'm that crazy? Hell, I wasn't with a D-boy all them years and didn't learn nothing."

Charice giggled. "Valid point. So, girl, what's going on? I haven't spoken with you in so long, and I've missed you. But I also know if you're calling me, especially from a new phone, then something is up."

"Does Ryan know any hitmen who can off someone in prison?"

"Uhh, I'm gonna pretend like I didn't just hear that and this conversation never happened."

"I'm just joking, Charice, although a girl can wish."

"Please don't make me disconnect this line!"

I rolled my eyes at my scared friend. "Okay, but something is up. Apparently, you-know-who is trying all kinds of things to get out of his little situation, including snitching on his business partners."

Charice made an *awe* sound in realization. "So, now the family could be exposed?"

"Right. And my husband wants to be involved to help resolve this foolishness. That is the last thing I want him to do."

"Have you told him that?"

"Would I be calling you if I hadn't and he didn't listen?" I asked smartly. "He's hell bent on helping the family, claiming to ensure our protection."

"That's risky as hell."

"You're preaching to the choir on that one, honey," I agreed, flailing my hand in the air.

Releasing a frustrated deep breath, Charice quipped, "T really needs to leave this alone. I understand that it's family involved, but you and the kids are the most important thing. Besides, what is the real possibility of him getting out of the current predicament? He's got life four times over."

Excitedly, I hit my steering wheel. "Yes. That's exactly what the fuck I'm saying, Charice. Like, there isn't a real threat. I know he's concerned, but he's going to make a mountain where there is only a mole hill."

"I feel you, girl," Charice said sadly. "I wish there was something that I could do for you. I know that's got to be hard. And then we're not near you or can even really communicate for now."

She was right about that. There was really nothing anyone could do, and I missed my girls so much. I loved my life with Terrence and the kids, but I hardly had any family in Evanston, and everyone who I was close to, outside of him and the kids, lived away from us. I couldn't communicate with them, for now, to keep us safe. It was a lonely existence, especially when Terrence did have some family in the area that he could spend time with and confide in.

"Honey, just hearing your voice is enough right now," I admitted as I pulled into my parking spot in front of my art gallery. "I just wanted to talk to someone about this craziness going on in my life. I needed some type of reassurance that I wasn't being selfish or not understanding toward my husband."

"Well, he should really let his cousin, the law enforcement, do his job when it comes to this situation. Isn't that why he volunteered to be a part of this whole sting operation in the first place?"

"My next point," I agreed. "Telling him that is a taboo subject. I'm itching to call Big Cal to ask him to intervene and keep T out of this, but if T found out I did that, he'd go berserk. He already feels a way about me communicating with him as is. Like as if I'd ever do something with his kinfolk."

Charice scoffed. "Really? There's literally nothing for him to be worried about when it comes to that. For one, that's his family and you are not that kind of woman. He knows that. For two, last time I remember seeing his cousin, bruh was not fond of cuteness, if you know what I'm saying."

Her dig sent me into a fit of laughter. Wiping the playful tears from my eyes, I shook my head. "Nope, girl. You know you're dead-ass wrong for that. I will not join in with you on that foolery."

"You know I'm right." Charice giggled. "That nigga is a straight-up Biggie song."

"Biggie song?" I asked, confused.

“Black and ugly as ever,” she said, and we both howled.

Holding my stomach from the cramping pain, I said, “See, you know what? I cannot fool up with you. Whew, chile. But you know Biggie said he still stayed Coogi down to the socks now.”

“Shit, that’s ’cause Biggie had a rap career and money. Ain’t a whole lot of women checking for no police detective with a barely-there pension.”

“Shit, these bitches be lucky to get a man that’s loyal. That pension will have them twerking a little sumthin’,” I joked, and this time Charice hollered hysterically in my ear.

“You know what, sis? You right.”

“Ryan done made you forget. A policeman with a barely-there pension is a downgrade for you, Mrs. A-list celebrity Real Housewife of New York, but a lot of these women would just be glad to say they have someone who has a job, let alone an actual career,” I explained, and Charice agreed. “But career, pension, and all, I gotta admit that nigga ain’t nothing cute to look at, though.”

Charice laughed. “See, look at you. Talking about me.”

“The truth is the truth. I can’t argue with you there.” I shook my head. “And like you said, he’s family, so I would never. Hell, if he wasn’t family, I still would never.”

“*That motherfucking part*,” Charice hollered.

We carried on for a little while longer. I couldn’t help it. I enjoyed joking and talking to my girl. I missed this and her so much; all of them. If there was one thing that I wish I hadn’t had to sacrifice in all this was my time with them. My girls had been so integral in my life, and then all of a sudden, they just weren’t. It was an unfillable void.

“Well, girl, let me get out of this car before one of my workers gets worried about me. I don’t need my warden husband getting upset with me for breaking protocol. We don’t need any more reasons to bump heads.”

"I understand, girl. Your secret is safe with me."

My shoulders slumped, knowing that our phone call was about to end. "Well, all right, girl," I said, downtrodden.

"I know. I miss your ass, too."

"I love you, girl."

"I love you too, and look, the only thing you can do is tell him the way you feel. If he insists on continuing that bullshit plan, just pray for the best and do what you gotta do to protect your man, your family, and yourself. All things aside, T loves the hell outta you, and though his mindset is ridiculous, he's only doing this because he loves you and he's just as scared of something happening to y'all as you are. And for that, you can't knock the man. He's doing what most men do. Real men anyway. Trying to protect his family, even if he doesn't see the detriment in it."

And that right there was why I had called Charice. Out of all of us, I knew I could speak to her safely and privately, but that she'd also give me very sound advice. More than ever, I needed that.

"Thank you, Charice. You know just what to say."

"And that's why you called me," she joked. "Go inside before the warden calls you to his office."

"Love you, girl."

"Love you too."

We disconnected, and I gathered my things and walked inside to start my day at the gallery. I didn't have all the answers I needed, but at least I had a sense of calm. Since I already knew Terrence was as bullheaded as they come, I also knew there was nothing I could say to stop him from doing what he felt he needed to do. That part pissed me off, but all I could do was keep myself calm and brace for the impact, whatever that impact may be.

Chapter Nineteen

Ryan

This was exactly what I needed. I had my iTunes, my LIFEWTR, a good pair of brand-new running Nikes, and complete and total isolation as I ran around the track. There was nothing better to relieve stress than good old-fashioned exercise, and believe me, I'd be out there all day if I could because I had a lot of stress to unwind. Hell, the way I felt, I could've run a fucking marathon. Running was the one thing I was great at. It took my mind off everything and everybody around me. When I was running, I was like one with the wind. My spirit felt free as my body ignited. I was the fastest running back in the league, and when I was in my element, nothing else mattered.

Nothing else mattered but . . .

I met this chick and she just moved right up the block from me . . . and she got the hots for me, the finest thing I need to see, but oh no, no, she got a man and a son, oh oh, but that's okay.

The lyrics to Nelly's song "Dilemma" flooded my ears.

"*Shit*," I said aloud, snatching my iPhone out of my arm strap to forward to another song. Instead, I pressed the damn fast forward button.

No matter what I do, all I think about is you. Even when I'm with my boo, you know I'm crazy over you."

I heard the chorus of the song crashing through the headphones.

"*Fuck me.*" I grabbed the damn iPhone again.

I was a die-hard Nelly fan, but today Nelly was on his way to losing a fan if I didn't get this damn song to change immediately. I hurriedly hit the shuffle button, glad that "Dilemma" was no longer playing on my iPhone and breaking my focus. I know what I needed—some good *hardcore* rap. Yeah, that was it. I could always count on my dude T.I. to put down some ol' gangsta shit for me.

Can't help but notice how you glowing. I can see in yo' face. Now I wonder if he know he close to being replaced.

The lyrics to "Why You Wanna" came blaring through the headphones.

Ugh. Hell to the fucking no. What the fuck? I thought as I snatched the iPhone out and just turned it off. Out of all the damn songs about rims, hoes, money, and dope this dude put out, I had to hear the one song he made about taking another nigga's woman.

So, it's Fuck with Ryan Week, I thought as my mind unwillingly replayed the event that led me to this moment of stress and mental anguish. . . .

The blood damn near drained completely out of me. Here I was, dick deep in my wife's ass, having the greatest anal experience of my life and one of the best climaxes in my life when all of a sudden, she called me Lincoln. My heart felt as if it was going to explode. I'd never in my life felt so low and hurt, yet so fucking angry at the same time. My body was fighting all kinds of emotions. It was the first time in my life that I actually wanted to put my hands on Charice and strangle the shit outta her. Out of all the shit in the world to do, she called me another man's name during sex—and not just any man. Lincoln.

"What the fuck did you just call me?" I screamed at Charice. I spun her around so fast she slipped and hit her back against the wall of the shower with a loud thud.

Instantly, her eyes filled with tears, and her body began to tremble uncontrollably. "I . . . I didn't . . . I don't—Oh my God," she stammered as she cried profusely.

I stepped up close in her face as she backed up with nowhere to go but against the wall. My eyes misted, and I could literally feel them burning from anger. "Are you fucking him, Charice?" I asked tensely as I slammed my bare hand against the tile of the shower wall.

"No! I—" She jumped, stuttering weakly.

I shook my head, cutting her off. "Oh my fucking God," I said, running my hands over my head. "You're fucking him," I yelled as I flung open the shower door and jumped out, wrapping a towel around my waist. "Unfuckingbelievable."

Charice jumped out of the shower and threw on her robe, following me as I stormed into my closet. "Baby, wait. No, you can't believe that. It's not true. Lincoln and I haven't been intimate since the night we made . . ." Her voice trailed off.

I turned to face her with anger in my eyes. "Go ahead and say it. Since the night you made Lexi. He was the last man to impregnate you, so I guess that's where your fucking devotion lies. I can't believe you. After all we've been through, you'd betray our marriage. Our marriage, Charice? For Christ's sake, we've lost a child together, and you do something like this?"

She wiped her tears and looked at me as if she could kill me. "Don't you dare bring Charity into this. You will not disrespect her memory. Now, I told you I didn't sleep with Lincoln, and I meant it."

"So, you just randomly called his name for no fucking reason—during sex, might I add—or were you just wishing it was him fucking you instead of me?"

"Baby, please. It's not even like that. I love only you. I've only been with you." She cried a river of tears.

I slid on my boxers and some jean shorts. "Yeah, okay. Yet you called his name while I was making love to you. I'm really supposed to believe that."

"Yes, you are. I'm your wife, Ryan. Do you really think I would do something like that to you?" she pleaded.

I looked at her as if she were crazy. "After all the ill shit I've done to you in the past, and let us not forget that last year you were Lincoln's fiancée, yes, I do believe anything is possible. Why should I not believe it, Charice? You called out his name while I was making love to you. Jesus Christ. I mean, this was a first for the both of us."

She swallowed a lump in her throat and attempted to grab my hand, but I snatched it away. Right now, I couldn't stand to be in the same room with Charice, let alone touch her.

"Baby, listen to me. I would never do you dirty like that. I wouldn't have agreed to be your wife if I hadn't forgiven you for all the things you'd done to me in the past. I put that behind me, just like I put Lincoln behind me when I became Mrs. Westmore."

I looked deep into her pleading eyes, and that's when it hit me. I laughed. "Oh my God. I know what it is."

Charice looked confused. "Wh . . . what?"

"This wasn't your first time being penetrated. Let me guess. Lincoln did it first," I said angrily.

Charice looked down, and her only response was to nod in agreement.

"Wow. You really had it bad for this nigga. I remember begging you the last time we were together when I was in college to let me try it. Hell, I remember begging you when we first got married. You were so against it, as if it was such a new experience for you, but you let Lincoln do it," I said, slipping on my Nike slides and white T-shirt.

Charice caught my arm as I was leaving the closet. "Baby, wait. Please. Don't leave like this. I'm so sorry. I was wrong. It's just that—"

"It's just what?" I asked angrily. "You were reminiscing on how good he used to fuck you instead of focusing on me," I hollered, snatching away from her.

She began crying heavily again. "Ryan, I love you. I don't want to lose you. Please tell me how to make it right," she begged as I grabbed my wallet and my keys.

"I need to go right now. I can't even think past my anger," I said, grabbing the bedroom door handle.

"Please, baby. Just promise me you won't do anything crazy. Just come back so we can work this out."

I laughed snidely. "Oh, you don't want me to do nothing crazy like kill your secret lover or go dick down some bitch to prove a point?" I threw over my shoulder.

"Ryan, I don't want you going to jail, and no, I don't want you to fuck somebody else because I swear on my love for Charity that I'm only fucking you."

Damn. She swore on her love for Charity. I knew that was one thing she'd never play about. That calmed me down, but not nearly enough. I felt like I was suffocating. I had to get out of there for a while, so I swallowed the lump in my throat and bounced.

I headed straight to Lincoln's house, because dirty little secret or not, I was going to kick his ass and let the fucking chips fall where the fuck they fell. I didn't know what the fuck was going on, but a huge part of me believed Charice when she said she wasn't fucking Lincoln behind my back. That gave me a little of my dignity back, but not much, because the fact still remained that for some reason, she was thinking of Lincoln during our lovemaking. The anger in me just wanted to be pissed about it and get dick deep in some throwback pussy to even the score, but the part of me that truly loved Charice wouldn't let me do that, nor would it let me believe that after all this time, those memories came up without any help from Lincoln. Somehow, some way, I knew that bitch-ass nigga had something to do with this. I felt it in my bones.

Not to toot my own horn, but before I settled down with Charice, I was the biggest playa out there right along with Lincoln and our old crew of NFL playboys. So, I knew when a playa card had been played. Knowing Charice and knowing Lincoln, I knew he said or did something that would trigger her to say some bullshit like that. *I absolutely knew it.*

However, God must've been on my side and his, because that fucker wasn't home. So, I drove around aimlessly for about an hour, trying to give myself time to cool off. I stopped by Starbucks and got a newspaper and a black coffee and just meditated. Once I started getting too many requests for autographs and photos, I left.

Being a celebrity was like that. Sometimes you just wanted to be normal because you had real life shit going on just like normal people, but you couldn't tell the media and normal people that. They felt you owed them. Don't get me wrong, I loved and appreciated my fans because without them, I wouldn't have had this fancy life that I lived, but the main people who'd be complaining were the people who never paid for one ticket to see you play or bought one product that you endorsed. They were what I called spot-a-celebrity fans. Every time they spotted a celebrity, they instantly became your biggest fan just for the sake of getting a picture or autograph to take back and brag to their buddies as if they knew you on some personal level.

Hell, I understood it. As a kid, I would've been happy to see any celebrity myself, but the key word was *kid*. There were grown-ass people still living pipe dreams.

They were the main ones who, if you turned down an autograph, wanted to get on every gossip blog and call up the entertainment news or newspaper to say how arrogant you were and that people shouldn't support you, so they could get their fifteen minutes of shine—when the only thing you needed was some fucking coffee and peace of mind because an hour ago, your wife called you another man's name while you were fucking. But I couldn't say that aloud like normal people because that tidbit would be on every media source faster than I could sprint down a football field. So, I learned that while privacy was a right I was entitled to, it was a privilege that I inadvertently gave up the moment I signed my draft papers with the Dallas Cowboys, first entering the NFL. Thus, I signed my final autograph and headed my ass back to my own house for solace.

When I got home, I found Lexi asleep in her bassinette next to our bed, and Charice was still in her robe from the shower, lying on top of our bed.

"Are you asleep?" I asked her.

"No," she answered, sitting up and facing me. Her eyes were bloodshot red, and her face drenched with tears. "I had Johanna take the boys to school today. She and the boys asked me what was wrong. I just said I had a touch of the stomach flu. I gave Johanna the day off once she dropped the boys off."

"Oh," I said as I sat on the bed.

"So, where have you been? Or do I have a right to ask anymore?"

"At Starbucks."

"Oh."

To break up the awkward silence, I dove headfirst into this conversation so it could be over and done with. "I am tired of dwelling on this, so I'll get straight to the point. I've already come up with the fact that something happened between you and Lincoln. If you're not cheating, something had to have happened between you two to make you act out of character. I know you. What happened in the shower, that's not you."

She exhaled slowly, reaching for my hand, and I let her take it. "I saw Lincoln this morning on my morning jog. He apologized to me for leaving me and started harping on all of these old feelings and emotions. I cussed him out, but he wouldn't leave me alone at first, and then he . . . he grabbed me and hugged me, trying to caress me like old times. I pushed him off, threatened to tell you, and came home. I guess my mind was so riled up this morning with him on my brain that I just said it. I'm sorry, baby. I swear to God it'll *never* happen again."

It took a second for everything she'd said to process, but when it did, I was mad as hell. I blew up. "*Wait a minute.* He grabbed you and held you? Are you serious?"

"Baby, calm down. I put him in his place—"

I jumped up. "*Hell no.* I'm going to be the one to put him in his place. You're married, and he's crossing the fucking line. I'm not going to stand for this shit, Charice. What if he'd actually kissed you or forced himself on you? *Hell to the muthafucking no,*" I yelled as I paced back and forth.

"Baby, please," she said frantically as she ran in front of me. "Just let it go. I know you want to whip his ass, but really, what would that accomplish?"

"Teaching him a lesson and giving him one hell of an ass kicking are a couple of accomplishments to start out with."

Frantically, she grabbed my hands, forcing me to focus on her words. "Yes, and momentarily those reasons will seem worth it, but professionally, it will cost you more than what the trouble is worth. You know I'm not cheating. You know what his M.O. is, and you know we're better than this. Don't give him the satisfaction of knowing he was able to penetrate our marriage. If we are fighting each other, then we won't have time to protect our relationship. It's the oldest and most used trick in the book—divide and conquer."

I wrestled for a few moments between knowing what she said was the truth and knowing what I felt in my gut I wanted to do. Begrudgingly, I forced myself to concede to what was for the best. "Fine. I'll leave it alone. For you."

Those were the last words we'd spoken about the incident. However, it sure wasn't the last time it was on my mind. I knew Charice wasn't cheating, but still it does something to a man's ego when his wife—hell, even a jump off—called another man's name. I won't lie. That shit affected me. I couldn't even have sex with Charice the way I wanted to because of it. I could get it up, but I couldn't get to the finish line. So here I was, running, trying to relieve some stress from the situation—and from having the fucking blue balls—and still only finding stress in simple bullshit like songs.

After running two additional miles, one and a half of them iTunes free, I still was in no better shape than when I came to the track. All I could do was imagine Charice sleeping with Lincoln, and I still wanted to whip Lincoln's pretty-boy ass. I decided to call it quits and head over to the center to check on my paperwork and hopefully get up on a pickup game of basketball.

As I got to the parking lot, Lincoln pulled up in his Ford F250 truck and hopped out with his duffle bag.

"Fancy seeing you here, Mr. Westmore. How's it going?"

All of my anger ignited as if I were having a true *Kill Bill* moment, and I shoved him into his truck. "Fuck you, Lincoln."

"Get your hands off of me," he said tensely. "I'm not playing with you."

Charice's words floated into my mind. *Divide. Conquer.* So, I calmed down. "Fine." I released him. "But I'm warning you. Stay away from me and stay away from Charice," I said, backing away from him with my chest heaving up and down and my eyes dancing with anger.

"*Woooo,*" Lincoln said cynically as he shook his head, laughing.

I paid his ass no attention. I just jumped into my SUV and let down the windows. Before I could back up, Lincoln called out to me.

"What, nigga?" I asked in frustration.

"You know, Ryan, if you're having girl problems, I feel bad for you, son. I've got ninety-nine problems, and a . . . *bitch* ain't one." He laughed and then turned and walked toward the track.

Son of a bitch, I thought. Jay-Z's "99 Problems," another song that was getting removed from my iTunes playlist immediately. As I pulled off, I knew this was definitely Fuck with Ryan Week.

Chapter Twenty

Charice

No, I didn't lie for Lincoln to protect him, so you can get that out of your mind right now. I lied to make sure my husband didn't end up in the penal system. With the way he reacted when I told him that Lincoln only *hugged* me, I couldn't risk telling him it went any further.

Shit, we were already having our share of problems as a residual effect from the whole incident. I'd noticed Ryan questioning my whereabouts more and more, and on top of that, there were the issues in the bedroom. Isn't make-up sex supposed to be the best sex? Key word *supposed*. The two times Ryan and I had attempted it had been the worst experiences in our lives. So, needless to say, we had enough on our plates to worry about for me to go confessing the whole truth and nothing but.

However, I felt so horrible for lying. I'd never lied to Ryan about anything the entire time I'd known him—aside from not telling him about Lincoln and me, which really wasn't a lie—and now that we were married, this was what I was reduced to. This was not how I had envisioned my marriage. I was mad as hell with Lincoln for forcing me into a situation where I'd have to lie to Ryan. Okay, sure, perhaps I had little room to be angry with Lincoln since I was lying to him in a major way, but Ryan was my husband, and my loyalty lay with him. The way I saw it, it wasn't like I was actually *lying* to Lincoln about Lexi. I just never told him. If I ever had to tell him about Lexi, I wouldn't deny that he was the father, but my goal was not to be put in the situation where I had to admit that.

Anyway, I was madder with myself for allowing Lincoln to get inside my mental like he had. Ryan actually took the whole situation a lot better than I expected and a helluva lot better than I would've. I couldn't believe I'd allowed myself to get so caught up in old memories that I would do some disrespectful shit like that.

I would never admit this to Ryan or anybody else, but a part of me—a very tiny, micro-morsel part of me—would always care for Lincoln. So, I guess that was why he was able to affect me the way he did. Just being honest, Lincoln was the first man I was going to actually marry, so of course I'd have some residual feelings, but *damn,* I never expected *that* to happen. I don't know. I guess a part of me liked to see him groveling for me. Hell, it made me feel better to know that he was enduring the same heartache he put me through. Still, there would be no more times like what happened that morning between Lincoln and me, and I put that on everything I loved.

To clear my mind of any thoughts of Lincoln, I stopped by the center before it opened. I wanted to do a little dancing for my exercise routine, and I had to come up with a new dance sequence for the girls. I'd been at it about ten minutes when my cell phone rang.

"Hello."

"Hey, baby," Ryan said.

"Hey, you." I giggled into the phone. "What are you doing?"

"Getting dressed to go meet Brendon about this new endorsement deal. Johanna will be in later today, so Ms. Lorraine from across the street is here to watch Lexi for us until she gets here, and I'm going to drop the boys off at school. I was just checking on you. You're still at the center, right?"

"Yes, baby. I am. When I leave here, I was going to do some grocery shopping and then head back to the house and go through the gazillion emails I know I have from the consulting firm."

"Sounds like you have a busy day." He paused as if something caught his attention.

Not wishing to hold him, I stated, "Well, I guess I will see you later on then."

"Why are you rushing me off the phone?" he asked quickly, his tone getting tense instantly.

That tone let me know that this thing brewing between us was definitely going to have to end. I couldn't take his condescending ways, and I hated being ridiculed on every word that came out of my mouth. As each day passed, his attitude got progressively worse, and it was slowly beginning to choke the life out of our relationship.

"Baby, we really need to go somewhere just me and you. We've got to—I don't know how to say this—reconnect."

"So, there was a *disconnect*?" he asked.

This shit was on my last fucking nerves. I rubbed the back of my neck. I couldn't do this shit right now. He was going to throw me off my mode, and I had to get this routine together for the girls.

"Baby, listen. I can't imagine how hurt you still must be, but we have to find a way to work through this. I just want us to be how we were before. Is that really asking too much?" I asked softly into the phone, trying to soften his mood.

After a few moments, he released a deep sigh. "I'm sorry, Charice. I've just really been buggin' lately. I know that you want to try, and so do I. It's just hard for me right now."

"I understand."

"Look, we'll talk about it some more when we both get home," Ryan said.

"I'd really appreciate that."

"Okay, well, I'm going to let you go so you can finish up."

"Okay, babe. I love you."

"Yeah, I love you too."

I drank a swig of my bottled water and stretched. Life with Ryan had been so blissful before Lincoln showed up and straight fucked up everything. All I wanted was my husband back. Lincoln could never, nor would he ever be able to come between us. The residual feelings I felt for him were just due to having my love scorned by him. What happened was because of Lincoln and his feeble attempt to remind me of a past that had long since died. So, it was simple. Stay away from Lincoln and stay out of drama.

At any rate, I was determined to get this routine together, go shopping, and finish my emails so that I could be free to discuss things with my husband. As I turned the music back on and began to dance, I heard clapping. I spun around and saw Lincoln.

"What the fuck are you doing here?" I asked angrily.

"What the fuck is up with you and your husband with these fucking attitudes?" Lincoln shot at me. "Damn. I was giving you a compliment, ma."

"I don't need no fucking compliments from you. What I need is to know how the hell you got in here before I call the police," I yelled with my hands on my hips.

"For what?"

"Breaking and fucking entering," I said, rolling my neck.

"Pipe down, ma. Rob let me in."

"I will not pipe down. Why'd he let you in?"

His condescending smirk turned into a light chuckle. "He's in his office, and he and I were going to work out together. He stopped here first, so I came to see you shake your groove thang while he finished up some paperwork."

Squinting my eyes, I spat, "I don't believe you."

Nonchalantly, he shrugged. "Call his office or go see for yourself then. Do you really think I would break in the center? I've done some foolish things in my past, but I think I have a little more sense than to break into a community center. I mean, if I really needed to see you that bad, you are only three houses down, ma." Lincoln chuckled.

Well, that tidbit was mostly certainly true, and it was highly unlikely that Lincoln would break in. He just got under my skin so badly, especially since all the drama popped off at my house.

"Fine. Stay in the center as long as Rob is here, but get the hell out of my classroom."

"Why are you so sensitive?"

"I'm tired of being bothered by you, Lincoln. Isn't that enough?" I asked in frustration.

"Perhaps, but see, your husband reacted out of character too. I know you all don't want me around, but attacking me off the rip and him pushing on me the first moment he saw me leads me to think something went down between you two and I'm smack in the middle," he said, walking in the classroom and shutting the door. He walked up toward me. "Be honest. Did you tell Ryan about last week?"

"Leave now," I commanded tensely.

"Oh, did I strike a nerve?" he pressed. "So, you actually told him, huh?" he continued in disbelief.

Disgusted, I shook my head at him. "Get out and stay out," I yelled, pointing toward the door.

He threw his hands in the air in surrender. Then, he turned and walked to the door. Once he reached the door and opened it, he snapped his fingers. "You didn't tell him about the kiss."

"What?" I asked, caught off guard. "I don't know what you're talking about, but you need to go, and you need to go *now*."

"Yes, you do. I know Ryan. If he knew I touched you that intimately, he would've been the one breaking and entering into my house. And I know you, Charice. If you had told him, you would've gladly gloated that in my face. You didn't tell him for a reason. What was the reason?"

"I got your ass." I walked over to my purse and picked up my cell phone. "Nine . . .one . . ." I said aloud as I pressed the buttons.

"*Hey. Hey. Whoa.* Don't do that. I'm going." He relented, and I paused with my thumb in midair, ready to press the next 1.

"I see you're serious about this," he said.

"As a heart attack," I said in a no-nonsense tone.

We stared at each other for a second, and when he saw I wasn't going to back down from my threat, he exhaled in defeat. I didn't really want to call the police on Lincoln, but I'd do what I had to do to keep my nose clean. That meant that these chance meetings between Lincoln and me were going to have stop immediately. With my marriage being on pins and needles, I didn't need anyone getting the wrong idea about us, especially not Ryan.

Just as he was about to walk out the door, Lincoln turned around with a serious expression on his face. "Just tell me one thing," he requested, looking intently at me. "Did you lie to Ryan about what really happened to protect him, or to protect your true feelings?"

The gasp that escaped me couldn't be denied. Lincoln knew both Ryan and me far too well, and that was going to pose a problem. Regardless, I had to stand firm. I didn't want to give him any tidbit of information so that he could have an opening, since he'd already proved he could take any opening and run with it.

Recovering quickly, I crossed my arms with a smirk on my face. "You know, Lincoln, what my *husband* and I discuss is none of your business. It's our marriage, and we are the only ones privy to the information discussed in it. For your information, however, I told Ryan. The reason he didn't *pummel* you is because neither of us has the time to waste on you. We have a life—*together*. Now, you need to get one of your own."

Lincoln looked at me as if I'd hurt him to the core. "Damn. Hmph. Well, I guess I was wrong. You have a nice day, Charice. I'm sorry to bother you."

"You have a nice *life*, Lincoln," I said harshly.

Just then, Rob walked up to the doorway. "Everything all right in here? You all look really intense. Linc isn't plaguing you, is he Charice?" Rob tried to joke.

"As a matter of fact, he is. Next time, leave your company in the car," I snapped, walking to the door and shutting it in both of their faces.

As they walked by the glass, Lincoln looked inside at me again, and I could feel his heart breaking. I looked away and sat down on the floor. As soon as I hit the floor, tears sprang to my eyes. I wish I could say they were tears of frustration or anger, but they were tears of loss. I felt just like I had the first time Lincoln and I broke up. The pain of *that* moment had come alive again for me in *this* moment as I looked at Lincoln's heartbroken face. So, the true question for me became, why did I even care?

Chapter Twenty-one

Lucinda

Well, I'll be damned. I'll be straight damned. Raul Garcia was the father of Maria's daughter, Rosemary, and my half-brother—turned out not to be my half-brother, but rather Nadia's half-brother—Emilio Jr. Ain't that some shit? My dad even had Eva tested, and luckily she was his child, but still, I could hardly believe that damn Raul wasn't lying. This had to be the most dysfunctional fucking family I'd ever seen in my life.

I was at my mom's house when my dad came back with the shit-face to deliver the gloomy details. He'd told us how Raul stood by Maria's side, gloating after the results, and how they were now a couple. He'd already filed for divorce from Maria, and now was asking for custody of Eva. He'd also put their house on the market and was officially living back in my mom's house. I really didn't feel sorry for my dad, but I knew that I would most definitely be back in court to get my child support reduced. Son of a bitch.

Now, what tripped me out was how the hell he was gonna ask for custody of a child while he was temporarily living with my mom. None of my siblings wanted him there, and I knew damn well he didn't expect anyone from my mom down to my siblings to be happy about him wanting to bring Eva into the household. Even my grandparents, who always stayed clear of my mom's business, didn't want my dad around my mom, let alone Eva. I just prayed my mom wasn't foolish enough to turn this temporary arrangement into a permanent solution. My dad didn't love her. He was just hurt behind Maria. Of course, I'd protect my mom at all costs, but I couldn't make decisions for her. She was still grown, and hell, she was *my* madre.

Probably the most hilarious part of this is—wait for it—Shanaya. She was pissed off with Raul after finding out about Maria and had taken his ass to court about her child support. It's so funny that when she thought Raul was her "man," she was giving me her ass to kiss. Now that she realized that Raul wasn't about shit, she was constantly calling me, wanting to hang out so we could sit around and have a "Raul-bashing session." I let her talk me into that mess one time. She called and said that Raulina really wanted to play with Nadia, so I met her at the park. The entire time, all she wanted to talk about was how Raul screwed both of us over and how we could plot revenge. I politely told her that she could do whatever she wanted, but I didn't discuss grown-up business in front of Nadia, nor did I have a reason to go after Raul. I already had my child support payments coming, and I had a man in my life that was good for me and to me. I wasn't looking for no drama.

Ever since then, I kept my distance from Shanaya and watched all the drama unfold between my dad, Maria, Raul, and her.

As for my child support reduction, I was absolutely correct. My hearing was today. As of now, I was pacing the house back and forth, waiting on Aldris. He was supposed to come to court with me. So, why was Aldris missing in action? He took a vacation day because Jessica was sick, so he'd been at Jennifer's house watching her while Jennifer was at work. I know you must think that's crazy for him to be over there, but I trusted Aldris. I was sure Jessica felt better being in her own bed, and I didn't want Jessica's cold virus taking root in our house, so it was a perfect solution. However, it was about 2:30 p.m., and I was definitely going to have to leave without Aldris if he didn't show up in the next five minutes.

Sitting on the sofa with my legs crossed in my black pencil skirt with my white button-down, three-quarter length–sleeve blouse, I held my black pump stilettos in my hand and looked at my watch for the gazillionth time.

"Damn it, Aldris, come on," I pleaded as his cell phone continued to ring in my ear with no answer. I hung up the phone, put it in my purse, and slipped on my shoes, then grabbed the keys to my new Maxima and headed to the courthouse before I was late.

By the time I got there, I was pissed because I still hadn't touched bases with Aldris, and I really didn't want to be back in court with this fool about child support. I still had my same lawyer, Attorney Cheatham, and thankfully the same judge, Judge Cutliff, was presiding over the case again. Those were the two pluses, since my support system wasn't in place for the day.

Before I entered the building, I called Aldris one last time and again got his voicemail.

"This is Aldris. Leave me a message," his recorded voice said.

"Aldris, I really hope Jessica is feeling better and that nothing has happened to her. At any rate, it's three fifty, and the case starts at four o'clock. I'm at the courthouse, and I hope you're either here or on your way. I really needed for you to be here with me today. I won't be able to hear your return call because I have to turn my cell phone off, but if you're on your way, I'll see you in a bit. I love you," I said and hung up.

"Hello, Lucinda," Attorney Cheatham greeted me as I came through the door.

"Hello, Attorney Cheatham," I said as we shook hands. "I thought Aldris was coming as well."

"Umm, his daughter is sick—"

"His daughter?" he asked in shock as he cut me off.

I'd forgotten this was news for everyone. Nodding, I answered, "Yes, he just found out he has a daughter with his ex-girlfriend. It's a long story."

He fanned in the air. "No need to explain to me. I just wasn't aware that he also had a child. Oh, well. We will be fine. This is just a formality. I'm sure your support will not be reduced that much. From what I hear, the young lady who was with Mr. Garcia the last time received a minimal amount of support. Judge Cutliff wasn't as understanding for her story, since she was lying under oath the last time around," he joked.

I let out a nervous laugh.

"So, tell me, nothing has changed with you, correct?" he asked.

"With me, nothing has changed that we haven't already discussed. I'm still making the same pay, and so is Aldris. We're not married yet. Oh, but Aldris does have to pay child support and has to take out life insurance for his daughter, so his pay has been reduced," I told my attorney.

"Wow, I really wish Aldris were here. I could've used that proof, since you reside together. It would've truly been beneficial."

I sighed in frustration. "You've got to be kidding me."

"I wish I were," he said. "But no worries. We still have the judge on our side with this one," he reassured me as we prepared to go into the courtroom.

Right at that moment, I could've choked Aldris. He knew I needed him today. Now, to hear that his information could have been beneficial to my case ensured that I was pissed all over again.

"Where's Mr. Fantastic?" Raul said to me when I sat down on my side. Maria and he looked at each other as they laughed at his dumb-ass attempt to be funny.

"You know what? You just sit there and figure out how you're going to take care of all these daggone babies you keep making. You're so pathetic," I said angrily.

"Oooouch. There must be trouble in Paradise." Raul chuckled. "What happened? Did the great black Adonis turn out to be nothing but Captain Save-a-Ho?"

"No, Captain Save-a-Ho is your ass. Sitting up there looking like a broke-down Ricky Martin. You may as well fuck men. You've fucked over enough women," I fumed as I stood up, ready to plow into his ass before my attorney sat me down.

"Don't feed into that. And you, sir, please refrain from speaking to my client," Attorney Cheatham said, standing in front of me.

The bailiff walked over. "Is there a problem?"

"No. I've got it under control," Attorney Cheatham said. "Just tell the plaintiff to refrain from addressing my client."

The bailiff looked over at Raul. "Sir—"

Raul put up his hand. "I won't say another word. I promise."

The bailiff nodded and walked off.

Once the judge walked in and everybody was sworn in, he looked up and laughed. "So, Mr. Garcia, we're back again. Son, how many baby mamas do you have?"

"Four, Your Honor," Raul answered as if that were something to be proud of. He was so ignorant. Let me rephrase that—*ig'nit.*

The judge shook his head. "That wasn't a question I really needed answered, but I'm curious about something else. You're working at Jiffy Lube with no intent to further your education—from your last testimony at your previous child support case—so how do you plan on taking care of the five children you have on that salary?"

"I'll make it work, Your Honor."

"You'll make it work," the judge repeated, shaking his head in disbelief. "So, I presume this reduction is in light of the new findings of established paternity for Emilio—"

"Excuse me, Your Honor. His new name is Raul Jr," Maria cut in.

"Wait a minute. You named your son after another man and now have changed his name after Mr. Garcia?"

Maria nodded. "Yes, sir."

"Yes, Judge Cutliff, the man who was presumably the father is actually Ms. Roja's father," Attorney Cheatham said.

The judge shook his head. "Wait a second," he said, removing his glasses and rubbing his eyes. "Let me get this straight. Ms. Rojas' father was married to Ms.—"

"It's Mrs. Rojas until my divorce is complete, and then it will be Ms. Cunningham, and soon after that, Mrs. Garcia," Maria gloated, smiling at Raul.

"Oh dear God," the judge said. "I'll say Ms. Cunningham to keep me less confused. So, Ms. Cunningham was married to Ms. Rojas' father. However, Mr. Garcia and Ms. Cunningham have a relationship that produced minors, Rosemary Rojas and Emilio Rojas Jr., whose names are now Rosemary Garcia and Raul Garcia Jr., and Mr. Garcia and Ms. Rojas also were once in a relationship, which produced minor child, Nadia Garcia."

"Yes," everyone said in unison.

"Trust me, Your Honor, Ms. Rojas knew nothing of this relationship and subsequent affair that her daughter's father and her ex-stepmother were having," my attorney said.

"Apparently, neither did Mr. Rojas," the judge quipped smartly. "Let's get this over with. I'm getting a headache."

"Judge, may I speak?" Raul asked.

"Go ahead," the judge allowed.

"Ms. Rojas makes significantly more than I do. I don't even make twenty grand a year compared to her nearly forty," Raul said. "Yes, I know she's enrolled in technical college, but she's also engaged, and my daughter and her live with her fiancé, who also makes about twice as much as she does," Raul said. "I can prove that she lives with him. I've submitted her attorney's letter about the change of address, notifying me formally where she was staying and with whom," he said as the bailiff retrieved his letter and took it to the judge.

The judge read it and smiled at me. I knew what the smile was for. Aldris was his cousin. "Ms. Rojas, are you still residing with Mr. Aldris Sharper?"

"Yes, Your Honor. He's my fiancé," I said, even though Judge Cutliff already knew this information.

My attorney stood. "Your Honor, but we have no proof of Mr. Sharper's income. Also, Mr. Sharper has a daughter for whom he must provide support and life insurance."

"I hope I'm not in court with you again, Mr. Garcia, claiming that her fiancé's child is also your daughter," the judge quipped.

"No, Your Honor, I knew nothing of this mystery child," Raul said tensely, then blurted, "Ms. Rojas took her out of daycare, Your Honor."

"Yes, Your Honor, she has. Ms. Rojas' current work hours make her available to take and pick up her daughter from school without the use of daycare services," my attorney added.

"Counsel, approach the bench, please."

I looked over at Raul and Maria, who were gloating at me. I could've knocked that smirk right off his face. I felt it. I knew this was not going the way my first case was.

With the judge finding out all these new positive things, it was sure to hurt my case significantly, and now I didn't even have Aldris there to help out my defense by providing proof of his child support order. I knew this day was not going to go well, and it had all started with Aldris' absence.

My attorney walked over to me and leaned toward me. "The judge is concerned. He doesn't want to reduce Raul's payments, but he also has to abide by the law. He just chewed my ass for not having Aldris' pay stubs and child support records. He's going to do what he can, but I'm afraid Raul has the upper hand this time, Lucinda. I'm sorry."

"I'm going to review this for a moment. Let's take a ten-minute recess," the judge said, banging the gavel and walked to his chambers.

We walked out of the courtroom, and then I went outside to call Aldris.

"Hey, Lucinda," Aldris answered.

"Where the fuck are you?" I said as soon as he answered.

"Just leaving the ER. Jessica's temperature wouldn't break, so I took her. I forgot to call you before we left, and you know I can't use my cell phone in the hospital," he explained. "What's going on?"

"I'm about to get my payments reduced because of your absence."

"I'm sorry, but what do I have to do with your child support?"

"We live together, Aldris. Raul brought the letter about the change of address to court. I had to admit that we live together and are engaged, and I had to submit our bills, which all have your name and not mine. The only good thing is I don't have proof of your income, but in a way, that hurts me because I also can't bring up the fact that you have child support of your own. With Nadia not being in daycare and me not having proof of bills that I have to pay, Raul could walk away from here paying little to nothing," I explained.

"Damn. I'm sorry, baby. I would've just left Jennifer at the hospital with Jessica if I'd known all of this."

"Wait a minute. Jennifer was at the hospital?"

He got quiet before he spoke again. "Yes, when I called her, she got off her job and came right over."

"So, you stood me up when you could've left, and you still didn't go outside to give me a courtesy call?" I asked, getting mad as hell.

"Don't say it like that. It wasn't like that. I was concerned for my daughter."

"Yeah, and *not* concerned about me."

"Are you asking me to choose sides, Lucinda?" he asked defensively. "Are you really telling me to choose between my sick daughter and your court hearing?"

"No, what I'm saying to you is that common courtesy, support, and respect for my feelings obviously comes second to your daughter."

"No, it doesn't. I've told you—"

"Jennifer was there to help watch her. You had another adult there with you. Nothing stopped you from calling me or being concerned except you."

"Lucinda, in hindsight—"

"You know, I'm so sick of your fucking hindsight. I need you to use your damn foresight. I don't have time for this. They're calling me back into the court." I hung up in his face.

Once inside, the judge took a deep breath and looked at me. "Ms. Rojas, let me first say that I am so proud to see you making something of yourself. Of all of Mr. Garcia's baby mamas, you are by far the only one with a good, sensible background who is trying to contribute to society instead adding to its diminishment. I feel sorry for your father and you for getting trapped in the web that Mr. Garcia has spun. I want you to continue to better yourself and to continue being the upstanding parent that Nadia needs in her life. It both sickens me and saddens me to have to do this, but unfortunately, by state law, I must reduce your payments."

"*Yes*," Raul and Maria cheered.

The sudden outburst caused the judge to bang his gavel. "That is enough out of you two. Shut up before I throw you both in jail for contempt," he yelled, pointing at Raul. "You know I can't do anything about this foolishness you have going on, and that absolutely sickens me. I despise you, Mr. Garcia. You are making a mockery of every good father who is honestly being taken through the wringer because of pure vengeance. Here, Ms. Rojas is only trying to better herself to take care of a child that you care absolutely nothing about, and you are excited because you're getting child support reduced for a child you helped create. I can't make you go out and find another job, but I swear I wish I could work you until your fingers bled to make you pull your weight for these children.

"Despite my personal feelings, the law is the law, in which we all must abide, even me," he concluded, taking a deep breath. "In light of the findings, I'm ordering Mr. Garcia's payments be reduced from three hundred fifty dollars a month to one hundred dollars a month."

"What?" I asked in shock.

"Your Honor—" my attorney protested.

"Attorney Cheatham, this is the best I could do. However, I will do this—I am putting this case up for review in six months. I expect to see Mr. Sharper here with all of your combined expenses."

"Yes, Your Honor." I nodded.

"That's not fair," Raul blurted.

"Did you say something, Mr. Garcia? Please say you did because my contempt order will be signed faster than these reduction papers."

"No, Your Honor." Raul sulked.

The judge shook his head at Raul and then looked at me. "Good luck to you, Ms. Rojas, and please return in six months with all of your information," he stated, and then he looked at Raul. "Mr. Garcia, you've got your payments reduced, but I challenge you to stand up as a real man and do what's best for all of your children. I want you to know this is not grounds to try to pull your little unemployment stunt again. You must maintain employment, and I suggest finding another job to contribute properly to the well-being of all your kids. If there is nothing else, this case stands adjourned." The judge banged his gavel. "Oh, and Ms. Rojas, congratulations on your pending nuptials."

"Thank you," I said, then we all exited the courtroom.

"Where's my mother at now?" Raul said smartly to me as we left the courtroom.

"If you'd call her sometimes you might know."

"Fuck you and her," he barked, grabbing Maria's hand as they left.

A dog and a bitch going to lay down and make some more fleas, I thought. I bid my attorney goodbye and headed over to my mom's house. I explained what happened to my mom and dad. I even told my dad that Maria planned on marrying Raul. Then, we listened to him rant and rave for a good fifteen minutes before he decided to go get himself a beer and watch television. I hoped my mom took in what she had witnessed. Emilio Rojas was no better than Raul Garcia. He just wanted to get in where he could fit in, or whoever's legs in could fit in between. I certainly hoped my mother hadn't fallen victim.

I didn't have time for their issues that day. I needed to run to the grocery store and head home to give Aldris a piece of my mind.

"Where are we going, Mami?" Nadia asked as we headed down the road.

"To the grocery store."

"Is my daddy really going to marry Ms. Maria?" she asked.

"I don't know, and how many times do I have to tell you to stay out of grown-ups' conversations?" I asked in frustration.

"I wasn't eavesdropping. I swear it. Papa was just yelling so loud we all heard it," she confessed.

I rolled my eyes. "Go figure."

"Where's my papi?" she asked.

"Raul is—"

"No, not him. Mr. Aldris."

"*Ay, chica.* I'm not sure. Home, I guess."

"Oh, okay. Can I have some Starbursts?" she asked me.

I smiled. "Yes, of course."

I knew she shouldn't have the candy, but it felt so good not have to worry about having only $35 in my bank account on Wednesday and still need gas money, milk, bread, and juice until Friday's paycheck, so every time she asked for the candy, I got her some. It was moments like this that made me proud of myself, not only as a woman, but as a mama. I really wasn't dependent on Raul's support, but it helped out. Now, with it being reduced, I was going to have to go over our finances, especially with Aldris having to shell out child support as well.

The reduction had me thinking over everything now, such as my new car. I knew I should've waited to get my Maxima, but Aldris insisted that I get another car after he found out my Honda was going to need $2,000 worth of work. I could've gotten my homeboy, Pedro, to do all the work for me and get the parts for about $800, but Aldris didn't want any "back yard mechanics" working on our vehicles. Shit, call Pedro back yard or front yard, I knew that dude could fix some damn cars, and he did it for dirt cheap. Aldris felt I should be riding in high style like him, but I just wanted a ride. Hell, my Honda Accord was ride enough for me, but since Aldris insisted I get something new with a warranty, I had opted for the Maxima. The only problem was that my old 2004 Honda Accord was paid for, and this brand-new Maxima came with a $300 car note attached every month. Aside from all of this, we had our wedding coming up, and we had expenses we still had to take care of with that. So, we had a lot on us right now that we had to pay out, and Raul's reduction couldn't have come at a worse time.

I pushed all of that to the back of mind and focused on my grocery shopping. I just needed a few odds and ends to carry us over until the weekend. On the bread aisle, I bumped into this guy.

"I'm so sorry." I turned to apologize.

"It's my fault really," Mike, Aldris' ex-best friend, said.

"Mike?"

"Lucinda?"

"Fancy seeing you in here. I didn't know Spanish Fly grocery shopped."

My blood boiled instantly as my eyes narrowed and I seethed, "Go to hell."

"Mami, who is he?" Nadia asked. "And who is Spanish Fly?"

I looked down at her. "He's no one, and that is none of your concern." I looked back at him. "This is my daughter. Don't do this in front of her," I said sternly.

A sorrowful look glazed his eyes "I apologize. I was wrong."

"In more ways than one," I mumbled.

Hearing my jab, he chuckled softly. "That's well deserved. Honestly, I was joking. I've heard some good things about you. My boy Rod hooked up with Alize after Pooch went down, and she kinda gave us the info on you."

Instantly, I burst into laughter. "OMG. I haven't seen her in like forever with her crazy self."

"And you better know it. She is still the same too. Ain't nothing changed." He laughed with me.

"So, what is she doing now?"

"Uhh." He paused, looking down at Nadia's big eyes. He leaned toward me. "Working at Magic City," he whispered. "It's driving Rod crazy."

"He may as well get used to that. Alize is always gonna be Alize."

"That is true," he concurred and sighed. "So, how is Aldris?"

"He's good," I said, flashing my diamond engagement ring. "He got a promotion, and we got engaged. I'm in college, and I work full time for an orthopedic doctor. We're both doing really well for ourselves."

"Damn. Congratulations," he said, gawking at the ring and smiling. "You may not believe this, but I am truly happy for you guys. I am a man who can admit when he's wrong, and for everything I said and did to you all—I was so wrong."

I smiled and playfully hit him. "*Ay, chico,* thanks. I can accept that, and I appreciate it."

He reached in his pocket. "Here's my card. Tell Aldris he can call me at any time. You know, if he wants."

I took the card and read it. "IT? You're a computer guru?"

"Yeah. I got it together, ya know? For my kids. I let my baby mama go so she can find who she's supposed to be with and decided to do something with my life."

"Well, congratulations to you, too. When a man comes into his manhood, it's worth the recognition," I complimented honestly. "And I'm positive Aldris would love to hear this and need the convo as well. You should know that Jennifer came back in town, and we just recently found out that *her* daughter is really *their* daughter."

With widened eyes, Mike asked, "For real?"

"Yep." I nodded my confirmation.

Stunned, he stood there for a moment before shaking himself out of it long enough to ask, "So, how are you dealing with all of it?"

"It's challenging to say the least."

"Well, don't worry. Aldris will work it out. He obviously loves you enough to make sure it all goes smooth." He motioned to the engagement ring.

"From your lips to God's ears."

Glancing at his cell phone, he looked back up at me. "Well, I hate to run, but tonight I'm on second shift and this is my lunch break, so I better head back. It was good bumping into you."

"You too. Take care of yourself, and I'll make sure I give Aldris the card."

"Thanks. Just make sure you keep my boy happy. Stay beautiful," he said and walked off.

I grabbed the bread and pondered his last statement. If Aldris Raymond Sharper knew what was good for him, he'd best work on keeping *me* happy. That was for damn sure. As soon as I got to the house, I was definitely going to remind him of that very fact.

Chapter Twenty-two

LaMeka

"Knock, knock." I tapped on the hospital room door.

"Come in," Tony's said weakly as I walked into the room. "Hey, you."

"Hey yourself. I was just dropping by to check on you," I said, sitting in the chair across from his bed. "How are you doing, Mrs. Light?"

"I'm all good, blessed, and highly favored. I'm just ready for the day he gets released," his mom stated, rubbing the top of Tony's head.

"Amen to that, Mrs. Light."

"What are you doing here today? I thought you were off," Tony asked.

"I am. Like I said, I was just dropping by."

His mom stood up. "I'm going to go to the vending machine. I'll give you two some space to talk." She kissed the top of Tony's head and left.

Once she left, I got up and pulled Tony's chart to review it.

"You're off and still acting like a nurse."

Smirking at him, I put his chart down. "It's a habit."

"No, it's not. That's you. You've always cared more than you should," he said, putting his head down.

I really didn't know how to respond to his statement, so I remained quiet. In a lot of ways, it was true. This same man tried to kill me, and here I was making sure his meds and his documentation were correct.

The night he woke up, he actually remembered everything that happened to him. He could barely talk from the tube that'd been his nose and throat, and he was very weak, but now only three days later, he was able to move and talk without assistance. He didn't have any residual effects from the gunshot wounds except scarring and stiffness. All the swelling had gone down, and all of his bodily and neurological functions were intact. He was doing so well they moved him from ICU but still wanted to watch over him, so he'd be in the hospital for a few more days.

The hardest thing in the world to tell him was that he was HIV positive. He took it as I would've expected him to—hard. He was suffering with bouts of depression, so I arranged for counselors to come in and speak to him. The doctors had also started him on the meds he needed to fight the virus. To help ease the burden, his parents agreed to let him stay with them and pay for his medical treatment. He had a strong support system in them. They were so happy he didn't die from that accident that I think they'd go bankrupt to make sure he remained alive. I couldn't say I blamed them. He was their only child.

"How are my boys?" he asked, breaking my train of thought.

"I thought you said you didn't want to talk about them?" I asked, surprised.

After Tony found out that he was HIV positive, he no longer had an interest in seeing our children. It was as if he'd checked out on everyone, especially the boys. It bothered me that he was distancing himself from them, especially since he nearly lost his life, but I didn't pressure him. I figured that he was mentally trying to adjust to what this new way of life would mean for him.

He sighed. "I was depressed, Meka. I'd just found out I have the fucking package. I didn't want to talk about the boys because I realize there is a possibility I won't live to see them grow up." His voice began to fill with emotion. "But until that day comes, I want to learn how to be the dad they need me to be. It's the only thing I can do to help me fight against this thing living inside of me," he confessed as a few tears rolled down his cheek. He hurriedly wiped them away.

Emotion gripped me. Tony had hurt me in the worst ways, even exposing me to this incurable disease, but when I saw him like that, it touched my soul. No matter what he'd done, I'd never wish this on him. That Tony had been replaced by drugs and alcohol, but this was the old Tony. This Tony didn't deserve this ill fate, and for that, sadness overcame me.

I walked over to him and patted the back of his hand. "Learn to let the disease live with you, not you with it. That will help you to be strong. As for the boys . . ." I switched gears to lighten the mood. "They are doing really good. Tony Jr. is really improving. He hasn't had any violent spells in months, his vocabulary is increasing, and he's interacting and playing more with LaMichael and all of us. He's even been on the honor roll in his first grade class. LaMichael is growing like a tumbleweed. He's going to be tall and fast just like you. He sure as hell can move fast for a one-year-old. I think he started running before he started walking."

He smiled and then suddenly got sad. "That's so good."

"What's wrong?"

"It's just that I've missed so much. I was so fucked up, and I did so many fucked up things—"

"Look, don't even think about that now. You have to concentrate on getting better—"

Tony grabbed my hand, interrupting me. "No, I have to say this, Meka. I fucked up so bad after the accident I had. I blamed you for all of my problems when the one person who was to blame was me. I chose to drink that night. I chose to get behind the wheel of that car. I had the accident. I chose not to go to college. I chose to get addicted to alcohol and drugs, and I chose not to be the man and father that you and my boys needed me to be. I degraded you, beat you, abused you mentally and physically, and I disrespected our love and my sons. I know I can never make up for what I did to you, but I can tell you that from the bottom of my heart, I'm sorry for everything I've ever done to you. I just pray that one day you'll be able to forgive me. I pray I'll be able to forgive myself," he apologized as tears streamed down his face.

Talk about being choked up. For years, I'd longed to hear those very words Tony spoke. Instantly, every burden I'd carried on account of him lifted off of me. It was as if my soul had been set free. For the first time in years, I saw the Tony Light that I fell in love with when I was fourteen, and I knew he was going to be just fine. I knew I'd be just fine.

With tears in my eyes, I reached over and hugged him. "I've already forgiven you, so let it go and deliver yourself. Forgive yourself because God forgives you, and so do I."

He gripped me tighter and cried in my shoulder harder than I'd ever seen anybody cry in my life. I just held him as all the anger, pain, disappointment, and hurt eased out of his body. He was cleansing his soul, and I was happy to be there to help him do just that. We both needed it.

"I'm so sorry, LaMeka," he cried. "I'm so sorry for everything. Thank you so much. Thank you for loving me and being there for me then and now."

Once he calmed down, I pulled back and handed him some tissue. He dried his face and started laughing. He was laughing so hard that I started laughing. "Why are you laughing?" I asked as we rolled in hysterics.

"I'm such a bitch," he said finally.

"It takes a real man to cry in front of a woman."

"And a real bitch-ass one to do it in front of his *ex*-woman," he countered as we both continued to laugh.

After we settled down, I took his hand again and caressed his face with my other hand. "Do you need anything?"

"No, I don't. Meka, I just wanted to tell you that I am proud of you for doing what you always wanted. Here I was, the one with the book knowledge and the scholarships, and I turned out to be a HIV positive junkie, and you're on the road to becoming a career woman. I'm proud of you."

"In a weird way, I have you to thank for that. If you hadn't forced me to leave you and do better, I probably would've still been living off the system and supporting your drug habits. I believe sometimes God allows things to happen in our lives that are so bad that all we can do is sink or swim. I learned to swim quickly, and so will you."

"Well, if I do, I'd be learning from the best."

A brief moment of silence passed between us before I stood up. "Well, you need your rest, and I need to run some errands and finish up my homework assignments."

"So, you're going to see Gavin, huh?"

His words hit me so fast that I gasped. Shock filled me instantly. The burning question on my mind was, how the hell did Tony know about Gavin?

He smiled as if he were reading my mind. "When I was in the coma, it was weird. I could hear shit going on around me, but I couldn't respond. It was like I was dreaming, but I knew it was real. Kind of like when you first wake up really groggy, and you know things are going on around you, but you're still in a fog. I heard you and Gavin talking one day in my hospital room. He was flirting with you and you—I don't know—you didn't seem to mind," he told me.

I'd heard of patients being in comas and being fully aware of what was going on around them, but I never really knew it was real. I guess now I knew.

Rather than address what he heard, I answered his initial question. "Um, I'm not going to see Gavin."

"Do you like him?"

"I really don't feel comfortable discussing this with you, Tony." I paced the floor. "Can we just leave the subject alone?" Thankfully, he relented. "Listen, I'd better head out. I'll be by tomorrow to check on you again. Would you like for me to bring the boys?"

He looked up at me and nodded. "I'd love that."

"Then it's settled. We will see you tomorrow. You get some rest," I said, patting him on the shoulder.

As I walked out of his room and down the hall, I began to ponder his questioning me about Gavin. How would Tony react to having Gavin in my life and around his boys? Hell, I was a step ahead of myself. Did Gavin even want to be with me? He probably assumed I had the package myself. I knew I was making all kinds of assumptions without discussing anything with Gavin, but this was not the typical baby daddy situation. You can't just drop the bombshell that the father of your sons is HIV positive right before you go get freaky with your new dude. Some shit just don't go together, like oil and water.

So, I had been avoiding him like the plague. I knew I was wrong for that, because Gavin really put his feelings out on the line for me. It was me who couldn't deal right now. For now, I just needed to avoid talking to him about this situation until it all blew over. Whenever the hell that might be.

As I turned the corner to get to the elevator, I ran smack into Gavin. "I'm sorry," I blurted, attempting to sidestep him.

"Unh-uh. No you don't." He grabbed my arm and brought me back. "I've called you a couple of times."

"I got it." I nodded my head and put my hands in back pockets.

"Did you try to call me back?"

"Gavin, I've been really busy—"

"Okay, so now you wanna push me away," he said, cutting me off.

"I'm not doing that." I looked around, making sure no one was watching us.

"So, what do you call it? Because I'm confused," he asked angrily.

"Can you keep your voice down?" I asked nervously, aware that our discussion was sparking a little bit of attention.

He looked at me sideways and then looked around. "Meka, I don't give a fuck about none of these people."

I was totally shocked. I'd never heard or seen Gavin upset before, until this moment. He was usually a laid back and collected person, no matter what the situation was. He proved today that everybody had a breaking point. A few people turned to look at us, so I grabbed him by his hand and pulled him into an empty stock room and shut the door.

"Damn, dude. Let the whole world know what's up."

"They shouldn't be in our business anyway. Look, fuck all that. We left off a great night at a very crucial point. Now, all of a sudden, you're acting like I have the fucking cooties. What is the damn deal, LaMeka?" he asked, his arms folded across his chest.

I was so gripped by fear I could barely look at Gavin. It wasn't because I was actually scared of him, but rather scared of his reaction to the news I dropped on him. I liked Gavin, and I didn't want him to reject me because of my situation. A part of me was stuck in limbo between wanting to be with Gavin and not wanting to dive into another relationship because of my dealings with Tony.

I just didn't think anyone could understand what I was going through.

Let's face the facts: my life was extremely complicated. I was a former domestic abuse victim living in a transitional home, with a mama who was a few months off of welfare, a sister who was HIV positive, two children—one of whom is autistic—with a junkie, HIV positive baby daddy. So, when I say I came with baggage, that was an understatement. Hell, my baggage was a ten-piece luggage set. How could I allow Gavin to get trapped up in my never-ending mess? Simple. I couldn't. He deserved so much better than what I could offer him.

"Gavin, it's just a lot going on with me, and I think it would be best if we just remained friends and co-workers," I lied.

He threw his hands up. "I don't even know why I give a damn. You know what—fine. If that's what you want to do, then do it. Keep on living your life for your babies' daddy and not having one of your own. Eventually, everyone around you will be living it up, and you're going to be alone," he fussed as he turned to leave.

I put my hand on his arm. "Wait, Gavin, don't leave upset."

"How do you want me to leave?" He snatched his arm away. "I like you, LaMeka, but you refuse to give me the opportunity to show you how much of a real man I am and can be for you. That's fine, because you have to want me as much as I want you. I'm on my grown man shit, and I ain't into these stupid-ass games, so when you're done playing, come holla at me. You just better pray that I'm still available, or rather that I still want to be available for you," he said harshly. Then, he snatched the door open and left.

Wow. I felt like I was just involved in Hurricane Gavin. He blew in, destroyed everything in his path, and blew right the fuck on out. The funny thing was I couldn't even be mad at him for cussing me out the way he had. I deserved it. I had allowed him to open up to me and gave him the hope that what we had started was definitely going to another level. Hell, it wasn't a front. It was going somewhere. I definitely wanted it to. It was just I had a lot to deal with, especially with Tony waking up.

It was my duty to be there for him and my boys. I just felt that God wanted me to help Tony through his situation so he could be on the road to being a better man. By doing that, I didn't have time to nourish a budding relationship the way I needed to, so why bother at this point?

However, Gavin gave me a lot to think about. Was I thrusting myself into Tony's life because of the boys, or was it really because I was too afraid to let go? Well, one thing was crystal clear: Gavin wasn't sticking around to find out what the answer to either question was. Who could blame him? Not me.

Chapter Twenty-three

Lincoln

Sometimes in life you have a moment of revelation. You have a moment that is so powerful that you have no choice but to stop and ponder over your life and the direction it's headed. That's exactly what I was doing. Don't get me wrong. I actually loved the fact that I was back in New Yitty. I was close to my family again, I could hang out in all my old spots with my old and new friends, and I was pulling down some serious bank with my new contract with the Giants, so for the most part, my life was good. The part that wasn't good was listening to Charice threaten to call the police on me and remind me yet again that she wanted nothing to do with me.

My plan seemed so simplistic: work hard, get traded, infiltrate Ryan and Charice's marriage and get my woman back. On paper, it made sense. It added up. However, in real life, my heart was tired of being shit on. Granted, I was the one who broke up with Charice, but damn, it hadn't even been a full year since we broke up, and she was acting as if what we shared never existed. I thought she would have had some lingering feelings for me, but that theory went out the door with the 911 call she threatened to make.

I loved Charice with everything inside of me. I honestly did. There was nothing I wouldn't give to be back with her. I just needed to know that some part of her, no matter how small, still cared for me. That's all I needed. If she gave me that inch, I'd walk the mile to prove my love. I'd walk a thousand more just to get her to be my woman, and I'd walk for infinity if she'd be my wife instead of Ryan's.

"You know, when you were a kid, you used to do the same thing when something bothered you," my mom said as she walked in the sunroom and sat beside me. "Except back then, it was a stoop, since we lived in the city. We've come a long way since Queens."

I chuckled. "I was just out here thinking," I said, patting my mom on the knee.

"I know. That's the only time you come out here, when something is bothering you. So, you want to tell me what it is?"

"I was just wondering if this move was really worth it. That's all." I stared down at the ground.

"That depends on why you moved. I certainly love having you around more, and I get to come to the home games."

"I love having you guys around more too."

"Yeah, well, you didn't move because of us. Is the team a right fit for you?"

I nodded. "The team is cool."

She pursed her lips. "Not everybody on the team is cool, and we both know it. Lincoln, I'm going to stop going tit-for-tat with you out here. Admit it. You moved up here to chase behind Charice."

"Why you gotta put it like that?" I asked, looking at her in shock.

"What? You thought I didn't know why you were so eager to come to New York? Lincoln, your favorite teams growing up were the 49ers and the Cowboys. So, why would you want to come back here to play for the Giants when you were already on one of the teams you loved?

Besides God, it's only two things in this world powerful enough to make a man make moves like that—money and a woman. I know you're getting a hell of a lot more money, but it's not as if you're hurting for it. That leads me to believe you did it for a woman, and the only woman who you've been with that meant anything to you was Charice. The same Charice you kept flying your ass back to Atlanta for after you all broke up."

Okay, so it was no use lying to my mom. She knew Ryan and Charice had gotten married and that Ryan played for the Giants. Hell, everybody in New York knew that unless they lived under a rock. He was the man with the five-year, $50 million feet. He was the highest-paid running back in the league and, notably, with the highest salary cap in franchise history. So, it was no surprise that even my mom—who only followed my games—knew that Ryan was the man in NY. Not to mention that there were billboards in every major city with pictures of Ryan, the quarterback, and me on them, advertising Giants games.

"You can't help who you love," I said.

"No, but you can help your own actions. Lincoln, this is unhealthy. You've chased this woman up and down the East Coast. She made her decision. She married Ryan. They are a family, and they're happy."

"I know that, Ma," I seethed, getting angrier by the second.

"Back your tone down," she snapped back quickly and sternly. A moment later, she turned soft eyes to me and spoke in a calming tone. "Listen, I know it hurts, but you have to face reality, son. Your reality is that Charice is long gone. I love her too. I wanted her to be my daughter-in-law and to see you all give me a bunch of grandkids, but I let that idea go, and now you need to."

Jumping up from my seat, I paced back and forth, trying to make sense of my feelings. "But, Ma, it's just something—I don't know, like down on the inside—that won't let me let her go. It's like I know we were meant to be together. I know it."

"I'm not saying you're wrong, Lincoln. I'm saying you have to let it go for your own sanity. Loving someone who doesn't love you back is always painful—"

"Don't say that to me. Charice does love me," I exploded in a fit of anger.

Instantly, she jumped up in my face. "No! You need to hear this. How do you know she loves you, huh? How has she shown it? By marrying another man? You're in love with a woman that's not available to you. Stop screwing with their marriage and stop chasing her."

I plopped down on the wicker sofa as I struggled to hold back tears. "Ma, you don't understand. I'd lay down my life for this woman. I need her so bad. I love her so much."

My mom reached down and hugged me as a few tears escaped my eyes. "I do understand. That's the same way I feel about your father because he's my husband. The difference is Charice is not your wife. She's Ryan's. You're going to have to learn to accept that, Lincoln. If you two were meant to be together, then God will make a way for that to happen. You just have to have a little faith."

They say there's a first time for everything. I'd never in my life cried over a woman, and Charice definitely was my first and only. As I sat there wiping tears that were impossible to withhold, I realized my mom was right. I couldn't continue this path of self-destruction. Nodding my head in acceptance, I spoke the words that my head and heart needed to hear.

"You're right, Ma. I have to let her go."

Placing her hand on my shoulder, she lovingly rubbed it for support. "Focus your energy on London. That will help you through. You're both hurting right now, and you both need each other."

“Ma, I don’t know how I’m going to do this. How am I supposed to raise London by myself?”

Lifting my face to hers, she assured me, “You don’t have to raise her by yourself. You have your father, your brother and his wife, and you know you have me.”

After a few moments of soaking in her words, I came to the conclusion that she was right. Standing up, I pulled my mother to me and hugged her as tight as I could. “Thanks, Mama,” was all I could muster up to say.

Understanding in only a way a mother could, she gripped me just as tight. “You’re welcome, baby. I love you.”

“I love you too.” I lingered in the hug for a minute. Then, remembering the time, I said, “Well, I better go. London’s furniture is being delivered today.”

“I can’t wait for her to come up here. I miss my grand-baby so much,” my mom said excitedly.

I smiled. “Oh, I know you do. She’s gonna be rotten.”

“She deserves it.”

She was right. London did deserve it. Okay, yes, the primary reason I moved on Ryan’s street was to be a thorn in his side and to disrupt his marriage. I’ll admit that. However, I also had a very good reason to purchase a house, since I had obtained sole custody of my little girl. I’d been going through a lot of battles behind my daughter lately—some being very unnecessary—but as fate would have it, I’d ended up with my daughter anyway.

I was never in a relationship with her mom. To be straight up, her mom was nothing but a jump off for me, but I’d never tell my daughter that. She was that chick in the back pocket who I knew would be around and be down no matter what. So, whenever I got tired of pretending to be a boyfriend to my girl at the time, I’d go and fall back on Lauren. That was until I jumped off and got her pregnant. That changed everything. We went through all kinds of changes. First, Lauren wanted to be a couple and get married so we could raise London together, and I wasn't feeling that at all. Then, I wasn't the best father at the beginning. Hell, I was a downright deadbeat, so Lauren grew to hate me. However, we both matured and became great parents for London.

Lauren ended up getting married to this one cat named Kyle. I have to admit it; she loved this dude like her life depended on it. For all intents and purposes, I actually thought he was a pretty good guy. He seemed to love Lauren and London just as much as they loved him. Last year, come to find out, after all these years, this dude had a wife and two kids in another state. His job required that he travel from Texas to New Jersey, so he had his life in Texas, and he had his life in New Jersey. The wife in New Jersey was the one who blew his cover. That was the craziest turn of events I'd ever witnessed. It was so bad that Lauren suffered a nervous breakdown and wasn't fit to raise London anymore.

Currently, London was living with her grandma, but she had cancer, so I stepped up to take full responsibility for my daughter. Lauren's sister, Rosalyn, tried to fight me for London, but I prevailed. So now, here I was, preparing to be a full-time dad in less than two weeks. I'd even moved my parents into another subdivision in Scarsdale so they could be closer to help me with London. So, I guess my mom was right. It was time to say fuck Charice and focus on London.

When I got to my house, I decided to relax my mind. I'd made a big sandwich and sat down to watch television. Just as I took a bite into my sandwich, my doorbell rang.

"Coming." I jogged to the door.

As soon as I opened the door, all I saw was a finger in my face. "Why did you send this furniture company down here to deliver little girl's furniture to my house? Are you playing some kind of fucked up game with me? How could you be so got-damned insensitive?" Charice yelled at me as soon as I opened the door.

"Whoa, whoa, whoa. Hold up! Damn," I spat defensively, putting my hand up to stop her tirade.

"I'm sorry, sir," the man behind her said. "We're the delivery company from Cite, and I believe we went to the incorrect house at first," the man stated, pointing down at Charice behind her back. "Should this delivery go to 246 or 240 Murray Hill?"

I sighed. "It's for this address, 246."

"My apologies, sir. I'll have the drivers pull up."

"Please pull around to the back," I instructed them, and he nodded and walked off.

"See, no harm from me. They had the wrong address, Charice," I said, looking down at her angrily.

Embarrassment shaded her face. "I'm so sorry. I didn't mean to yell—"

I cut her off mid-sentence, my annoyance evident. "What kind of man do you take me for? Do you really think I'd send furniture to your house for a little girl knowing what happened to Charity? Jesus Christ, Charice."

Bowing her head, she offered softly, "I'm sorry. It's just that earlier, with the center and all . . . I was wrong, and I'm sorry. I'm serious," she apologized, returning her gaze to me with complete sincerity.

Without a second thought, I forgave her and exhaled my anger away. "Apology accepted." While my heart was skipping a beat that I actually had Charice standing in front of me, I decided to follow my mom's advice and my earlier decision to leave her alone. "Now, if you'll excuse me, I have to tell these men where to put these items."

She nodded but continued standing there with a look of curiosity on her face.

"Why are you looking at me like that?"

She shook her head. "I'm sorry. I was just confused about the little girl furniture. So, you're decorating a room for when *London* visits? That's so thoughtful of you. That's sure to make her feel right at home."

"Yes, it is for her." Pausing for a brief moment, I added, "Actually, London is coming to live with me."

Her widened eyes snapped to me in sheer surprise. "You're shitting me?"

"No shit," I said as I watched the delivery men begin to unload. "Listen, you can come in and wait if you want. I'll tell you about it, but I have to get these delivery men situated."

Lo and behold, she walked in my house. Now, I was stunned by this move, but it struck me that she must really be thrown for such a loop that she forgot I was her public enemy number one. I showed her to my family room and directed the delivery men to London's room.

"Umm, you can set up the bed against this side," I instructed, when out of nowhere, I felt someone beside me and looked down. It was Charice.

"No," Charice said, pushing her way through and interrupting me. "That's so backward, Lincoln. Her room would be turned sideways then, and she'd be looking toward her bathroom."

I turned to her. "Well, then you fix it up."

She fanned me out of the way. "Men have no sense of design. That's why I came in here in the first place. Look, place the bed here," Charice began as she directed them with the bed, dresser, armoire, desk, and nightstand. Within an hour, the furniture setup was complete. I had to give it to Charice; she'd hooked up London's room.

"Thanks, because I was really lost," I told her as we made our way back to my family room after the delivery men left. "I was thinking of painting her room pink."

"She would shoot you," Charice quipped.

"What's wrong with pink? She's a girl."

"Nothing is wrong with pink for babies and bedspreads. She's ten, Lincoln, not one. Come on. If you're going to do feminine colors for a pre-teen, I would say paint her room a soft lilac tone. She has high-end furniture, for Christ's sake. You have to bring it out. Get her a theme like Egyptian, not princess. To keep it girly-girl for you, you could buy her the lilac and hot pink bedroom comforters and throw pillows with the girls' Egyptian theme. I think she'd like that."

"Shit, I should've hired you," I said, putting my head in my hands. "I know nothing about little girls."

"That brings me to my next question." She sat beside me on my sofa. "What the hell happened to make Lauren give you custody?"

"Am I that bad of a parent?" I asked, shocked.

"No, I didn't mean it like that. That came out wrong. I mean with your schedule and all. Nawimean?"

Not wanting to get in a dragged-out conversation about the details, I kept the explanation to the point. Shrugging, I admitted, "Long story short, Kyle had another wife and kids in New Jersey, and Lauren suffered a nervous breakdown because of it."

For a long while, she stared at me blankly and then laughed. "Boy, you are so full of it." I just looked at her with a serious expression. She calmed down and swallowed. "Holy shit. You're serious?"

Realizing she wanted more details, I told her the story about Kyle's double life, his decision to move to New Jersey and stay with his first wife, Lauren's breakdown, and my custody battle with Rosalyn. Throughout it all, she sat there tentatively, listening to every word I spoke. A few times, she *ahh*ed and *oooh*ed and even patted my thigh as I found the courage to tell her everything that happened. This was the Charice I knew and remembered.

This was the Charice that I loved. However, I pushed my feelings back because this was also the Charice that was married to Ryan.

"Oh my God, Lincoln. I had no idea. How is London taking all of this? I know she must be completely devastated," she said, holding her hand over her heart.

"Yeah, she is. Right now, she's staying with her grandma in Texas. I would've let her finish out the school year there, but Ms. Maureen has cancer, and on top of that, she has to deal with Lauren and her breakdown. So, I figured it was best to bring London up when I got settled."

"Oh my God," she gasped. "I didn't know Ms. Maureen had cancer. How far along?"

"It's the beginning stages, but she's going through chemo, which is a battle for her itself, so London is really having a hard time. I check on her every day. Rosalyn is there helping out, but you know I won't feel comfortable until my daughter is here with me," I explained.

"Wait, so who's going to help you? You have mini-camp, regular camp, the full season, and not to mention all the other obligations with your endorsement deals and non-profits. She can't go with you to all of those places."

"Are you volunteering your assistance?"

She got quiet and put her head down.

"It was a joke, Charice." I chuckled. "I understand that you can't. My parents are going to help me."

She looked confused. "From Queens?"

"No, from Scarsdale. I moved them near me."

"Oh," she said in realization. "How are your parents, anyway?"

"My dad is still a jokester, and my mom is still my mom, feisty and loving." I smiled, happy that she'd asked.

She smiled demurely. "Yeah, she is. I'm glad to hear they are doing well."

"I'll tell them you asked."

Looking down at my uneaten sandwich, she stood. "I'm sorry. I've interrupted your lunch. I need to get back to the house and let you finish."

"You weren't any bother to me. It felt good to have someone to talk to for a minute. I really appreciate it."

She nodded as I started walking her to the door. "About earlier, I'm sorry. I was very extreme, and I shouldn't have been. I'm talking about when the delivery men came *and* at the community center."

My heart skipped a beat. She cared. Charice never apologized unless she cared about your feelings. "I forgive you. Besides, I was wrong too. I shouldn't have bothered you. It's just good to see you doing your thing with the dancing. I know you love it."

She turned to face me, and her face was lit up with excitement. "I really do. It's a dream come true for me."

"Well, congratulations." And I meant that. I was honestly happy for her.

Her smile warmed my heart. It felt good to feel on decent standing with her.

"Thanks, and congrats with London. I'm sure everything will work out for you two."

"Thanks. I hope so. You're welcome to visit her if you like. She asks about you all the time."

Covering her heart, she cooed, "How sweet. Well, tell her I said hello."

"I'll do that," I said, reaching for the door. I had to lean toward her, and her body tensed up. I resisted the urge to bend down and kiss her. Still, I couldn't stop the flirting that flowed out of my mouth. "Don't worry. I won't bite. Not unless you want me to."

She swallowed hard and licked her lips. "I better go."

With that, I pulled the door open, and she walked out. The next thing that happened had to be straight out of a movie scene. Just as she stepped on my front porch,

Ryan drove by, and it seemed like everything went in slow motion. He ripped his shades off in shock to see Charice coming out of my house. Instantly, he jammed on brakes, barely throwing his SUV in park in the middle of the street, hopped out, and ran full speed to my front door. He damn near knocked Charice over as he ran up on me and punched the shit out of me.

"Didn't I tell you to stay away from my wife, muthafucka?" Ryan yelled.

I felt my busted lip, and rage swelled up in me, so I popped his ass right back. He stumbled back and nearly fell, holding his jaw.

"What the fuck is your problem?" I yelled.

"Ryan, baby, please. It's not what you think." Charice grabbed him.

He turned to her. "Why the fuck are you even down here, Charice? Huh?"

"It was a mishap with his furniture delivery. They came to our house instead of his," she explained frantically.

"Listen to your wife before you get fucked up, bruh," I shouted angrily. "She's telling the truth."

"You shut up. I bet you loved it. Maybe you could cop another hug on my wife. I shoulda kicked your ass at the track. If you ever hug my wife or touch her again in any shape, I will not stop until you find a bed in the nearest hospital," Ryan yelled.

"The best thing for you both to do is to leave my house. Nawimean?"

"With pleasure," he grunted, turning around. "Come on, Charice." He grabbed her by the arm and damn near dragged her to his SUV.

Slamming my door in a fit of anger, I swore that was the last time that muthafucka was gonna get a punch off on me. If he ever touched me again, I was gon' put that bitch to sleep.

Walking into my kitchen, I grabbed an ice pack to throw on my swelling lip. Then I plopped down on my sofa in the family room and cut my television back on. I sat back, nursing my swollen lip when it dawned on me what Ryan had said. Suddenly, I sat straight up.

"Didn't he say I only hugged Charice?" I asked myself aloud. I laughed. *Yep, he sure did,* I thought, answering my own question. He had no idea I kissed her. So, she lied. Wow. If she lied then, she lied for a reason. I smiled to myself. *Oh, Charice, you done fucked up now. You have surely fucked up now,* I thought as I closed my eyes and stroked on my manhood, thinking about all the times Charice and I had made love together. With that tidbit of information, all that shit my mom had spoken went straight out the window. *Well,* not all of it. There *was* always more than one way to skin a cat.

Chapter Twenty-four

Trinity

Okay, so I went a little overboard with the comment about Big Cal. I was just so fucking pissed with Terrence about this whole Pooch shit. I was tired of him being caught up in this mess with his cousins. Wasn't he the one who always said he had me and not to worry about Pooch? If he kept fooling around with Tot, he was going to have to work overtime to protect us because Pooch and his goons were gonna find us. That was for *damn* sure.

Terrence had really put his hands on me. In addition, I was still struggling with the fact that I tried to shake it off because, in a way, I felt responsible for his reaction. I knew Terrence was jealous, and what I said about Big Cal and wearing that skimpy outfit was just my little payback to him for getting involved with this Pooch shit again, but I realized that what I did was extremely insensitive and dangerous.

I know what Charice and I discussed, but Terrence's insistence to continue this plan coupled with him putting his hands on me angered me more with each passing day, especially with the physical part. I'd made my stance on that known because I hadn't said another word to Terrence since the day Tot and Big Cal left. I was so furious with Terrence that I'd resorted to avoiding him altogether. This was made possible because I'd slept in the guest bedroom for the past two nights. I wanted Terrence to understand that hitting me was not ever going to be a part of his solution. I'd rather grow old alone than to be with another man who was going to use his "manly power" to break me down.

This night made night three, and I had no intention of interacting with Terrence. He needed to remember how it felt to be without me. As I slipped on my silk nightgown and put my hair up in a ponytail to get ready for bed, there was a knock at my bedroom door.

"Come in," I called out assuming it was one of the kids.

"I can't believe you let me in this time," Terrence said, entering the room and shutting the door. "I won't take long. I just wanted to give you the news."

Damn. Had I known it was him, I wouldn't have. "Actually, I thought you were one of the kids." I turned to face him, leaning on the dresser. "What's up?"

He put his hands in his pants pockets and cleared his throat. "I just thought you'd like to know that the presiding judge over Pooch's case took the bait. He just got a hundred-thousand-dollar bonus in unmarked bills. Pooch's plea bargain is a wrap."

"So, it's done?"

"Should be." He nodded.

"Good for you." I turned around and brushed my ponytail, uninterested in further conversation. Sure, I was relieved Pooch was still locked up, but we still had unresolved issues. While I appreciated the news, I felt that he'd addressed the Pooch situation without addressing *our* situation.

Frustrated, he let a deep sigh. "Come on, baby. I did this for us."

"I know," I said with a slight attitude.

"Li'l mama, part of me taking care of you means that I have to make sure that Pooch never gets out. Do you think I really want to stay involved in this foolishness?"

I turned to face him again and shrugged. "I don't know, Terrence."

He walked up to me, and I backed up. He stopped in mid-stride and frowned. "Why are you backing away from me?"

It was a defense mechanism. Ever since Pooch attacked me, I didn't take too kindly to men walking up on me. Normally, I wouldn't have reacted to Terrence walking up on me, but after the incident the other day, my senses were heightened all over again.

He rubbed his forehead. "Do you think I'm gonna hurt you? Come on, baby. I would never hurt you. What happened in the kitchen . . . that was a freak reaction. I'm so sorry for that." He pleaded, "Can't you forgive me?"

Tears overcame me as I listened to Terrence's plea. I could see the hurt reflected in his eyes, and it matched mine. "Terrence, it's not that I don't forgive you. I know you didn't mean it, and honestly, I feel partially responsible for the way you reacted, but you have to understand I can't go through that again. Not with you or Pooch or anybody else."

Terrence's expression looked as if I'd hurt him to his core. He walked up on me, slowly embracing me as I allowed him to hug me tight. I cried into his chest. His wifebeater was soaked as I wrapped my arms around his waist and released all my emotions.

"Don't you know I'd never hurt you? I love you, Trinity. Seriously, I would never put you through the shit that Pooch put you through. I rescued you from that. Why would I put you back through it?" he declared, stroking my hair.

"Deep down, I believe that, but I'm scared, Dreads. I'm scared to go back to the way I was before, and I'm scared because you keep staying involved with crap that involves Pooch. I don't want anything to happen to any of us. I don't want to live my life without you, Dreads."

Dreads lifted my chin and stared into my eyes. "Aww, li'l mama. Listen to me. On the real, don't even talk like that. If there's one thing you'll never have to do, it is live without me. Ain't no way I'm letting that happen, so don't worry about that at all. I did this so that we don't have to worry about Pooch no more. Now we don't, so we can focus on our kids and us." He cradled my face. "Starting with you moving back into our bedroom. Will you please come back?"

He wiped the tears from my eyes, and I allowed his words to sink in before I nodded my agreement. "Yes, I can do that. I've missed you."

He smiled and kissed my forehead, my nose, and my lips. "I've missed you too, li'l mama," he said as I jumped back and looked down. He laughed. "Yeah, we've both missed you."

Giggling, I wrapped my arms around his neck. "Well, I guess I'll have to take care of that, huh?"

He pulled me close to him, wrapping his arms around my waist. "Yes, you have to put in some overtime because this is an all-night job."

"I can handle that," I whispered sexily as I leaned in and kissed him.

Suddenly, he gently pushed me back and leaned his forehead against mine. "Wait."

"Why? What?"

He looked at me intently for a few moments as he held me close. Then, he sighed and sucked his teeth. "I have to ask about you and Big Cal."

"Baby, please. Okay, I was wrong for saying what I said. In fact, it was downright fucked up. I know it. But I only said that to push your buttons. I didn't mean anything behind it, and I am very sorry."

His eyes closed as he soaked up my apology. "Yeah, I get that, and I appreciate it. Looking back, I realize you only said it out of anger, but that's not what bothers me."

I furrowed my brow. What was he referring to? “So, if it’s not that, then what is it?”

He shrugged. “I don’t know. Your—*closeness*. Big Cal reacts to you as if . . . like . . . I don’t know, like he wants you for himself, and sometimes it just seems like . . . you know . . . you don’t mind.”

“What? Are you serious, baby? You can be so jealous—”

He put his index finger to my lips. “It’s not jealousy. Okay, some of it is, but I’m not imagining how close you all got when you were with Pooch. I’m not seeing double when I see how Princess adores him damn near as much as she adores me. I’m not hearing shit when I notice how often he has to compliment your beauty, and I know I didn’t misread the fact that you have his cell phone number and email address in your phone. So yes, the fact that you two are close bothers me, but what bothers me even more is the fact that I didn’t know it.”

Hearing his take caused me to take a pause and ponder his words. I guess it did look weird to him, but still, he should know that we would never betray him like that. Big Cal and I did get kind of close while I was with Pooch. He was so fucking paranoid over losing me that the only nigga he trusted me around was Big Cal. That was until Big Cal told Pooch I looked good, and Pooch chin-checked him. After that, he wasn’t allowed near me without Pooch being around.

After Pooch was arrested, we exchanged contact information so that I could keep my eye on Pooch. Yeah, we talked on the phone every now and again just to see how each other was doing, and yes, we sent email forwards to each other, but Terrence made it seem like we were secret lovers. Good grief. Aaron and I were cool friends. That was it. Terrence was my husband and Aaron’s cousin.

"Terrence, baby, look. Aaron and I are cool. Yes, we've been cool since my days with Pooch because he'd always encourage me that things would be better for me one day. In hindsight, I realize now he was telling me in a roundabout kinda way that you all were getting ready to make your move so I could be done with him. But Aaron and I are only friends."

He eyed me suspiciously for a few moments. "Are you sure about that?"

Now I was getting heated. I'd already apologized, explained my actions, assured and re-assured him of my feelings, and he still doubted me. That was extremely hurtful. I put my hands on my hips. "Terrence Reginald Kincaid, are you asking me if I've cheated on you with your cousin? Is that really where this is going?"

He rubbed his face in frustration. "No. I know you haven't done that. I'm just asking . . . I mean, nothing happened between you all when you were with Pooch, right?" he asked nervously.

Wow. He actually went there. Sick of the bullshit, I decided to dead this once and for all. "I can't believe you, but since you want me to spell it out, no, Terrence. I had a hard time cheating on Pooch with you. Do you really think I'd be bold enough to sleep with Aaron too? Really?" I shook my head, annoyed, turning to walk away.

Terrence lightly grabbed me by my waist and pulled me back to him. "Don't get upset with me, please. I'm only asking. It's hard for me, Trinity. I spent serious time away from you while I was locked up on account of Pooch, and the only woman I could think of was you. Then, I find out that you are in love with the same nigga who got me locked up. I went through so much hell to get back to you and to be with you, so it bothers me when I see that you are close to another nigga, even if that nigga is my kinfolk."

As irritated as I was, I couldn't deny that I understood that. I was just appalled that he'd think something like that. "We're family, Terrence. No, nothing has ever happened between Aaron and me except friendship. That's it."

He exhaled and nodded. "Thank you for clearing that up for me."

"I'm just shocked that I had to."

He put his hand over his chest. "I know it may seem small or even shocking to you, but I needed to know this. I had to be sure."

There was no use arguing over this, so I let it go. I couldn't change how he felt. I could only let him know that his feelings amounted to nothing but some bullshit he'd imagined.

"Fine. You had to be sure. So, are you better now?" I asked, a little aggravated.

He nodded. "Yes, I am." He kissed me. "Don't be mad. Just try to understand where I'm coming from."

Rather than argue, I agreed. "I understand."

"Thanks, baby." He kissed me again. "So, can we have make-up sex?" he asked, all eager like a kid in the candy store.

"As you wish, baby."

He smiled. "I'm going to let you gather your stuff, and I'm going to our room to run some bath water. We're going to bathe together, and then we can get down to business." He rubbed his hands together and ran out.

I smiled, but on the inside, I was upset. *Me and Big Cal? Amazing. Simply amazing.* My feelings were hurt, but I had to shake it off. Dreads had gone through a lot, just like he told me, but still, how low of a person did he take me for? Wow. The more I pondered that, the more it hurt. It hurt badly.

Chapter Twenty-five

Pooch

I was the king of the world. That's what I felt like anyway. Shit was getting back on point for me. I had my dope game back up and running, so I was gettin' that paper. This little life sentence was starting to feel like a little cake walk. I had Chocolate Flava and Adrienne doing the running for me, and that shit was going smooth as hell. Flava had Adrienne doing all kinds of shit for her. Yeah, Wolf didn't know it, but Flava had turned that chick out. Flava told me she called her up, and they hung out as girls. She said she bought her and her kids some things they needed since her ex-husband wasn't doing shit for them and Wolf couldn't. That next weekend, she invited Adrienne to her house for a little girls' night out type of deal. They got tipsy, and she got her to spread them legs for her. She said that bitch was pouring like buttercream. Ha!

Flava said that Adrienne was a little embarrassed the next day, saying she'd never done that before with a female, and that she only did it because she was hot and lonely waiting on Wolf to get out. Flava told her not to worry about it, and they could keep it between them. Lo and fucking behold, this bitch agreed. So, Flava was gettin' a taste of that buttercream any time she wanted. Flava said that shit was so good that she made sure she did a little something for her kids once a week just to make sure that bitch kept them legs spread. She even convinced Adrienne to do a threesome with me once I got released. Since I was the mastermind that kept everybody paid, Adrienne agreed and begged us not to tell Wolf she'd agreed to it. The shit muthafuckas do for money.

Here on the inside, I had my little clique that kept me protected and made sure we collected our ends in a timely manner. I kept it simple. My clique had five niggas, including myself. I called 'em, lieutenants. The main chief officer was my man Wolf. He had that inside connection with the guards, you know, to make sure nobody ever saw shit going down. Then, it was my dude Pit from the laundry room. After he made good on that original demand, I knew I could trust him. And I liked the fact that that nigga was discreet as a muthafucka. The warden still didn't know who had offed the phone dude. Pit was my payment collector, so to speak. Then, there was the dude across the hallway, who hipped me to the fact that Cock Diesel was gay. His name was Nitro, but I called him Info. That nigga kept his ears to the floor and his eyes on the prize. He always knew who was plottin' or plannin' before that shit was even finalized. It made it real easy to infiltrate and put a halt to anyone tryna take over my operation. Lastly—and I know this may come as a surprise—was Cock Diesel. I didn't particularly care for his undercover gay affairs, but I saw this dude knock out two muthafuckas that were twice his size in one fight. I mean, one-hitter-quitter muthafucking punches. Literally. So, nut muncher or not, I had to put this nigga down on my team. But I had made it clear: save your nut-bumping activities for your cellmate. He was a little embarrassed that I knew, so he agreed without further discussion. Good. It was hard enough knowing that shit without having to debate it 'cause he wanna be in denial. Cock Diesel was the clique protector. Enough said.

Now that I had a few ends to break off to Lisa, she was tryna throw that pussy to me left and fucking right. This bitch got so slick with it that she would be hiding in the supply room after her shift ended so that when I went to pick up my meals that she hid, I could get some pussy then too. Instead of dinner and a movie, I was getting dinner and some pussy. I mean, she was throwing that gushy stuff so much that I even turned it down once. Now, I'm all for risk-taking, but this bitch was losing her mind over this king dingaling and money. Some shit had to be exercised with caution. I had to make sure my only link to pussy kept gainful employment with the federal prison system, and the way this bitch was gettin' loose, she'd be fired before my appeal could get approved. Once I broke it down to her, she understood. No lie, I wanted to get down with her every day, hell three and four times a day, but more importantly, I needed to get out of this muthafucka, so I didn't need more dings on my record.

Everything was looking up for me. I had a new dope boy clique, three bad bitches doing whatever the fuck I wanted and needed, and my paper was stacking up real nice. Now I was meeting with my attorney to see what the deal was with my plea bargain. Yep, I was pulling a bitch-ass move by being a snitch, but this wasn't no five-to-ten, out-in-three-for-good-behavior type of bullshit I was doing. This shit was life plus more, so you can call me a snitch if you want. I called this shit survival.

"Vernon." My attorney greeted me as I sat down at the table in front of him.

I grabbed his hand and shook it. "'Sup, Stein," I said as the guard shut the door. "What's good?"

"Nothing much. Have you been taking care of yourself?" he asked.

"As best I can for a locked-up nigga. So, tell me, is that gonna change?" I asked him, trying to move this conversation to the point.

He sat back and inhaled nervously. “We had a minor setback—”

I sat forward, shaking my head. “I don’t wanna hear no bullshit, Stein. This deal was as solid as pure gold. Platinum, in fact. Ain’t that what you told me?”

He loosened his tie. “Yes, and I believe it still is—”

I put my hands up. “Whoa, whoa, *whoa*. What the fuck you mean you believe it *still* is? What the fuck happened, Stein? You said this shit was 99.99% guaranteed.”

“Vernon, if you just let me explain—”

“Explain what!”

“Judge Watson denied it. He wasn’t convinced that you had enough information on the person to force a trial or conviction,” Stein stated. “That doesn’t mean that we can’t try again. You just have to give up more information.”

With a sinister laugh, I looked at him like he was a fool. “Are you shittin’ me? I’m already dodging the grid for this bullshit I was already tryna do. Ain’t no fuckin’ way I can give you any more information. Besides, I’m positive Tot is laying low now that I got busted. Shit.” I hit the table, creating a loud thud.

“Vernon, I’m trying everything possible to make this happen for you.”

“So, what about my appeal?”

“Those things take time—”

Anger coursed through my veins, and I jumped up and grabbed him by his collar. “I don’t want to hear about time and shit. Get that appeal done like yesterday and get me outta here.”

“Oh . . . oh, okay,” Stein said nervously as I let him go. He gathered his things. “I’m going to call Sonja on Monday with an update.”

“Bet,” I said angrily, and I sat back down.

Once he left, the CO came to get me and walk me back to my cell. How dare that fuckin' judge deny me? Did he know who the fuck I was? As soon as I got out, I swore I was putting a hit out on that fuckin' peckerwood. My blood was fuckin' boiling. This was supposed to be the happiest day of my life, and now it was the worst. The only thing that could truly calm me down was gettin' my dick rocked. That would relieve some pressure. But Lisa didn't work weekends and Flava wasn't coming up this weekend, so I was gon' be a pissed off all weekend.

When I got back to my cell, I nearly lost my fuckin' lunch. Back in the corner, where the guard couldn't see behind the bunks, Wolf was letting Cock Diesel suck his dick.

"What the fuck?" I hollered as they scrambled up. "Come on, man. Not you too, Wolf?"

"I'm sorry, Pooch, man. I was on a dry spell. I just needed to relieve some pressure. I swear the whole time I was picturing Adrienne doing it," he said nervously.

Cock Diesel just laughed. "Pooch, you need to chill, dude. We all gotta ass of time to serve, and I look at the shit like this—a hole ain't nothing but a hole as long as my dick gettin' serviced. Wolf needed a favor. I serviced it."

I shook my head as I peeped Wolf's seeds on the floor. "Y'all is a bunch of gay muthafuckas around here. Fuck that," I said, turning to the bars. "Do y'all. I gotta get up outta here. *Guard*."

"Pooch, don't say nothing," Wolf pleaded.

"I ain't ruining the rep of my clique. Just stay away from me right now. *Guard*," I yelled, and this woman walked up. "Who are you?"

"A CO, fool," she said.

"I see that," I said smartly. "You big ugly bitch," I mumbled under my breath.

"What did you say?"

"Nothing."

"I'm here to help on the weekends. What do you want, inmate?"

"To go to the yard."

"Okay, but you shoulda let your CO take you when you came back. I'll be nice this time," she fussed as I backed up. Suddenly, I had an idea, and I reached up to feel if my package was still in place. It was there.

Once she let me out to escort me to the yard, I turned to her. "You ever fuck with any of the inmates?"

"Hell no. Besides, I like pussy."

"So, you ain't never had no dick?"

"Yes. Shut up. Why am I talking to you?" she said, shaking her head.

Okay, it was time out for playing with this bitch. "Look, I got five hundred bones. You can have it if you let me fall in that kitty right now." Yes, I was desperate. I was all set to give that grip to Stein, but after I got his news, he wasn't gettin' shit.

She laughed. "Yeah, right."

I patted my chest. "Check it."

She paused, then she reached up and saw the funds. The next thing I knew, we were headed to the stock room. "I can suck it. My girlfriend will know if I've been with a nigga. You clean, right?"

"Shit yeah," I said, thinking to myself, *Hell, I'm sacrificing too, 'cause you uglier than a summa bitch.*

She pulled down my pants and eased that shit in her mouth. I grabbed the back of her head, and my eyes rolled back as I pretended that this was Trinity. My mind floated back to my last birthday with Trinity. Gawd damn. I think I shot off so much I walked around with the limp dick for at least three days. That girl knew she could put a hurtin' on me. I missed her ass something awful. She knew just what to do to make me feel—

"Damn, inmate. You taste real good and sweet," the CO said, breaking into my thoughts.

"*Fuck.* Shut up and keep working it. You fucking up my concentration," I said angrily, squeezing my eyes tighter. The last thing I needed was to hear her loud, manly voice talking while I was trying to get my dick rocked.

She got quiet again, and I put my thoughts back on Trinity. Within seconds, my nuts drew up, and I knew it was 'bout time to explode. Big Bull tried to move back, but I gripped her head in place. For five hundred bones, she was gon' drink all of this to the last drop.

"Ahhh, Trinityyyyy," I hollered as I forced all my nut down the back of her throat.

She jumped up, coughing. "Muthafucker, you damn near choked me. Oh my God, and you made me swallow it. Where's my fucking money?"

I zipped up my pants, laughing. "Right here." I threw it at her.

She counted it. "Who the fuck is Trinity? My name is Danielle."

"Don't worry about who Trinity is. And to me," I said, looking at her nametag, "you are just CO Brown."

"Whatever. You ready to go to the yard?"

"Yep. Thanks for the service."

"Let me know if you need that service again, especially for that kind of grip," she said as she let me outside and walked off.

Hell no, I thought as I cringed at what I'd done. I couldn't believe I was so hard up that I let Big Bull put any part of her body on me. But I was so pissed about my news that I needed a release or else I'd probably murder somebody up in there. Damn. I had to hurry up and spring this camp. I was used to fucking dime pieces and now, I was reduced to women who looked like men. Damn. It made me wonder how long it would be before I had my jimmy shoved down Cock Diesel's throat like Wolf and his cellmate. *Hell no. Never*. Big Bull and a dime piece did at least share the fact that they were women and had pussies.

Despite everything, I was still stressed. I couldn't believe that fucking Judge Watson didn't take my plea bargain. These fuckers were serious about making me rot in this bitch, but it wasn't going down like that. Something had to be done, but what? I kept pacing and thinking to myself about what I could do when it hit me. I had to stack this paper up quicker. I had to get Stein to extend Watson an olive branch and give Watson some paper. Like I said, there wasn't shit a muthafucka wouldn't do for money.

Chapter Twenty-six

Aldris

It was times like this that I wished my old man was still alive to talk to. I loved Lucinda with all my heart and soul, but she was on my nerves in a major way. Every time something went wrong or not the way she wanted it to go, she was always at a category 10. There was no in between with her. She didn't know how to let some shit go. Either the world was right with her, or she was against the whole world. Arguments with her weren't riffs or discussions; they were battles and wars bound to leave scars and wounds. That's how she rolled.

She'd laid into me so hard about missing her court hearing until I wished I would've just called Jennifer to come home and left. Admittedly, I was wrong in how I handled the situation. I'd promised her that I'd be there for her, and I didn't even bother to notify her that I wasn't coming. That was fucked up on my part; however, I didn't think that was the issue. I believed that even if I had called her and told her I wanted to stay with Jessica, even though Jennifer was there, she would've still been at a category 10. I knew it was hard for her to deal with the fact that Jessica and Jennifer were now a part of our lives, but at the same time, I owed it to my daughter to be there for her just as much as Lucinda expected me to be there for Nadia and her.

Nowadays, it was like walking on pins and needles around her, especially since our wedding date had to be pushed back until September so that we wouldn't overextend ourselves financially. I wanted to ask my mom for more help, but Lucinda didn't want to hear of it. My mother had already ponied up five grand toward the expenses, and Lucinda didn't want to overburden her. Those were the things about her that I loved. But since the wedding was pushed back and we were doing this on our own, she had the shittiest attitude. I got blamed about the car note she now had, and if I spent what she considered to be too frivolously, she was at—say it with me—category 10. Sometimes I just wanted to hit the mute button on that woman's mouth, I swear.

Today, I'd taken a personal day to stay home and relax. We'd implemented a new computer system at work, and I had been working twelve- and thirteen-hour days for the past two weeks, trying to make sure everything was running correctly and helping to work out the kinks, so I was tired as hell. Now that everything was running smoothly, I decided to take a day for myself. Nadia was in school and Lucinda was in class, so that was an added bonus. I was category free for a while.

I'd been lounging around, eating a big bowl of Cap'n Crunch and watching rap videos and ESPN when my cell phone rang.

"Talk to me," I answered.

"I know you're not at work answering your cell phone all ghettofied like that." Jennifer laughed.

I laughed. "Nope. Personal day. I needed it."

"Yeah, you did. You've been burning the midnight oil."

"Exactly. So, what it do, Jenn?"

"Lay off the rap videos," she joked as I wondered how she knew I'd been watching them. "Anyway, I was on lunch, and I was gonna roll over to your job and drop off those DVDs of Jessica that I'd promised to give you."

Excitement took over. I finally got to see all my baby girl's firsts. "Just swing by here and drop them off."

She paused. "Is Lucinda there?"

"No. Look, don't worry about it. She'll be cool. You're just bringing me some home videos."

"You know she hasn't been a fan of mine since she caught us in that hug at your house, so I don't want no mess out of your fiancée," Jennifer said matter-of-factly.

"It's cool. Don't even trip. Besides, that was an isolated situation," I said to defend Lucinda.

"Okay. Yeah, right," she said condescendingly. "I'm on my way."

Once she arrived, she walked in and handed me a small bag full of DVDs. "Here you go."

"Thank you so much." I grabbed the bag. "I know you went out of your way, and you didn't have to use up your lunch to bring this, but I appreciate it."

"It's no big deal. I have my brown bag lunch. I have to watch this physique."

"Well, do you want to sit down and eat? Since I did ask you to drive all the way over here to drop this off, it's the least I could do. Besides, you can watch the DVDs with me."

"I don't know about that. I don't want your fiancée to go *ham* on you," she said, chuckling.

"Girl, please. It's not even like that. Come on in. Cop a squat and have a drink."

She walked in and sat in the LaZBoy. She wanted a bottled water, so I retrieved it for her. Then I put in the first DVD as she removed her sandwich and fruit from her bag to eat.

"This is the DVD of her birth," she said between bites.

I looked over at her. “I have a question. Why do you keep saying Lucinda is going to go ‘ham’ on me and shit as if I’m some kind of pussy?”

She drank a swig of her water, recapping it as she laughed. “Well, Aldris, if the shoe fits.”

“What the hell is that supposed to mean?” I asked, a little irritated.

She sighed and rolled her eyes. “Don’t be getting all sensitive. You know it’s the truth, Aldris. You black men kill me—”

I put down my bowl of cereal. “Okay, here we go playing the race card again. Does it always have to come down to that?” I said, shaking my head. I got so tired of people judging us because Lucinda was Latina and I was black. Damn already.

She wiped her hands and shook her head. “No, I’m not knocking interracial dating. But keep it real. If a black woman was bitching and moaning as much as Lucinda does, you wouldn’t even put up with it. However, here she comes—long hair don’t care, light and bright so she gots to be right—and you won’t even open your mouth. You all put up with shit you would never put up with from a woman in your own race just to keep your ‘exotic’ dime pieces on your arm. That’s all I’m saying.”

“Bullshit.” I shrugged her off. “I just deal with it because she’s my fiancée. It’s a give and take relationship.”

She pointed at me. “You’re a punk. You’re scared she’s gonna cut off the pussy supply, so you hold back from checking that ass.” She laughed.

“You’re stupid.” I shook my head, remembering Jennifer’s off-color comedy. It definitely wasn’t for everyone. “You ain’t changed a bit with your shit-talking ass.”

“I call it like I see it. You know that.” She drank a swig of her water. “Look, on the real, this whole situation with you, me, Jessica, and Lucinda is new. We all have to adjust, and she just can't be on ready-set-go all the time. But she's never gonna know when enough is enough if you keep pacifying her ass. You're gonna have to man up."

In a way Jennifer was out of line, but I couldn't really argue with her. She may have been joking and fucking with me, but there was also a lot of truth in what she'd said, so I couldn't be mad at that.

Coming out of my thoughts, I glanced up to see Jennifer coming toward the sofa where I was seated. "I had to rush to the hospital because Jessica was coming so fast," she said, pointing to the screen. "It was very quick—painful but quick," she said as I watched the delivery on the screen.

I was in awe. It was as if I were transported back in time. Even though I wasn't there, this moment was very real for me, and I almost got choked up.

"Damn." I cleared my throat. "This is amazing."

Jennifer turned to look at me. "You all right, beetle bug?" she asked.

My solemn emotions were replaced with laughter. "Hell no. I haven't heard that nickname in ages. Do you remember that car?"

"Do I? OMG. You thought you were the shit with that beat-up jalopy. Nobody could tell you that bug wasn't the shit."

"It was the shit. Man, please. You know you liked it."

"No, I liked when you got rid of it."

"I wish I still had that old thing too. I'd hook that shit up." My eyes darted away from her as I reminisced on the true value of the old, dusty car.

She smiled, patting my knee. "It still hurts, doesn't it?"

Exhaling, I admitted, "Yeah. That car reminded me of my old man. It was his first car. Shit, I miss both of them."

Giving my knee a squeeze, she said sympathetically, "It's like that sometimes. You'll always miss him, Aldris, but just know he's in a better place."

Nodding, I agreed. “Yeah, he is,” I said as I looked at her. “We’ve known each other a long time, huh?”

“Yeah, we go back.” She leaned back against the sofa.

There was a brief moment of silence as the realization consumed me that Jennifer and I had finally turned a corner with communication. That thought made me want to discuss more as we figured out this new way to co-parent and be friends.

“Can I ask you a question? I’ve wanted to ask this but just never felt comfortable enough to ask it.”

She gazed over at me knowingly. “Let me guess. You want to know what happened to the child I was pregnant with by my ex-husband.”

“Yes. You never talked about that child. I assumed he must’ve taken him or her.”

“No,” she said, tears prickling her eyes. “Actually, I slipped and fell during my seventh month, and the baby was stillborn. He got choked by the umbilical cord.”

“Oh, shit.” Of all the things to hear, I wasn’t expecting to hear that, and I immediately embraced her. “I’m sorry. I didn’t know. After all of that, he still left you?”

That’s when I felt her silent tears falling on my chest. “Yep. I’ve learned that it doesn’t matter what you go through with a person. If they don’t love you, they just don’t.”

Guilt. For the first time since Jennifer had reemerged in my life, I felt guilty for how I’d treated her. It was a very sobering feeling to see myself in the same shoes as her ex-husband, and for the first time in a long time, I finally understood the depths in which I’d betrayed Jennifer. I didn’t like it, not as a man, and especially not as the father of a little girl.

I lifted her face toward mine. “Well, I’m sorry for all that I’ve done, and again, I didn’t mean to bring that up.”

Faintly, she smiled. "Thank you for that," she said, the sincerity shining in her eyes. "And no worries about bringing that up. It actually feels good to talk about it to somebody."

We sat there in a silent embrace as we continued to look at the DVDs of Jessica when she was a few days old. The more I saw the video, the more I realized how much valuable time I'd truly lost and how every moment was indeed precious.

Bam! I heard something slam and I scrambled to get up.

"What the fuck?" I asked, rubbing my eyes.

Jennifer sat up and stretched. "What time is it?" she asked, looking around.

"Time for you two motherfuckers to tell me why you are cuddled up asleep on my fucking sofa," Lucinda yelled with her hands on her hips. "So, is this how it is, Aldris? You just gonna disrespect me in *our* house?"

Shit. Somewhere along the way, Jennifer and I had fallen asleep on the sofa watching the DVD. What's worse than Lucinda finding Jennifer in our house without Jessica present was the fact that we fell asleep still embraced in that hug. Fuck me. Now, Lucinda was home, and category 10 was about to be off the fucking radar.

Jennifer jumped up, looking at her watch. "*Oh, fuck.* It's been two hours. My lunch was over an hour ago. I've got to call my boss and let him know I'm on the way."

"No, you've got to tell me why the fuck you're in my house. So, you just gonna be in here on my man and act like that shit is just a normal part of your day?" Lucinda screamed at Jennifer.

Jennifer put her hand up. "Listen to me. It was an honest mistake. You need to talk to Aldris, but right now,

I have to talk to my supervisor," she explained as she snatched up her cell phone and dialed her job.

I looked at Lucinda, and I swore I could see steam coming from her nostrils. Okay, this looked bad as hell, but it was so innocent. I knew better than to approach her, so I just kept my distance to explain the situation.

"Look, baby, I know how it looks, but it's nothing like what you're thinking. Jennifer came over to drop off some DVDs of Jessica."

"Why the fuck didn't she just drop it off and keep it moving? How the hell did that turn into you two curled up on my sofa together asleep?"

"She was originally gonna just drop them off at my job, but I asked her to come over here to drop them off—"

She stepped back in shock and immediately cut off my explanation. "Ooooh. So that's what we do now, Aldris? Invite bitches to our house and spend time together. I can't believe you invited her. *You invited her?*"

"It wasn't an invite. I simply asked her to bring the DVDs here because I wasn't at work," I said, trying to calm down the intensity of the moment.

"Yeah, okay." She shrugged sarcastically.

Just then, Jennifer walked back in the living room and grabbed her purse. "Lucinda, I'm sorry. It really was nothing. We were just watching the DVDs," Jennifer said as she began walking to the door. "Again, I'm sorry."

Lucinda's mouth fell open, giving Jennifer a look of sheer disbelief. "So, you just bold enough to breeze your ass to the door like it's all to the good? Bitch, you done tried me—"

Knowing Lucinda was about to pop off, I jumped between them. "Stop, Lucinda," I yelled, blocking her from grabbing Jennifer just in time.

Jennifer looked at us wide-eyed as I held Lucinda's arm in the air. "Oh, hell no. I am so *glad* I've got to go to work. Aldris, handle her. She done lost her fucking mind," Jennifer yelled angrily as she snatched the door open and stalked out.

As soon as the door slammed shut, I was met with a huge slap across my face. I grabbed my face in pain, and before I knew it, I was up in Lucinda's face. "Oh, hell nah. What the fuck is wrong with you? Now, I'm not hitting you, so don't be putting your hands on me. Don't you ever put your fucking hands on me." My voice thundered with anger.

Suddenly, tears rolled down her face. "You had that *bitch* in *my* house, curled up on her like you were a couple, and you're checking *me*? Wow." She stepped back, running her hands through her hair, completely aggravated with me and this situation.

Pacing back and forth, I yelled, "You won't let me explain. Since she came out of her way on her lunch break to bring the DVDs, I told her to stay and eat her lunch here."

"And that *still* doesn't explain you two being cuddled up."

Frustrated, I tried to knead the tension out of my neck before I continued. "As we were looking at the videos, I asked about her baby with her husband, and she explained she lost the baby. She started crying about it, I hugged her, and we must've dozed off. That's it. I put that on everything I love," I explained, slapping my hands together in a sense of finality. I was over done with this whole scenario.

"So, every time this bitch has an emotional moment, you're gonna be hugging on her? Let God be her comforter, not you. That's not your role or position. Play your fucking position, which I thought was my fiancé," she screamed.

Her words triggered a flashback in my mind. I remembered Jennifer being in the same position with me when we were engaged. Only then, she was justified in her assumptions. Still, I never wanted to make Lucinda feel like I'd made Jennifer feel. That thought alone caused me to reevaluate how I was handling her in this moment.

With a growing sense of understanding, I tried to grab her hands to center her, but she snatched away from me. "It was just a natural reaction because we're friends."

"Well, excuse me. I signed up to be engaged to Aldris, not Captain Save-a-Ho!"

This back and forth wasn't helping anyone, so I opted to end this argument. I'd explained the situation, and all we were doing was going around and around the details. I decided to be the bigger person and just accept this as completely my fault.

Releasing a deep sigh, I walked up to her, grabbed her hands, and stared into her eyes. "Lu, I was wrong, and I promise that I won't do it again."

She looked away, and then looked back at me as if what I said didn't even matter to her. "Really? Because if my memory serves me correctly, this is time number two." She held up her index and middle finger in the peace symbol and paced the floor with tears in her eyes. "Do you even love me anymore, Aldris?"

"Yes! Of course I love you. You're my fiancée."

"Then why do I feel like I'm the baby mama and Jennifer is your fiancée? Ever since you found out about Jessica, it's been all about you, her, and Jennifer. It's like fuck me and Nadia," she cried. "If you don't want us so you can have your ready-made family, then just say so."

Although I knew this was my fault, I was blown away. Was she really fucking serious? I fought so hard for us to be together in the first place, and she acted like this wasn't what I wanted over a fucking hug? You've gotta be fucking kidding me. She acted as if I was dicking down Jennifer. I mean, it *was* fucked up, but *damn*. It was in no sense a betrayal. I was so sick of her blowing shit up to a hundred when it was really only a ten. I had to get the fuck away from Lucinda for a little while before I said some shit I knew I'd regret.

"You know what? I need to go. Mike invited me to play hoops with him today, and I think I need to take him up on his offer. We need some cool-down time."

"Fine. Leave then, motherfucker. Maybe I'll *leave* too."

I tensed up and turned to look at her. "What the fuck does that mean?" I asked, looking at her as if she were crazy. She had my blood boiling. Then, I thought about it and shook my head. I couldn't entertain this shit right now. "You know what? Never mind." I grabbed my keys and walked out, leaving her standing there with her mouth agape.

I needed to be around my dude Mike and get a man's opinion. I had to admit that even though I was pissed with Mike about the whole incident at my mom's house, I was happy as hell when Lucinda trotted in the house with his number. He'd made a lot of changes in his life, and it was like we never skipped a beat, only this time he was a lot more mature. I was ready to release some stress by whipping some ass on the courts while at the same time getting some much-needed advice from him on how best to relieve the pressure of this situation between Lucinda and me.

"Mr. Fabulous finally joins us," Mike said as he called time-out.

I went up to him and my boy Rod and gave them a one-arm hug. "What's up, fellas?"

"Nothing much. Glad to have you back in the circle," Rod said.

"It's good to be back." I laughed.

"This is my cousin, Sam." Rod introduced us. "He's going to be our fourth so we can beat you and Mike in some basketball, baby."

Rod was amusing. He knew me and Mike had handles. "Whatever, son."

Mike laughed. "Yep, it's time to school these clowns." He playfully hit my chest.

Rod looked at Sam. "You ready to do this?"

"All day, baby."

We began playing the game with fierce intensity. We were truly street balling—throwing elbows, pushing, charging and all. It ain't no fouls in street ball. We were having a blast. Then these fools started shit-talking.

"You don't want none of this, you pussy-whipped muthafucka," Rod said in my face as I defended him.

"Shit, nigga, please. Alize wears the pants in your house," I shot back as Mike and Sam laughed.

"Fuck you, boy," Rod said as I snatched the ball away from him and shot a three-pointer.

"Oooh, that shit wasn't nothing but net my nigga," Mike said, slapping hands with me.

Rod called time out, and we went and sat on the bench to drink water and wipe our sweat.

"So, you're really going to do this marriage thing, huh?" Rod asked me between swigs. "I mean, I feel you. Lucinda is a bad bitch."

I pushed him. "Man, watch your mouth. That's you and Alize who play like that."

Mike fanned him off. "You know this fool just dumb."

Rod shrugged. "What? My bad."

Just then, Sam's cell phone rang. "Sorry, fellas, I'm up. I've been waiting on this hot piece of ass to call me for two days. I'm 'bout to go tap this."

We all laughed. "All right," we said, throwing up deuces.

"Hey, dude, I gotta get my stuff out your car so I can ride with Mike," Rod called out as he got up to go to Sam's car.

Mike looked at me. "That's a damn fool. Rod ain't never gonna change."

"Hey, never say never. You did." I hit him in the chest.

He nodded. "That is true. So, let me ask, can a brother at least get an invite to the wedding since I'm not gonna be in it?"

"Yeah, man. I'll make sure you get an invitation," I said, putting my head down.

"What's up with the long face? You should be excited."

Taking a deep breath, I let out, "I am."

"What's going on, man? This is Mike, baby. Talk to me."

Without Rod and Sam around, I took the opportunity to open up to Mike about the current situation with Lucinda. "Man, this shit with Jennifer, Lucinda, and me is getting outta hand. Ever since Jennifer and I worked out our differences and became friends, we are cool as hell. We have no problems raising our daughter together as an extended family, and Jessica is the light of my life, man," I explained, pulling out my wallet and showing him a picture that Jessica and I took together.

"But my issue is Lucinda flips the hell out every time Jennifer and I are around each other. Like today, I asked Jennifer to bring over some DVDs of Jessica. Well, Lu was in class, so she wasn't there. Anyway, Jenn and I sat there looking the DVDs and joking. We started talking about some serious shit, she got to crying, and out of comfort, I hugged her. Somehow, we fell asleep, and then Lu came home. Even though I explained it to her and apologized for what happened, she was crazy mad, slapping me and shit, trying to fight Jennifer and stuff. I mean, just doing a bunch of crazy bullshit. Not to mention the sideways shit flying out of her mouth.

"I know this was an extreme situation, but it's been like that with little shit too. *Why is she calling you? Why do you have to drop what we're doing to run over there?* It's crazy, and I hate to say it or even think this way, but a part of me feels like I'm pulling away from her because of it. It's weird because I love her so much," I explained as I leaned back on the bench, happy to get that shit off my chest.

Mike nodded as he took it all in. "Well, I know first-hand that the wrath of Lucinda can be a volatile one."

I chuckled, remembering their fallout. "This is true."

Then, he got serious and patted my shoulder. "Look, man. I hear you. But be that as it may, I learned that Lucinda is a good woman, and I know she loves the shit outta you, Aldris. That's hard to find, and you found it twice—once in Jennifer and once in Lucinda. I know Lucinda is a firecracker—"

"Shit, more like a stick of dynamite," I cut in. "Or a block of C4."

He laughed. "Yeah, I agree with the block of C4, but she loves you. When I saw her in the store, she had a glow on her face when she showed me that ring. It was like that smile came from her soul. I also saw the turmoil in her face when she said that Jennifer was back and Jessica was your baby. I think you have to find a way to balance enjoying your daughter with the life you already have."

"I am," I yelled, offended. I couldn't believe this fool was actually on Lucinda's side!

Mike gave me that "get real" look. "Really? Even with you discussing this situation, not once did you say, 'we did this or that as a family.' It was clearly your life with Jessica and Jennifer, and then your life with Lucinda and Nadia. Of course, Lucinda is gonna feel threatened. You were engaged to Jennifer and you all share a child. Look at the picture you took. Granted, it didn't have Jennifer in it, but it didn't have Nadia in it either, and if Lucinda is gonna be your wife, Nadia is your daughter too."

Did I just get my hat handed to me by my best friend? Ain't this a bitch? Times had *definitely* changed. I couldn't believe he was with Lucinda on this one. "Wow. You really think I'm doing that?"

"I think you're *allowing* it to happen," he said, wrapping the towel around his neck. "Look, I'm the last person to talk to about making a relationship work. It's cool to do your thing with Jennifer and Jessica, but try to make Lucinda feel like she's a part of Jessica's life too, and not just the woman her dad is marrying. 'Cause the one thing I do know is Lucinda is completely in love with you. Don't fuck it up."

I was about to talk more when my cell phone rang. I knew that ringtone. Usher's song, "There Goes My Baby." It was Lucinda. I sighed and looked at it.

Mike looked at me and hit my arm. "Answer it," he said, then grabbed his water and walked off.

"Hey, baby," I said into the phone.

"Aldris, please come home. I'm sorry," Lucinda apologized in a tear-strained voice.

Chapter Twenty-seven

LaMeka

"*Surprise*!" Everyone yelled at Tony as I rolled him inside the front door. A couple of his nurses were there, as well as my mom, his parents, Pastor Gaines, and our kids.

He smiled gleefully and looked back at me. "What the hell is this?"

"It's for you. It's your surprise welcome home party."

His parents walked up to him, and each hugged him for a long time.

"I love you so much Mom and Dad," he said.

His mom pulled back, and instantly, the floodgates opened. "I'm just so happy and blessed to have you home. Thank you, Jesus," she shouted, hugging him again with tears streaming down her face. She choked up damn near everybody in the room.

Tony had successfully completed his drug and alcohol rehabilitation, and he was on a consistent medical treatment program for his HIV. He was still a little weak from his surgery and in some pain, but he was doing very well, all things considered.

He slowly stood up and looked around. "Thank you all so much," he said to everyone. "I owe all of you so much, and I put my right hand to God that I will get my life together this time."

"Dada," LaMichael said as he toddled away from my mom.

Shock filled Tony, and instantly, tears fell from his eyes as LaMichael staggered toward him and he picked him up. I grabbed Tony Jr., and Tony hugged all of us in his embrace. "Yeah, little man, it's Dada," he cried. "I swear to God I'm going to do right by y'all. I love you little boys."

That's when everyone's floodgates opened. It was so emotional and cleansing to know that after all Tony and I had been through, we could stand there together as a family. That was God's work.

"Enough with all this crying. This is a party. Let's go ahead and turn up some music and get this food together. I know my son. He's ready for some fried chicken, collard greens, macaroni and cheese, and cornbread," Mr. Light said.

Tony pointed to his dad, nodding his head in agreement. "That's what I'm talking about, Daddy."

While Tony mingled and played with the boys, I took the opportunity to call the two people who were on my shit list: Misha and Lucinda.

"Misha, where you at?" I asked as I stepped outside the house. "You were supposed to be at Tony's parents' house for the welcome home party."

Misha huffed. "So, he actually made it out of the hospital? Damn. Was that nigga a cat in a former life? He got fucking nine lives, I swear."

I gasped. "*Misha*. I know you don't care for him, but all things aside, Tony has changed. He's better now. There are no more drugs and alcohol. He's going to do right this time, and he needs all of our support, especially since he's living with HIV."

"Yeah, that I gave him, so why the hell would I want to hang with his ass? Really, Meka? You are the loony one.

Gavin has called here three times to speak with you this week, and you've been so far up Tony's ass that you can't even see that you're passing over a good man. If you want to throw your life away dealing with that lowlife nigga, then go ahead, but don't ask me to. Hell, I was trying to get rid of the nigga, not be his damn buddy," Misha said nonchalantly.

"You know they are locking people up for intentional manslaughter behind that shit you did, so you might not want to get too loose-lipped about it," I said.

She sighed, and I could practically see her rolling her eyes through the phone. "So what? Are you gonna tell on me? Please. This is me and you talking. I know he's li'l Tony's and LaMichael's daddy, but damn for real, sis, you need to let that nigga go."

"Goodbye, Misha." I hung up to dial Lucinda's number.

"What's good, chica?" Lucinda answered her cell phone.

"I know what ain't good."

She gasped. "*Ay, lo siento*. My bad, Meka. I forgot all about Tony's welcome home party. Girl, it's just so much going on right now between Aldris, Jennifer, and me. Not to mention that foolishness between my dad and Raul. My mind has been all over the damn place. I'm sorry."

"So, do you think you can still come? I think it would mean a lot to Tony to see his old crew of folks who were with him before he got hooked on drugs," I pleaded.

"I wish I could, but I'm at the skating rink with Nadia. I promised her I'd do a mother-daughter night with her."

I sighed, disappointed. "I understand."

She let out a slow and deliberate sigh. "Meka, check it, mami, I understand that Tony is different, and he needs support, but don't you think you're too involved in this? I get that you want to be there for him, I do, but I'm just saying maybe you should back off just a bit. I saw firsthand what you went through while you two were together, and I really don't want to see you hurt again."

I threw my hands up. "Is that why you're not here because secretly you don't want to deal with Tony?"

"Chill, chica," she said firmly. "I honestly forgot, but you're avoiding my comment and my question."

"I don't have time for this. All I asked was for a little support from you. You have plans with Nadia, so do your thang. I will be just fine," I said with plenty of attitude. Actually, a lot more than I really needed to give to her because I knew Lu meant well.

"Fine. Do you, boo. Holla," she huffed and hung up in my face.

I hung up my phone and slipped it in my front pocket, heading back inside. Everybody was making their food, so I grabbed my plate and started too. As everyone laughed and joked around, I really didn't feel up to it. I was disappointed in my sister and gut-checked by Lucinda. Of course, there was a part of me—the hurt and scarred part—that wanted to tell Tony, "Adios, muthafucka." Yet, I also understood that a lot of the way Tony used to be was because of his depression and substance abuse issues. The real Tony—the one I fell in love with—would never have done the things he did.

Don't let that fool you, though. I missed Gavin and all the possibilities of what we could be, but emotionally, I wasn't ready for Gavin. I had so much to clear up in my own life and in my own mind about my relationship with Tony that I knew it'd be unfair to date Gavin at this point in my life. Unbeknownst to my sister, I'd actually called Gavin back once that week and explained just that to him. He felt as if I was hiding under a false sense of obligation to Tony. Ugh. Was I really that wrong for wanting to be there for my babies' father? Everyone was so against Tony, as if he'd personally violated them. Hell, I was the one who got degraded, beat on, cheated on, and left to raise two boys on my own, so if I could let that go, then they should too.

I sat out on the screened porch with my plate. I wanted to be by myself so that I could think about what I wanted to do about Gavin and Tony.

"Can I sit out here with you?" Tony asked, coming out the door.

"Sure." I jumped up and grabbed his plate for him so that he could step down.

"Thanks. It's hard to move around still," he said as he finally sat down. "But I ain't complaining, though. I could not be moving at all."

I giggled. "That is very true."

"Guess who called me?" he said, taking a bite of his macaroni. "Mmm-hmm. Girl, you were always the best at making macaroni and cheese."

"You know how I get down, for real," I joked. "Who called?"

"Ryan. I haven't heard from that cat since I started wilding out with them drugs and shit. I understand. He has a reputation to uphold. He couldn't uphold that hanging out with junkies and dope dealers."

I nodded. "Yeah. A lot has happened since then," I said, reflecting back on the events of last year with Ryan and Charice.

"So I heard. I can't believe what happened to little Charity. And how the hell did he go from playboy to married to Charice? Was I that zooted?"

I chuckled. "Man, that's a long story. In between that, there is another dude Charice was engaged to named Lincoln. I'll have to tell you about that shit one day."

He put his fork down and looked at me. "Lincoln? As in Lincoln Harper? Ryan's-best-friend-from-the-Cowboys Lincoln?"

I looked at him weird. "You know Lincoln?"

"Yeah, I met him when I went on that nine-day vacation with Ryan right before I got really strung out. That nigga was something else, just like Ryan. Man, how the fuck did Charice hook up with him? And you said they were engaged? I'm surprised them two niggas didn't kill each other."

I laughed. "Yeah, like I said, it's a long story. It's a lot of shit that's happened over the past year. You wouldn't believe half of it. Hell, *I* wouldn't believe half of it if I didn't know these people personally."

"I can tell. Lucinda is in college with a good job and engaged. Pooch is locked up. Trinity is gone out of state, and Ryan and Charice are married. Man, I feel like I was in a coma or some shit and I'm just waking up." He shook his head in disbelief.

"I guess in a way you are, huh?"

There was a long pause as I awaited his response. When I looked over at him, he was staring directly at me with the most sincere look on his face. I could tell that this conversation was about to switch up into something very serious.

"Yeah. In more ways than I'd ever imagined." He placed his hand on top of mine.

"Umm," I said, unsure of what he was doing.

He smiled at me and held my hand tighter. "I love you, LaMeka. Despite all that I've put you through, you've been right here for me as if I'd never hurt or betrayed you. I've done so much fucked-up stuff to you that it's a blessing you'd even be in my presence, let alone be there for me the way that you've been. I'll always be indebted to you for that. Always."

"You don't have to be indebted to me. It's just important that you get through this, you know?"

He turned to look at me and placed my face between the palms of his hands. "I need you, LaMeka. I can't make it through this without you—"

I interrupted him. "I'll help you. You know that."

His eyes shone as the brightest smile appeared on his face. "I know I have your help, but can I have your heart? I know that I don't deserve it, but I would love the chance to be the man you've always wanted and needed me to be."

He couldn't be asking me what I thought he was. I coughed to clear my throat, which suddenly was extra dry. "What exactly are saying, Tony?"

Eying me sweetly, he grabbed my hands. "I would like for us to be a family again. I want to be the man you need me to be. Maybe one day I could be your husband even," he said, getting choked up. "I know that I have HIV, but I've done some research, and if we both use protection—the male and female condoms—and as I continue to take my medications on time and on a consistent basis, the chances that you'd contract it are extremely slim. I know I'm asking a lot of you, and I understand if you need to think about it, but I love you, and I want to be your man again. You and the boys are all I have in this world to live for."

I damn near drank all of my tea in one gulp. He really went there. He was asking me to make the ultimate sacrifice and put my health at risk to be his woman again. As a woman with a sister who was HIV positive and a future medical professional, I knew that many people did this sort of thing. He was also right about the intercourse. Sex practiced extremely safely, combined with a strict medical treatment plan, could be successful at ensuring that the virus wasn't passed to the non-infected person.

Then, there was so much he didn't know, like the fact that my sister gave him the virus. He just accepted that he had it because he'd slept around with junkies and used drugs. He never questioned how he contracted the disease. Shit, he was so messed up that he thought he was the one who gave it to Misha. Only my mother and

I knew differently, and I would never in my life tell him or anybody else anything different. Not to mention that he thought I didn't like Gavin since I wasn't dealing with him. Not the case. I had my concerns about interracial dating, and I came with some extreme baggage, but seriously letting go of the possibility of being with Gavin wasn't something I was ready to do just yet. Yes, I was putting him off and denying myself that chance, but I'd convinced myself it was only temporary, until I could help get Tony better and up on his feet. Now, Tony was asking me to be a family with him.

Hell, I didn't know. Maybe I should. What man wanted to deal with all the things I had going in my life? Yeah, Gavin may have thought he wanted to try, but he didn't know my entire situation. To me, being a nurse was not just a job—it was my life. For him, being a nurse was a profession—just a part of his life that he got to leave at the ER at the end of his shift.

Perhaps God had spared Tony so that we *could* be a family. There were always sex toys and masturbation if I chose not to have intercourse with Tony. Truth be told, a woman could please herself ten times better than a man if she knew just how to please her erogenous zones. At any rate, I did love Tony, and we did have sons together, so maybe . . . perhaps . . . it could work.

"Don't answer now." Tony sealed my lips shut with his index finger. "Just think about it and let me know." And with that, he picked up my fork, scooped up my macaroni and cheese, and fed it to me.

A little bit of cheese drizzled on my chin, and he bent over and wiped it off with a napkin, then he kissed my chin where the cheese once was. I caressed his face. It was the first time in a very long time that Tony had actually been this nurturing to me, and it felt good.

He rubbed my chin with his thumb and looked me in the eyes. "I love you, LaMeka, and for the first time in my life, I can honestly say I know what it means to truly love someone."

I just sat there and finished eating, in awe of the man that Tony was trying to become. The only question in my mind was, was I really ready to let him be my man regardless of the possible consequences?

Chapter Twenty-eight

Lucinda

Sometimes you have to do what you have to do to preserve what you've got. I usually didn't try to smooth shit over—or as I'd like to say, back down—when I felt I was right, but for Aldris, I went against the grain. I had every reason to go ham on him for that shit, but I had to learn to trust in my relationship and my love with Aldris. That solo fact made me pick up the phone and try to salvage our relationship. I was trying to mature and be the better person.

I must say that it actually seemed to pay off. Aldris was very apologetic about his actions when he came home, and I swear to God, the make-up sex blew my fucking mind. We talked about some things that were kind of bothering each of us, and of course, my explosive attitude was his main concern. For me, it was his failure to communicate with me when it came down to Jennifer and Jessica. I must say that the conversation allowed me to get a lot off my chest, and since then, everything had been pretty copacetic around the home front.

I could honestly say this new, reserved Lucinda had taken over in all aspects of my life. Raul was late with his child support, but instead of dialing him up and going off, I kindly sent him a certified reminder letter. Hell, he was only paying me $100 a month, and the *puto* couldn't be on time for that. I did get my money five days later, but it was all right. He had to face the music on it.

Even my girl Meka tried me. Here I was, making a valid point, trying to help that chica out, and she went off on me. The old Lucinda would've immediately cussed her out and went off about that crackhead baby daddy she had, but no, the new me just charged it to the game. I'm not gonna pretend that I was completely sold on this transition, because going off was easier, but I tried because I realized that my way wasn't always the best, nor was it healthy. As my abuela would say, you can catch more flies with honey. So, I was learning the essence of being sweet.

In effort to be *sweet*, today was deemed united family day. Aldris, Nadia, and I met up with Jennifer and Jessica at the park so we could all spend time together as a *family*. We made it into a big deal, where we each made a dish and brought drinks, while Aldris cooked burgers and hot dogs on the grill. We were loaded with plenty of toys and a radio for Nadia and Jessica on our fun day. Surprisingly, everything had been going well. Nadia and Jessica were having the time of their lives, playing with each other and with Aldris. Jennifer and I didn't have much conversation for each other, but we did listen to the music and talked about current events. I even played good hostess while Aldris was on the grill and chatted it up with Jennifer instead of hanging around him and leaving her by herself.

"All right, who wants me to make them a plate?" Jennifer asked once Aldris put the last of the burgers and dogs in the tray.

"I do. I do." The girls jumped up and down.

As I stood up to make Nadia's plate, Jennifer stopped me. "You can go ahead and fix your own plate, Lucinda. I've got Nadia."

"Thank you," I said, stirring the baked beans I'd made. "Nadia doesn't eat potato salad," I said before she put it on her plate. I didn't want her to think that Nadia was intentionally not eating the food she made.

She turned around in shock. "Are you serious?"

"You seem surprised. It's a lot of people who don't eat potato salad. I actually don't eat it either, but I can tolerate it a little better than Nadia can."

She giggled. "I guess it's just a black thing then. We love potato salad."

Was this bitch trying to imply that we didn't like potato salad because we were Latina? Oh, so she thought she had a common link to Aldris, huh? I had something for that ass.

I shrugged. "Aldris doesn't eat potato salad either."

Jennifer frowned and instantly turned to look at Aldris, who instinctively put his head down. "Since when? I distinctly remember Aldris eating my potato salad."

I put my hand on my hip. "Yeah, Aldris, since when do you eat potato salad? You always told me you didn't like it either."

Maybe he was just trying to appease this heifer, 'cause I know my man, I thought.

He coughed, looking up at me nervously. "Well, I'm not a fan of potato salad, so I usually don't eat it. Jennifer's potato salad was the only person's I've eaten and actually liked."

Jennifer snapped and did a little dance. "That's right. I remember you telling me that you hated your mom's potato salad and not to tell her."

"And you still better not tell her that." He pointed at her as they playfully laughed with each other about their inside information. "I love my mom's cooking, but just not her potato salad. I don't know what it is that you put in yours that makes it so much different than anybody else's."

"If I told you, I'd have to kill you. It's a top-secret family recipe."

"Well, you learn something new every day," I said.

Okay, so I guess I didn't know Aldris that well, or at least not that he loved *Jennifer's* potato salad.

Jennifer turned to face me. "You should try it, Lucinda. I guarantee you'll love it," she said as she set the girls' plates down in front of them.

Instead of replying, I handed her their juice drinks and then asked Aldris what he wanted. Fuck that potato salad.

"Umm, give me two burgers with the usual and everything else," he said as he grabbed a beer out of the cooler.

I made his plate of two cheeseburgers with extra mayo, ketchup, mustard, and onions, then put a big helping of baked beans and chips with a smaller portion of potato salad. Yes, I was being a little bitchy. I had to find out that my fiancé was in love with his ex-fiancée's potato salad all out in public, making me look like I didn't know my man. Okay, I was gonna chill. I'm just saying, though.

I set the plate down in front of Aldris.

"Thank you, baby." He rubbed his hands together. "This looks good. Lucinda makes the best baked beans too, Jennifer."

She raised her eyebrows. "Oh, really?"

I smiled and nodded as I rubbed Aldris' back. "Yep, I do. My baby just loves them."

Take that, you potato-salad-making heifer.

He nodded. "Yep, and now that she taught my mom how to cook them like she does, I get them at home and at my mom's house."

Jennifer shook her head. "You can't be giving another woman your secret cooking tips, Lucinda. Now you have no leverage because he can get the same meal at his mama's house."

I was glad my back was turned so she didn't have to see me roll my eyes. So what if he could get the same damn baked bean recipe at Ms. Lily's house? I knew damn well I had something Ms. Lily couldn't give him: this Spanish Fly.

I made my plate, and to show I was a bigger person, I put some of Jennifer's "world famous" potato salad on my plate. Jennifer and I ended up sitting beside each other because Aldris was sitting between the girls.

"Hmm," Jennifer hummed, biting her burger. "You finally learned how to grill." She laughed, looking up at Aldris.

He instantly burst out laughing. "Forget you, man."

"What is Mommy talking about, Daddy?" Jessica asked.

He hugged her. "Mommy is just being funny."

"I like funny stories, Daddy. Can we hear it? Please, oh please?" Nadia asked, laughing as he tickled her.

Jennifer put her hand up. "Okay, Nadia coaxed me into it. Well, when your father and I were in college, I used to cook for him all the time, so I asked him to grill for my spring break cookout at my apartment." She began laughing again. "But here's the thing. I asked him first, 'Do you know how to grill?' and he said, 'Oh, yeah,'" she shouted exuberantly, and by this time, she and Aldris were doubled over in laughter.

Personally, I didn't see shit funny as I drank the rest of my beer.

"So, the day of the cookout, I was getting everything prepared and having fun with my friends. I asked Aldris when he was going to throw on the burgers, so he got up and lit the grill and nearly burned his eyebrows off. He had so much daggone lighter fluid on the coals he could've started a forest fire. We put new coals on, and I asked him if he wanted me to take over, but he swore it was an accident and that he was good. That first batch was literally blackened burgers. Those things were burnt to a crisp. That's when he admitted it was his first time cooking on the grill. I took over the reins to spare the rest of the food we had and made his butt stand there and learn how to grill hamburgers, barbeque chicken, and hot dogs. That's how your daddy learned how to grill," Jennifer said in hysterics as Nadia, Jessica, and Aldris all joined in.

"So, you taught him how to grill, huh?" I asked after they'd died down.

She nodded. "Yeah, I did."

"I guess you shouldn't have shown him your cooking secrets," I said.

She looked over at me, and I stared right back at her with the straightest yet shittiest expression on my face. *Yeah, bitch, you just got served,* I thought as I took a bite of her potato salad—which I hated to admit *was* the bomb.

Aldris began coughing instantly and got up. "Gotta get another beer."

She laughed it off. "Good one. That potato salad is good, huh?"

"Yes, it is. You deserve your props."

"Thanks. Your baked beans are good as well. I'll have to tell my Aunt Lorraine somebody has the same recipe as she does. She must've let her secret get loose."

No, this bitch didn't. Okay, score two points for her. I just laughed mine off too.

"Great minds just think alike, that's all."

"Yeah, but it's always best to be original." She winked at me.

"Dessert, anyone?" Aldris asked, interrupting my response to that smart-ass comment Jennifer made.

"Yes, Daddy," the girls yelled in unison as they got up so he could give them slices of the chocolate cake I had made.

"You do have one up on me, though, Lucinda. I'm not much of a baker," Jennifer admitted, getting up to get some cake.

This time, it was Aldris' turn to make jokes. "I should tell the story of how you tried to bake me a birthday cake, since you want to put me on blast about grilling."

"Hey now, I tried. So what if it fell and it was a little dry?" she joked.

"A little dry?" he asked, mocking her as he looked at me. "Baby, that thing was so dry, I had to drink a gallon of water just to swallow it, and two gallons once it hit my stomach."

"It ain't that funny," she mumbled.

"Oh, you can dish it, but you can't take it." Aldris handed both of us some cake. "You know what they say about turnabout."

"Whatever," she said, before taking a bite of my cake. "This is really good, Lucinda."

"Thank you." *Now, tell your Aunt Lorraine to top that, biotch!*

We all sat there, making small talk and joking with the girls. It dawned on me that I forgot to tell Jennifer about Nadia's birthday party.

"Before I forget again, you and Jessica are invited to Nadia's birthday the Saturday after next at Jumpin' Jamboree."

"Do you mean next Saturday?" she asked me.

"No, the Saturday after the next one coming up," I repeated.

She looked up at Aldris. "You forgot to tell her. Jessica's birthday party is at Putt-Putt that same Saturday."

Aldris hit his forehead. "I completely forgot to tell you, Lucinda. She told me that last week. Maybe we can move Nadia's party to Sunday." He looked at me apologetically.

Okay, now I was just about to get mad, because why the hell should I be the one to move my child's party just because Jennifer told him last week? I'd been talking about Nadia's party all month. Besides, there were no Sunday openings, and I'd already paid half down for it.

"Umm, no. Sunday is full. Besides, I've already put a down payment on it. What time is Jessica's party? I'm sure they aren't at the same time. We'll just be some partying people that day," I said in an attempt to make light of the situation.

"It's from one to three p.m.," she answered as Aldris and I looked at each other. "What?" she asked.

I exhaled, rubbing my forehead. "Nadia's party is at one, from one to three."

"Okay, so what are we going to do? Because I've already paid for the Putt-Putt party. Sunday is no good for me because I have a mandatory meeting that day for work, and I'm helping my friend cook for this dinner party she's having," Jennifer explained.

To me—and probably to Jennifer, too—the real question was, what was Aldris going to do, because the girls could see each other any time they wanted to. In fact, I was positive we'd have Jessica all day that Sunday, since Jennifer just put it out there that she'd be busy. So, the question became, who was going to sacrifice their child's party, or whose party was Aldris going to miss? We both turned and looked at Aldris.

Aldris sighed and put his hands up. "Listen, let's not get in a huff over this. This is what we'll do. Both girls will have their party. Since it is truly my fault for not relaying the information, I will be the one to do the running around. I will just have to split my time between both parties. I will go to Jessica's party first and spend about an hour there, and then spend the second hour at Nadia's party. That way, I won't miss either of my girls' special day." He tickled both Nadia and Jessica. "Is that fair?"

Jennifer and I looked at each other and nodded. "Fair enough," we said in unison.

"Good. Now, I'm going to take my little ladies over here and play with the Frisbee. Come on, you guys."

"He's really good with the girls," Jennifer said.

"Yes, he is," I agreed and began to clean up. "I really hate that Nadia will miss Jessica's party."

"Same here, but I'm sure they will talk each other to death about it. The most important part is that Aldris gets to spend some time with each of them."

"Exactly."

Aldris played with the girls for a little bit as Jennifer and I packed up all the food and toys. Then, Aldris came and loaded both our cars, then we said our goodbyes to Jennifer and Jessica.

"Whew! I am worn out," Aldris said as we drove home.

"We all are." I turned, looking at Nadia, who was already knocked out. "Nadia beat us to the punch, though." I laughed.

Aldris rubbed my thigh. "I thank you for doing these family days with me. I know it's been rough having to adjust to Jennifer and Jessica, but I think we're all coping much better."

"Yeah," I said, thinking to myself that it was a lot harder than rough, but life was so much easier when I wasn't arguing with Aldris, so I kept that tidbit to myself.

Aldris ran his hand up and down my thigh. "You know I am tired, but since Nadia is asleep, I'd love to get into something when we get home."

I licked my lips. "I'm sure we could think of something to get into." I leaned back again and looked out my window.

"Spill it. What's on your mind?" Aldris asked.

Damn. He was beginning to know me all too well. I looked at him and shook my head. "Don't get upset. It's just that I want you to keep your promise and share the day with both girls."

"I figured that was going to come back up," he said.

"I'm not fussing, Aldris. I'm just saying—"

"I'm not going to disappoint Jessica or Nadia," he cut me off. "I give you my word. Nadia is just as much my daughter as Jessica is. I just wish that you would see that I feel that way," he said a little tensely.

Staying true to my no-arguments pact, I threw my hands up in surrender. "Okay. Okay. I believe you. You asked what was on my mind, so I told you. You gave your word, so I'm cool with that."

He looked over at me. "You sure about that?"

"Drop it, Aldris. Yes, it is what it is."

For the rest of the ride home, there was nothing but silence between us.

Chapter Twenty-nine

Ryan

"Baby, please talk to me. Ryan, are you awake? I know you're awake. Baby, please," Charice kept repeating as she gently continued to stir me.

Hell no, I wasn't asleep. How could I be with her yapping in my fucking ear and pushing on me? I didn't want to talk to her. I wouldn't even have been in the same bedroom with her if she hadn't cried and begged me to stay in there. Yes, I was still pissed off about finding her at Lincoln's house. How was I supposed to believe that they didn't have shit going on when she was calling me his name during sex and then I find her waltzing out of his house? How would she feel if it were me?

I was beginning to wonder if this relationship was even worth the fucking trouble anymore. I loved Charice, I did, but the fact remained that the more I looked at shit, the more it was apparent to me that she had feelings for Lincoln. She could tell me she didn't until she was blue in the fucking face, but one minute she couldn't stand him, and the next she was sitting in his house. Yeah, I understood how the story went down. The delivery company fucked up the address, and she assumed Lincoln was being cruel. I got that. What I didn't get was why my wife was in his house, especially since I didn't observe one damn delivery truck in his yard when I drove off. Okay, so she said he told her the story about how he was awarded custody of London. Yada. Yada. Yada. Who cares? I felt sorry for Lauren, but that was Lincoln's business and Lincoln's problem. The true question was, why did Charice care? I'll tell you why. She still had feelings for that nigga.

I didn't know if she thought I was dumb or blind or both, but I knew when a woman had feelings for a man—especially Charice. One thing I was not going to do was put my heart on the line for her, after all these years, then watch her rebuild a relationship with Lincoln. I just didn't know what to do about it, so I'd been ignoring her all week because I was so angry and so hurt. A part of me was hoping if she felt that I was pulling away from her, she would straighten up and realize what she had in me. But, an even bigger part of me was just plain damn hurt. I'd never truly loved another woman more than I loved Charice, and I didn't know how to deal with that. I'd be damned if she was going make a fool out of me the same way Iris did. My pride, my ego, my confidence, and my heart were all being shattered by the one woman I never thought would hurt me. Charice. My wife.

"Ryan?" Charice said through a tear-strained voice. "It's been a week."

"Charice, it's three o'clock in the damn morning. Go to sleep." The harshness in my tone made my position known as I refused to face her.

Ignoring that fact, she continued her plea. "I haven't slept in a week. All I want to do is make things right between us again. I'm your wife, Ryan. How could you continue to treat me this way?"

Now, that made me get up, and I nearly jumped out of the bed. I was so pissed off. "Are you shitting me? I can't believe you're fucking for real right now. You're the one sneaking over your ex-fiancé's house and calling out his name during sex. What the fuck are you talking about, you can't believe I'm treating you this way?" I yelled, the anger in my heart evident.

She huffed as if she were just completely fed up. "I wasn't sneaking around, and I don't know how many times you want me to apologize for calling out Lincoln's name. *My God*. Sometimes you act as if you've never done shit to me. The amount of shit I've had to forgive you for pales in comparison to your reason for being angry with me."

I was fired up now. Well, if you push the right buttons, you start to see a person's true feelings. Now, she was going to see mine. "Nice, Charice. Real nice. Wasn't it you who said you'd long since forgiven me for my past?"

She put her head down and nodded. "I wasn't trying to bring up old stuff—"

"Yep. I do believe that was you," I spewed, interrupting whatever excuse she was about to drum up. "I remember hearing you say it. At least I wasn't married to your ass then. Hell, we weren't even together then."

Looking at me as if she were tormented by my pain, she mouthed the words "I'm sorry" as if they were lodged in her throat. Still, I wasn't letting up. I was determined to make her understand that all of this was her fault and not mine. I refused to take any blame for the state of our marriage.

"During this marriage, I've been nothing but fucking supportive, faithful, and loving, and you treat me like this?" I yelled, pacing the floor.

Desperately, Charice jumped up and walked toward me. "Baby, that didn't come out right. I'm just frustrated—"

I threw up my hand, thwarting her words again. I was on fucking fire, and if she wanted the gospel, I was here to give her the sermon from Alpha to Omega. "I've forgiven you for fucking and almost marrying a man who was supposed to be my best friend, not to mention accepting his daughter as my own even after I lost my only little girl. Then, you have the audacity to throw up *my* past—"

Charice put her hand up defensively. "Wait a minute, baby. Maybe you're going a little—"

Oh, she had the nerve to want to get defensive? Oh, hell naw. "Oh, please. At least the majority of my dirt was done when you were nothing more than a jump off to me."

As soon—and I mean as soon as—I said that, I regretted it. Sure, I was pissed, but I never wanted Charice to feel like I ever thought of her as a jump off. I was doing my dirt because of the type of person I used to be, and because of that, I did treat her like a jump off, but I never truly viewed her that way. Deep down, I always cared for Charice because I knew she was real, that she loved me, and she was the mother of my kids, so for me to say that was just downright cruel. I felt bad instantly. Despite all that was going on, she was my wife.

Charice gasped so loudly that I thought her heart stopped. Crocodile-sized tears began to fall, and she couldn't even speak.

Realizing that I'd fucked up, I rubbed my hands across my face. "*Shit*. Charice. Oh my God." I walked toward her. "Baby, I'm sorry. I didn't mean—" I reached for her trembling hand.

She slapped my hand back, and in one swoop, sucker-punched me. "*Fuck you,*" she hollered. Charice put her robe on and grabbed her pillow.

"Wait. Baby, what are you doing?" I asked, running over to her, still holding my throbbing cheek. Damn. She hit harder than a nigga.

"Since I'm so unworthy to be the great Ryan Westmore's wife, I'm going to move into the guest bedroom until I can find me, our sons, and my bastard daughter a place to live. I didn't need you to help raise your kids when I was a—how'd you say it? Oh, yeah, *a jump off*—and I don't need you now."

"*Wait*," I yelled, blocking her at the door. "No, I was wrong. I really don't feel that way. I never did. I was just hurt and talking out of the side of my neck. C'mon, babe." I caressed her shoulders.

"Get your hands off of me," she said tensely. "You made your feelings very clear, and for once, I'm listening. I can't believe I thought anything about you had changed. You are still the same self-serving son of a bitch you were in high school. If the only reason you married me was because you wanted your ego stroked to say you'd won me from Lincoln, or because you were fighting demons because of your lack of involvement in Charity's life before she died, then please don't do me any favors. I'm done begging for love from any man, but *especially* from you," she yelled and stormed out of the room.

As soon as she did, I heard Lexi crying and went to the nursery to check on her, but Charice was already in there. "We probably woke her up. Let me rock her to sleep. She likes that," I said, reaching for her, but Charice clutched her tighter and walked away.

"Stay away from me and my baby," she said angrily.

"*Charice*."

"*Ryan*."

Man, if looks could kill. Rather than argue in front of Lexi and upset her any further or risk waking my boys, I walked to the door and turned to leave. "Lexi is my daughter, and you're my wife. That hasn't changed."

"Not yet anyway," Charice said and slammed the door in my face.

Great, Ryan. Just great. You idiot, I thought. I walked back to our bedroom, dejected. Rather than force her into my arms, I'd probably pushed her right back into Lincoln's. I sat on the bed, thinking about what I could do to turn my marriage around. Then, I noticed my cell phone blinking. It was weird because I hadn't noticed it before I went to bed.

I picked it up and read the email. A smile spread across my face. This was sure to clear things up. My plans had been finalized. Charice was now the owner of her own dance studio. I was going to make her lifetime dream come true. There was no way she'd hate me after this. No way.

Chapter Thirty

LaMeka

"Hurry up," my mom and sister yelled at me.

"Okay, I am. I just . . . wow, I need a minute," I said nervously.

"Well, I don't, and this boy is heavy." My mom laughed as she held LaMichael in her arms.

I took a deep breath and slid the key into the lock on the front door of my new house. We all walked in, and it was simply amazing. I barely remember my sister shutting the door as we all let out a sigh of awe. It was such a relief to see one of my lifetime dreams come to fruition, and this was even sweeter because it was truly mine, not mine and somebody else's or mine and the loan company's. I held the keys and the quick deed in my hands. This was LaMeka Roberts' house.

As the thought came over me, I turned into a bucket of water. I'd accomplished something. After all I'd been through, I'd actually accomplished something in my life that was worth something.

"What's wrong, sweetie?" My mom asked as she rubbed my back.

"Yeah, Meka, is something wrong with the house?" Misha asked, grabbing my hand.

I wiped my eyes and began to laugh. I mean, I laughed so hard that they began to laugh, until we were all doubled over in laughter.

"What the hell is so funny?" Misha asked, laughing.

"Hell if I know. I'm laughing at y'all," my mom said as she wiped tears of laughter from her face.

"I have no idea why I'm laughing, but I know that nothing is wrong. Everything is turning out just right. *This is my house*," I yelled, jumping up and down like a big kid.

Misha looked at my mom and hit her. "Who house?"

"My house!" I screamed.

"Who house?" Misha and my mom screamed together.

"My house."

"Damn, is this the Mercedes-Benz Stadium?" Gavin asked as he came into my house.

"Gavin? What are you doing here?"

He nodded toward Misha and put his hands in his pockets. "A little birdie told me that you closed on your first home, so I thought I'd drop by to check it out and congratulate you, but I think I ended up at a Falcons game or something," he joked, making all of us burst out into laughter.

"I haven't been in the neighborhood a day and I already got singing canaries." I looked at my sister with a side eye.

"Well, who is this handsome man? That's my question," my mom asked, making Gavin blush.

"I'm sorry. Mom, this is Gavin Randall. He works at the hospital. Gavin, this is my mother," I introduced.

"He's also the dude that Meka keeps running from," Misha blurted as she began to roam the house with the boys.

My mom turned to me. "Oh, so *this* is the young man?"

"Mom, can you please go with Misha and check out the house? Thank you," I said, not offering her an opportunity to say no.

"It was nice to meet you, Gavin. Stop by *often*."

"Well, Mama Roberts, I will do that—if LaMeka allows me to, that is."

She waved her hand dismissively toward me. "She don't mind. Trust me. And as long as you bring me some wine, I don't either."

Gavin flashed her his million-dollar smile behind a chuckle. "I promise I got you next time. I've got that bottle of Moscato on ice just for you."

Glancing over at me, my mom gently tapped my arm. "Oooh, girl, I like him. He got a little color in him."

"Mama, please don't start with him. He already thinks he's Cablanasian," I pleaded, shaking my head in amusement.

"Gavin, it was nice to meet you," she said, shaking his hand. "I'm going to explore the house with my other daughter, and I'll be waiting on my Moscato."

"I've got you." He laughed then turned to face me. "So, you're a homeowner now. I had no idea you were in the market, but of course, how could I? I'm happy for you. Congratulations."

I folded my arms and smiled. "Thanks, Gavin."

Suddenly, there was an awkward silence between us. He stood there, rocking back and forth with his hands in his pockets, and I stood there with my arms folded, sliding glances between him and the floor nervously. What could I say to Gavin? Oh, by the way, I like you and all, but let me tell you everything going on in my life and how I'm considering getting back into a relationship with my babies' father? Yeah, I didn't see that going over too well. We'd kept it strictly professional at work, or rather he had. To be frank, besides hello and goodbye, Gavin only spoke to me about work-related issues. He'd even stopped calling me, but I knew for a fact that Misha was calling him and keeping him on ice, so to speak. How'd I know? Well, besides that same little birdie telling me that she was doing so, I had to admit that I'd actually reached out to Gavin once. I missed his companionship, friendship, and his sense of humor. Hell, I missed him.

I was an introvert except with my family, my girls, and Tony. And Gavin was the only person outside of that circle to get me to open up. After Tony hit me with his request, I broke down and called Gavin, but he didn't answer. I assumed it was because he no longer wanted to be bothered with me on a personal level, so I left him alone. Now, here he was, in the middle of my foyer, staring at me and me at him with so much to be said, yet so little being said.

"LaMeka."

"Gavin." We both started in unison before a nervous laugh passed between us.

"You first," I said.

"Naw, ladies first," he coaxed, rubbing his hands together and licking his lips.

I nearly lost it. Every time I saw that man lick his damn lips, it sent chills down my spine. Why did he have to be so fucking fine? I was standing there, ready to give him the gospel, and he looked scrumptious as hell in black denim jeans, black Jordans, and a black-and-red Jordan T-shirt. To top it off, he smelled so damn good.

Okay, Meka, just keep your composure, I thought.

"I . . . uh . . . ooh," I stammered, fanning myself as I took my gaze down to the floor instead of at him.

Apparently sick of the bull, Gavin grabbed my hand and walked me down the hall. He gave me a questioning stare as if to ask which room, and I obliged him, nodding toward the room that was in fact going to be my bedroom. Once inside my bedroom, he shut the door, locked it, and we both sat on the carpeted floor.

"What's good, mama?" he asked, grabbing my hand and interlocking fingers with me. This time, I didn't pull away. In fact, for the first time since I ran off to check on Tony, I let him to comfort me.

I shook my head slowly from side to side as we both leaned against the wall. "There's so much you don't know, Gavin. So much."

He turned my face to look at him. "Then tell me. Meka, I've been trying like hell to tell myself that I don't want you and that I don't care about you, but on the real, my heart is beating real slow without you. I keep asking myself why, because it ain't like we actually got involved in a real relationship, but I can't tell my heart how to react. Something inside of me has clung to you, and you've got my heart and mind stuck on you. Then, it's like we ain't even how we used to be. Before we tried to explore our feelings, we were damn good friends, but now, we are just two people walking on eggshells around each other, and I don't even know why. I'm trying. Hell, I wanna try. I wanna try this with you, but you've gotta tell me—*something*."

His eyes held such longing, like he was making a last-ditch plea for me to open up to him. Out of nowhere, tears started rolling from my eyes and down my cheeks, and I couldn't stop them.

"Come here," he said sweetly as he brought me to him and held me. "Let it out, baby. Let it all out on me."

I buried my face in his chest and held onto him tightly. I continued to cry until my tears subsided into little more than whimpers. "Thank you. I probably seem so weak to you right now. Hell, I don't even really understand why I was crying."

He lifted my face. "The strongest person in the world has to be vulnerable sometimes, Meka. It's just finding that place and that person who you are comfortable enough to be vulnerable with. I'm glad I could be that person to you. It shows me that I mean enough to you for you to let me see you like that. And I'm glad, too, because you're the only female I've ever allowed myself to verbally express my feelings to, and that's probably because you're the only one who has managed to make me care enough to do that."

I didn't know what the hell came over me, but I leaned in and kissed him. Then, I pulled back quickly. Caressing me in his arms, he gently brought me back to him and kissed me passionately. That damn white boy could kiss his ass off. The next thing I knew, I was on my back, with Gavin on top as he explored my protruding breasts and softly kissed the nape of my neck.

"Umm, Gavin," I moaned.

"Yes, baby?" he whispered in my ear.

In a flash, I heard Tony Jr. running, and I pushed Gavin up. "Oh, damn. I forgot we weren't alone in this house."

"I got a house we can go to," he offered, pulling out his keys.

I pushed him playfully and laughed. "No. We need to *talk*."

"My bad. You're right. Let me get myself together."

I grabbed him by his hands after we'd sat up again. "So, let me tell you about the woes of LaMeka. If you hear the whole story, then you can decide for yourself whether you want to be bothered with me. I owe you that much."

Brushing my cheek with his hand, he turned soft eyes on me. "Thank you for realizing that."

So, I told him the whole story. I began with how I met Tony in high school and how we began dating. I took him through my pregnancy with Tony Jr., Tony's car accident, dropping out of high school, Tony Jr.'s autism, and living on the system. I continued on with my pregnancy with LaMichael, to Tony's alcohol and drug abuse, then his verbal and physical abuse, and all the way through Tony's cheating and my near-death experience. I also told him how I found out Misha's and Tony's HIV status, and that I was still HIV negative.

The entire time, he listened attentively, caressing me at times and encouraging me to continue when I wanted to break down. It felt so good to talk to him in a much different way than speaking with my mom, my girls, or Pastor Gaines. I didn't know what was so different, but for the first time, I really felt a release like I could put all my cares on him and trust that he could make me feel better.

"So, that's my whole story," I said softly. "You can run now."

He stood up, then stood me up. He wrapped his arms around my waist and pulled me into his arms. "Run where?" he asked and bent down and kissed me. "I'm here if you let me be."

"You're not freaked out by all of this?" I asked cautiously.

He smiled. "Misha has been feeding me tidbits here and there, and honestly, I figured out some things on my own, but I just wanted to hear it from you. That way, you could know that none of that shit matters to me. I still want you."

Wow. I was at a loss for words. It never dawned on me that Gavin may already know these things. Of course, I had no idea that my big-mouth sister had spilled some of the business to him, but I could expect that from her. She'd wanted me to be with Gavin ever since she first met him. She had a thing for white boys. Her ex-boyfriend Vince was biracial, and she'd actually hooked up with a nice guy of the Caucasian persuasion named Bryce from her HIV awareness seminars. He was also HIV positive, contracting the virus when he was a child from a blood transfusion after he was in a bad car accident. But anyway, I was more shocked that Gavin actually wanted to be with me and deal with all the drama that I had to take on day in and day out.

"Are you sure? I mean, Tony Jr. is getting better, but having an autistic child isn't like dealing with someone with a broken arm. You can't patch him up, give him some painkillers, and send him on his way. This is everyday life for me. My sister, who has HIV, is everyday life for me. Dealing with Tony, who is my kids' father, is everyday life for me. How can you honestly say that you want to deal with this *every day*?" I asked him as I stood back with my arms folded.

Reclaiming my hands in his, he stared in my eyes. "I can't argue with you, because you have a valid point. But, Meka, I understand the things you're going through. Part of the reason I understand is because I am in the medical field. I may not be used to it, and I ain't gon' lie, it will take adjusting, but can't you let me decide if I want to try? I totally get that you can't date openly and freely because of the sensitivity of all the issues surrounding your life, and I know that with Tony Jr.'s autism you can't have people in and out of his life. I'm not trying to hit it and quit it. I'm saying to you that I like you. I really, *really* like you, and I care about you, and I want the opportunity to see where this friendship could take us outside of just friendship."

He was right. I had pretty much decided that no one was going to deal with me because of all the factors in my life, so I'd given up on allowing anyone to try. When it came down to it, I didn't want to be hurt. I'd been through hell and back with Tony, and I refused to go back down that road or any road like it. Love was something I desperately wanted, but it was also the same thing I was deathly afraid of. The question that remained was, should I try for that love with Gavin or rekindle it with Tony?

"What's on your mind?" Gavin asked as I shook my head of my thoughts as I walked into my master bathroom.

Sitting down on the edge of my Jacuzzi tub, I patted it for him to sit beside me. "I just wanted to tell you something. Something that I wanted to be sure was a bit more private."

Being the ever jokester that he was he said, "Damn. I thought you was about to invite me in the tub with you. I wasn't gonna turn that shit down either."

"You are so freaking stupid, Gavin," I said, laughing and playfully nudging him. "I was just giving us a place to sit since I don't have any furniture yet."

"I know. I'm just messing with you, Meka. What's on your mind? I'm open to answer any questions you may have."

I put my hand on his thigh. "No, you've answered enough for a while. It's just that I have to tell you that my kids' father asked me to consider being back in a relationship with him. He wants us to try to work things out as a couple and raise our family together."

He didn't readily respond. It was as if he were taking a moment to consider his next words. "So," he said with a deep exhale. "What did you tell him?"

"Honestly, nothing. He wanted me to think on it."

"So, did you think about it?"

"It's all I can think about these days."

"What did you decide?"

"I don't know. I want to be completely honest with you, Gavin. A part of me will always have love for Tony because of who he was to me and who he will always be to my sons. Then, the other part of me—the side that remembers those last few years of hell—wants to run like hell."

He looked at me curiously. "I hate to ask the obvious, but is he asking you to put your health at risk to be in a relationship with him? I mean, HIV or not, he is still gonna have those urges. If you're together, you run the risk of exposing yourself to the virus."

Nervous energy caused me to bite my lip before I confirmed his question. "That's exactly what he's asking. Well, he wants us to be well protected to reduce the risk, but he's still asking to be in a relationship with me—sex included."

Gavin's head fell forward, but he turned a side glance to me. "Are you serious?"

"Very serious."

"And you're still thinking about this?" he asked, looking at me as if I were crazy. "Shit, Meka, hands down your answer should've been no. Hell, not even just no, but hell no."

"You're just saying that because you want me."

Gavin was on his feet, glaring at me, his evident anger searing out. "This ain't about me," he said boldly. "It's about you. It's about what you want. Hell, more importantly, it's about what you need and don't need in your life. Are you kidding me right now? Okay, of course I want you, and I want you to want me too, but damn that. You have a life, LaMeka. God blessed you with a second chance to start anew. And what about the boys? Who's gonna look after them and raise them if you both have the virus and pass from it? Why in the hell would you fuck up your life and the boys' lives for Tony? What has he sacrificed for you?

"Sometimes the best thing a person can do for another one is to let them go. That's how he can show that he's matured and that he cares. It'd be different if he contracted the virus from a blood transfusion or through birth, but this dirty bastard was out there on drugs and screwing any and everybody without protection, and now that he's been spared, he wants to drag you back down the rabbit hole with him because of his mistakes? Hell no. *Fuck that*. He's wrong, LaMeka, and you ain't doing a damn thing but giving God your ass to kiss if you agree to this damn foolishness."

Talk about getting hit with *real* talk. I hadn't even thought about what he was saying because I only saw it as a way to mend our family and get Tony back to the man he needed to be. However, Gavin was right. What *had* Tony sacrificed, and who was to say that he would keep his promise to change? Who was to say that I wouldn't catch the virus if I agreed to this relationship? For a hundred reasons why I should consider being with Tony, there seemed to be a thousand more why I shouldn't.

Kneeling in front of me, Gavin kissed my hands. "Meka, you are worth so much more than what you're giving yourself credit for. I know you feel obligated because that's the God in you. You're a real woman, a ride or die, and I admire that about you, but sweetheart, you have to live your life for you—not me, and damn sure not Tony. If he truly loves you, he'll understand that you have to find your own happiness and that you still have a purpose and destiny to fulfill for yourself and the boys. I'm just asking you to step out on faith and do what's truly in your heart to do."

With that statement, my entire perspective changed, not just about myself, but about my feelings for Gavin, and my heart literally sang. Yeah, I know it sounds like the old cliché, but I swore I heard bells, whistles, explosions, and applause. I couldn't even deny that if there was anybody I should be giving my time, energy, efforts, and possibly heart and love to, it was Gavin. He wasn't even my man yet, but he made me better. Gavin felt like that missing piece I'd been waiting for.

I bent down and caressed his cheek. Then, I leaned toward him. "So, I guess I should do what my heart tells me then," I said, sealing my decision with a kiss.

As our lips touched, I knew this was different. This was the kiss that said *I am your woman*, and I knew he felt it too. Exhaling deeply, we both let the kiss consume us. It was sweet and loving, yet not overly sexual. It was what I needed. I couldn't fight this anymore. I wanted this pretty, fly-ass Cablanasian man named Gavin Randall.

"Girl, I ain't never been kissed like that before."

"Well, maybe it's time to get used to it," I said, staring up into his eyes.

Licking those sexy lips, he smiled with a twinkle in his eye. "So, whatcha saying to me?"

I wrapped my arms around his neck, interlocking my fingers as we gazed deeply as if we were peeking into each other's souls. "I'm saying that I want to give us a chance at something more than just friendship."

"We can definitely do that," he whispered as we kissed again.

Pulling out of the kiss, I hugged him gently. "Thanks for waiting on me."

"Don't thank me, baby. I couldn't go anywhere if I tried," he said, stroking my hair.

Then he looked toward the door and said, "We've been in here a minute. Your mom and sister are probably wondering what the hell we're doing back here."

We giggled knowingly.

"We should go out there, but I need to know what I need to move in the house for you," he said.

"You're helping me move?"

"Damn, baby, you really ain't had a real man in your life. That's my job. You're my girl for real now, and as your man, my job is to make your life easier."

He was right. I hadn't had a real man, but he didn't have to tell me twice. "Umm, well, it's not much actually. The furniture in the transitional home is the property of the church, so the only things I really have are a couple of TVs, DVD player, a gaming system, and boxes of clothes. I went to Rooms-To-Go and bought furniture for the dining room, living room, family room, and four of the bedrooms. They are supposed to deliver everything tomorrow. I was really coming over to make sure everything was in order and to clean."

"All right then. I'll move what you do have at the other house, but if you're ready to start cleaning up, give me some gloves and you got me. I'll even spring for lunch."

Looking at him, I couldn't help but smile in admiration of him. *This is my man. Damn.* It felt good as hell to say that.

We walked out, and my mom and sister were standing in the kitchen, with LaMichael on the countertop and Tony Jr. sitting on the floor, playing with his toy.

"Damn, I was wondering what happened to y'all. I wanted to come back there and check, but I was kinda afraid of what I might see," Misha joked.

"Girl, please. We were talking."

"Oh," they said, looking at us as if they wanted to ask but were trying hard not to.

Putting them out of their misery, I announced, "Oh, and we're a couple."

Misha jumped up and down. "It's about damn time." She hugged me then Gavin.

"Whatever." I laughed. "We're going to get the things out the car so we can all start cleaning up."

Misha fist-bumped Gavin. "Handle that, playa," she joked.

Gavin gave her that look. "Oh, I got this, Mish. Trust."

"Come on, baby. Don't let Misha start you on that foolery," I said jokingly as Gavin wrapped his arms around my neck from behind and we walked through the house to the outside.

"All right, baby. I have a bucket with cleaning agents in the—" I was saying as we stepped out on the porch, but I stopped short and nearly choked on my words as we were met by Tony, who was walking up my front porch.

"My bad. I came over to see the new house and help out. I guess you already have help," Tony said snidely as he stopped in mid-step on my front porch. "Let me guess. You *must* be Gavin?" he asked with a hint of jealousy in his voice.

Gavin nodded as he held me tighter in his arms. "Yep. You *must* be Tony."

Tony sniffed, flicking his nose. "Yeah, I am. Meka's sons' *father*," he stressed.

Gavin nodded. "I'm aware of that. And I'm Meka's *man*."

At that moment, I knew it was the beginning of the bullshit.

Chapter Thirty-one

Lucinda

I was completely swamped with claims and coursework. At times, I wanted to throw in the towel because being a fiancée, mother, and student were all full-time jobs within themselves. If I could figure out how to get paid to do all of them, then it wouldn't be so bad. On top of that, tonight was one of those nights where Nadia was being extra clingy, extra needy, and extra aggravating. I really needed a break.

Aldris' time had been split somewhat lately. His job had him stretched thin, and then trying to balance home and Jessica with the time that he did have left was taking a toll on him. It was still a bit of an adjustment for all of us. I tried to remain understanding and supportive. I didn't want him to think I was being selfish when it came to his child. It really wasn't that at all. I just had to get used to it. I'd never been in a relationship with a man who really put forth an effort to take care of his outside children, so I admired and struggled with it at the same time for two totally different reasons.

"Hey, baby." I answered the phone excitedly.

"Hey, mami," Aldris said. "I was calling because I have a meeting that is gonna run later than expected, so I should be home around 6:30 or 7:00."

"Aldris, I really needed you home tonight. Nadia is in one of those little baby moods, and I am just swamped with trying to submit this paper and homework, and my claims at work are off the chain."

"I understand, baby, I do, but I don't have a choice. If I did, you know I'd much rather be at home helping you than here."

Rubbing my forehead in frustration, I threw out, "I know."

"Did you cook?"

I looked at the phone as if he were crazy. "*Cook?* Please, Aldris."

"It was just a question. I'll bring something home for us."

"All right. I guess I'll see you later on."

"Yes, baby. I love you."

"Love you," I said before hanging up.

"Mami." Nadia came running into the kitchen. "Can I have some cookies?"

"You haven't eaten dinner. You have to eat first."

"Well, you haven't cooked," Nadia said smartly.

My *mommytude* took full effect as I turned to her, and I had to catch myself. She was trying my patience. "I know that, little girl. I'll make you a sandwich. Then I want you to sit and study your vocabulary words while I do some work."

"I want pizza," she whined.

"You'll get what I'm giving you," I fussed, turning to open the refrigerator door.

Just then, the doorbell rang. "Oh, good grief. Who could this be?"

Closing the refrigerator, I trotted to the front door. Peeping out, I was surprised by who I saw standing there. "Mike?" I asked as I looked out of the peephole.

"Yeah, Lucinda. It's me," he answered before I opened the door.

I waved for him to come inside. "Hey. Come on in." I shut the door behind him. "You have to excuse my appearance. I wasn't expecting company," I apologized, staring down at my cotton jogging pants, spaghetti-strapped tank, and flip flops, with my hair in a messy ponytail.

"If that's a bad look, then you ain't never hurtin'," he joked.

Folding my arms, I giggled. "You so crazy. What brings you by?"

"Aldris. He told me to meet him here because he and I were supposed to go and shoot some hoops. Is he at home?"

"He must've forgotten. He's actually still at work. He had a late meeting and won't be home until about 6:30 or 7:00."

"Mami. Mami," Nadia shrieked, running into the family room. "I want my sandwich. I'm hungry."

I blew the strand of hair that fell in my face in frustration. "I'm sorry, Mike," I said, turning to Nadia. "Rudeness. I am speaking to Mr. Mike. I will make your sandwich in a bit. Now, go in your room and go study. That's the last time I'm going to tell you that."

Nadia huffed and walked off. "You better tighten up," I yelled after her.

Sensing my tension, Mike patted me on the arm. "I have three. I've been there. You look like you could use a break."

Exhaling, I let out a frustrated scoff. "Oooh. Can you tell? Aldris was supposed to come home so I could finish up my coursework before I signed into work, but that's not going to happen, and Nadia—as you can see—is being a little unruly."

"She's just being a kid and getting on Mommy's nerves. I think they have radar that signals them to act foolish when their parents are stressed," Mike joked.

"They probably do. As much as my mom said we got on hers, I can believe it."

"I'll tell you what. If you don't mind, I'll call in some pizza for you guys and pick it up. If you need me to, I'll watch Nadia for you until Aldris gets home. It seems we won't be playing hoops tonight, and I don't have shit else to do."

"You don't have to do that." I shook my head even though I really wanted to jump at his offer.

He eyed me. "Are you sure? I don't mind."

Considering the night I was having, I decided, *what the hell*?

"Okay, you've twisted my arm." I laughed. "Umm, we like Pizza Hut meat lovers."

"You want some wings?" he asked.

"Cool with me."

"What is Nadia working on?"

"Her vocabulary, spelling, and subtraction."

"Cool. I can handle that."

I called Nadia in the room and explained that Mr. Mike was going to help her. Mike called in the food, and I sat in the breakfast area in the kitchen with my laptop, finishing up my research paper. I ain't gonna lie. Mike's help with Nadia was a huge relief. He even took her with him when he went to pick up the food. By the time they returned, I had submitted my paper and my homework. I made everyone's plate, and then we sat in the family room to watch television and eat.

"Thank you so much for your help, Mike. I really appreciate it. You just don't know," I said gratefully then bit a piece of my pizza.

"Ain't no thang. You know we play cousins," he joked. "So, did you get anything accomplished?"

"Yep, I finished my research paper and my homework."

"All right now, miss lady. Give me some. Plow-dow," he boomed with a fist bump to me. "Nadia knows all of her spelling words, and she's got to practice on three vocabulary meanings, but she'll get it."

"Yep." Nadia giggled. "Mami, Mr. Mike told me that I'm the best and nothing less," Nadia quoted.

"That's right, little lady, and how do you get to be the best?" he asked her.

"By studying for the test," Nadia shouted with exuberance as they fist-bumped.

I laughed. "Wow, I think you missed your calling. You should've been a teacher."

"Hey, there's always time to go back," he said, and I nodded, shocked by his assessment.

"Mami, can I go in the back and watch Nickelodeon?" Nadia asked.

"Sure. Just make sure to bring your plate back to the trash can, and it's after six, so no more juices, only water."

"Okay, Mami. See you later, Mr. Mike," she said as she grabbed her plate and her remaining juice and headed to the back.

"Good. Now I can get my real drink." I picked up the empty soda can. "You want a beer?" I asked Mike.

He shook his head. "No. I know Aldris only drinks that damn Coors Light. I can't stand it."

I put my hand on my hip. "Oh, hell no, he doesn't. I stopped that shit. Coors Light is not my cup of tea either, so I got him hooked up on that Bud Light."

Mike laughed. "Are you serious? Oh, man. I love Bud Light. In that case, bring me one."

I returned with two bottles and handed him one. "Here's some *real* beer for you," I joked.

"Thanks. I appreciate it." He popped the top. "And you drink the bottles too?"

"Hell yeah. Never the can," I said, after taking mine to the head.

"And with no cup? You are some kinda girl."

Shrugging, I confirmed, "Uh, yeah. You ain't messing with no little prim and prissy chick with me. I am a beer-bottle-drinking, pizza-and-wing-eatin', Sunday-night-football kinda chick."

"Stop it. You like football?" he asked, amazed.

It was my turn to stare at him as if he had horns growing out of his head. "Do I like the best sport in America? Hell yeah. I'm a fan of several teams, but you know I'm gonna always go with the home team dirty birds as my favorite."

"I'm a home team fan too. Aldris is such a traitor. He likes—"

"The Baltimore Ravens." I finished his sentence. "I mean, I ain't gonna lie, they had some legends. Ed Reed was a straight beast, and Ray Lewis will always be the man. I have much respect for their game, but Aldris is rootin' for the wrong birds."

Sharing in the laughter, he quipped, "Damn. You really do follow football."

"Hell yeah. I made Aldris sign up for the Sunday Ticket just to have access to all the games on Sundays. I'm telling you, all day Sunday, Monday, and sometimes Thursday nights, I am unavailable."

"Aldris is a bigger basketball fan. That's why he's rooting for the wrong team. I like basketball, but it ain't really my thing. I like to play it more than I like to watch it."

"Yeah, I'm with you on that. I follow it more now because of Aldris, but I'm all football. I live on CBS, NBC, ESPN, and FOX during the season. And you know I have to make sure I have the NFL network and Showtime so I can see—"

"Inside the NFL," Mike shouted with me as he jumped up and down in his seat. "Me too. Get the fuck outta here," he hollered in sheer amazement.

"Man who? Phil Simms and Boomer have me freakin' rolling," I joked as Mike sat back down, looking at me in wonderment. "I like to watch ShoBox too. I was intrigued with the whole Marquez versus Vasquez matchups."

He looked at the bottle. "Are you sure you're saying this, or is it just the bottle? I love boxing too. Do you watch MMA?"

I drank a swig of my beer and set it down. "What? All day. UFC, Pride, and Strikeforce are in constant rotation on Saturday nights."

"We've gotta plan some fight nights. Man, Aldris didn't tell me his lady was such a down-ass chick. You like one of the damn fellas. I ain't never met a woman who actually liked watching MMA or boxing, and it ain't too many that I know who truly like football. Most of them just like seeing the men in their uniforms."

Beer almost spewed from my lips as I laughed. "Well, now that *is* an added bonus."

He pointed at me, giving me the side-eye with his lip pursed. "Aht. Look at you now."

"Shit, Aldris knows. He's my papi, but I have to give credit when I see a nice-looking man in some football tights now. He ain't trippin' as much as he fawns over Keri Hilson and Rosalyn Sanchez."

He nodded. "Yeah, those are two bad chicks there," he recalled, looking up as if he were daydreaming. "And you said Ms. Sanchez's name just like she does. I think it's the accent that gets the men," he joked.

"It's all part of the Latin charm for men and women." I giggled, turning the television station.

"Must be."

"You finished?" I asked. After he nodded, I threw our plates away then came back and grabbed a guitar. "There's nothing on the tube, so I guess I can play one round of Guitar Hero on the Wii before I sign on to my job, if you don't mind."

"You play Guitar Hero too?" he asked, shocked.

"Yeah. It's usually just me and Nadia because Aldris hates it. He'd rather play NBA Live or Call of Duty on the PS4. That's cool, but of course, if it's sports, I'd rather play Madden or boxing. But my favorite is this damn Guitar Hero."

Mike stood up. "Well, prepare to battle. I am the Guitar Hero master," he challenged me as he grabbed the other guitar.

I pointed at him. "Are you challenging me, Bruce Leroy?"

He laughed loudly. "Oh, you'll see who the last dragon is once I'm through with you. Strap up, lady."

"Ay, chico. You better bring it." I turned on the Wii and set up the game. I looked over at Mike, who was smiling at me. "What?" I asked.

"I'm just in shock. It is so true that you cannot judge a book by the cover. Lucinda, you're all right." He nodded, resolving that he'd misjudged me.

It was the first time I saw Mike through different eyes. We were actually more alike than we thought, and I realized I'd misjudged him as well. "Aww, thanks, Mike. So are you," I said as the game started. "But I'm still gonna whip that ass."

We stood there playing Guitar Hero for what had to be thirty minutes. Nadia had come back and sat on the sofa, watching us play, and we were all laughing it up and having a good time when Aldris floated into the family room with two boxes of pizza.

"Hey!" Aldris had to yell loudly to us over the noise.

I paused the game, and we all calmed down with the laughter and talking.

"Hey, baby," I greeted, smiling at him.

"Hey," he said, looking back and forth between Mike and me. "Mike?" he asked, puzzled.

Mike snapped his fingers. "Oh, man, I came over to scoop you up. Remember, you were going to shoot hoops with me?"

Aldris sighed and snapped his fingers. "Oh, yeah, man. I totally forgot. My bad," he said to him as they slapped hands together.

"Oh, no worries. Lucinda's been a great hostess." Mike smiled back at me.

I fanned him off. "*He's* the one that's been a big help."

"Yep, Papi, he helped me study, and he and Mami have been battling on Guitar Hero," she said and then whispered, "But Mami's winning."

"I heard that." Mike nudged Nadia playfully. "Sheer luck," Mike hollered.

Aldris nodded. "Oh, okay. Wow. Well, I appreciate it man. Lu, I called you to find out what you all wanted to eat. I see now that you were occupied by the Wii. I settled for pizza."

Gasping with a balled fist to my mouth, I apologized. "Oooh. I shoulda called you. Mike bought Nadia and me pizza already, but at least we have a meal for tomorrow."

He set the pizzas down on the coffee table. "Yeah, I guess you're right. Well, did you manage to get any work done?"

"Yeah, I did. Thanks to ol' Mike here." I play-boxed with Mike. "He watched Nadia for me while I finished my paper and homework. Speaking of work, I have to sign on—although I was thoroughly enjoying kicking your tail," I joked with Mike as he moved into one of my play punches. "Stick and move."

He laughed, fist-bumping me, and then he pulled the guitar off. "Until next time. You won the last dragon this time," he teased as I did a little victory dance and he laughed.

"Y'all are just bosom buddies now, huh?" Aldris commented.

"Man, Lu is a trip. I told her we have to plan fight nights and some tailgate parties when the football season starts," Mike said excitedly.

"Yeah, in that regard, you and Lucinda have a lot in common," Aldris admitted with a shrug.

"Yeah, we know," Mike and I said at the same time, then looked at each other and pointed. "Jinx. Double jinx. Triple jinx," we rattled off together, howling.

"Jinxy twins." Aldris put his hands up. "I'm pretty tired. I'd love to chop it up with you, man, but I need to eat and chill, and you know, spend a little time with my family."

Mike and he slapped hands. "A'ight, dude. I feel you. Holla at you later." He grabbed his wallet and keys.

I walked him to the door. "Thanks again. Whenever you're free again we have to get up on that Wii or PS4. You know, to even the score," I said sarcastically.

He fist-bumped me. "Oh, most definitely. Bud Light's on me. I'll holla at you, Lu. Be easy, mama," he said as he walked out, and I waved at him.

I turned around, and Aldris picked up the pizza boxes. "Seems like you and Mike are fast friends. The best of buddies."

"He's real cool. We're cool." I shrugged.

"I'm glad you all are getting along. After I eat, I'll battle you on the Wii."

"No thanks. I know you hate it. Plus, I have to work. Enjoy your dinner," I said to him and walked back to my office area.

A few minutes later, Aldris walked in and kissed me. "I didn't get a kiss or nothing. Just thought I'd give you one."

"My bad," I apologized, then began working again. I looked up and noticed Aldris staring at me. "What?" I giggled.

He shook his head. "Nothing. I'll leave you alone," he said and walked out.

I just shook my head and wondered what the heck he was acting all strange and weird about. I didn't have time to delve into it, though. It was time for work. As I got logged in, I giggled aloud as one of the songs from Guitar Hero came on my iTunes. Mike was a straight clown. Who knew he and I would end up being friends?

Chapter Thirty-two

Trinity

To Terrence, everything was back to normal, but for me, I still had a chip on my shoulder. It was one thing to think that Big Cal might've been attracted to me and even me to him, but to ask if we'd actually had an inappropriate relationship was a low blow. Hell, it wasn't even the ask that was the most hurtful. It was the fact that he accused me of such, to the point I damn near had to take a lie detector test. Like, he really didn't trust me, after everything we'd been through together. Wow.

Now that he claimed the Pooch situation was handled, I was even more on pins and needles. He looked at shit from his lens, but I was the one who'd been in a relationship with Pooch. I knew how he operated and how he thought. When Pooch found out whatever plan had failed, he wouldn't stop until he found out the reason and the culprit behind it. What kind of leverage did Terrence have that this scheme wouldn't eventually be linked to him? That was my whole point. I knew that he was intelligent and a forward thinker, but Terrence held a different level of comfort than I did when it came to Pooch. He only dealt with the people who dealt with Pooch. I dealt with *Pooch*. I knew his mindset better than anyone else, and that included Terrence.

The calm that we were now experiencing felt eerie to me. By now, I figured we'd have heard something besides just that the bribe worked. The fact that we hadn't heard anything was what gave me pause. Pooch may not have been as intellectual as Terrence, but he was still a street nigga. They didn't fight fair. And being honest, for all of Terrence's intelligence, Pooch was the one who got him locked up first because that's how grimy niggas operate.

Terrence wasn't that type of dude. He didn't give a damn about what the next man had going on as long as he could get his. Pooch wasn't like that. He cared. He wanted it all, other niggas be damned. It was that attitude that made me wonder what the fuck was going on behind the scenes that we didn't know about. We'd covered our tracks the first time, but the second time might not be so easy. And that was the part that led me to my current conversation.

"To what do I owe the pleasure of this phone call?"

"Big Cal, I need information on Pooch," I said, getting straight to the point.

"Hello, Trinity. How are you? I'm well. Thanks for asking."

"Yeah, okay. Now that we got the pleasantries out of the way, what is the update?"

Aaron paused. I couldn't tell if he was upset or simply pondering what to tell me. The pause made my tension escalate instantly.

"What is it?" I pried nervously.

He hissed before sucking his teeth. "I shouldn't be speaking to you about this."

"And why the fuck not?" I hollered, upset that he was brushing me off. "That's the exact reason you gave me your number."

"I understand that, and all things considered, it was the right thing to do at the time."

"So why isn't it the right thing to do now?" I asked before he could finish.

A harsh and loud breath escaped him. “Trinity, have you talked to T?”

“He told me about the payout. That’s it. Why? Does he know something else?”

“Trinity,” he blew out in frustration.

“*Aaron*,” I said sternly.

“Oh, I’m Aaron now?”

“That’s what ya mama named you,” I said just to be a bitch.

“Look, you really need to talk to T about this. I’m not trying to get into no shit with him about this phone call.”

Wait. What? What the heck did our phone call have to do with Terrence? And why was he all of a sudden shutting down information to me? Then it hit me.

“Terrence told you not to talk me about anything concerning Pooch, didn’t he?” I asked, heated as hell.

“Bingo. And I have to report only to him. He’s my cousin. It was his wish.”

“Well, I’m your cousin-in-law, so you better tell me something, or else I’m just gonna call and ask about the case myself.”

“You wouldn’t risk your family like that, so calm down. Besides, it ain’t shit for you to call up there for. Shit quiet ’cause ain’t shit going on. The judge is taken care of. It’s been handled, Trinity, so chill.”

I knew that I would push him to spill the beans if I threatened to call, but a part of me still didn’t believe what he had said.

My quietness must have clued him into that fact. “I’m serious, Trinity. It’s handled. You can breathe easy,” he said convincingly, causing me to relax for the first time in weeks. “Besides, I love my cousin, but you know if some shit was really popping off that I’d call you. I know my cousin has your back, but I do too. And on God, I’d never, ever let anything happen to you and those babies. For real.”

His words were comforting. Big Cal had always tried to be a source of support when I was with Pooch. It was silent, but it was there. I could see how upset he was when he couldn't be there for me, like when Pooch beat my ass for being with Terrence that time. But when he could intervene with Pooch's antics, he did. I'd always be grateful to him for that. Besides me, he was the person who knew Pooch the best, so I trusted his word for it. If Big Cal said that everything was cool, then everything was cool. So, I did as requested and decided to chill.

"Thanks for the reassurance. I appreciate that."

"Anytime, Trinity. Now, get off this phone and enjoy those babies."

I laughed. "Thank you, Big Cal."

"Who's that? My mama named me Aaron," he joked.

After our laughter subsided, I said, "Well, thanks *Aaron.*"

"Anything for you. You're welcome."

We disconnected the line, and for the first time in a very long time, I felt like a weight had been lifted from my shoulders. I decided to take Big Cal's advice and breathe easy. I was no longer fearful of Pooch. He'd lost, and we'd finally won. Finally.

Chapter Thirty-three

Pooch

Man, I was one grumpy muthafucka. Lack of sleep, being locked up, and not locating Trinity was fucking with me something awful. The real culprit, however, was that ever since I caught Wolf and Cock Diesel together, I'd been sleeping with one eye fucking open, on the real. I wasn't tryna wake up in the middle of the night to Wolf having a midnight snack at my expense. *Shit.* Wolf tried to explain that shit to me again, but I didn't need or want to hear it. My only words about that shit were to do whatever he fucking wanted, but to be clear, to keep it with Cock Diesel and don't be messing up my muthafucking money.

Wolf was the one nigga who I felt I could really be down with, and now every time I looked at his punk ass, my stomach hurt. He was constantly tryna stay on my good side by doing every little thing I asked. I could tell that bitch to jump up and down like an orangutan like Eddie Murphy did ol' girl in *Coming to America,* and he would do it. He was that desperate to keep that shit a secret. That's what I didn't respect. If you didn't want your shit in the streets, then don't be doing shit that was gon' embarrass your ass.

At least Cock Diesel was admitting his shit. He still kept his dime piece at bay, but every nigga in this joint knew that he would give it and take it any way he could get it. I could respect that shit, though. If you sucked dick and packed breadcrumbs, be courteous enough to let it be known. Cock Diesel wasn't punkin' nobody for ass. There were enough admitted shit packers and plenty more undercover booty lovers to keep him satisfied, so Wolf wasn't shit but a notch on his belt.

The truly fucked-up part was that I was gonna put Wolf down with Lisa to keep his dick sucked until he went before the parole board next year. But he fucked that all up. Ain't no way in the hell Lisa was gon' wrap her lips around my dick after putting her mouth around his, and he been lettin' Cock Diesel smoke on the pipe. Fuck that. That was like being around secondhand smoke to me. Secondhand gayness. I was already around that shit twenty-four seven. I didn't need to be that close to another dude, even if it was only secondhand.

Hell, for all I cared, Wolf could've claimed Cock Diesel as his boyfriend, since Flava was makin' sure to keep Adrienne on ice for me until this plea bargain went through. And I did believe that Adrienne was startin' to get fond of ol' Flava, too. Every time I talked to Flava, she was talking 'bout some shit her and Adrienne did together or with the kids. Flava said ol' girl was open like the 7-Eleven for her nowadays, and I couldn't even be mad at that. From what I used to hear about how Flava got down in the bedroom, she'd probably make me forget Trinity's ass.

Speaking of, sometimes I straight forgot that my whole purpose of getting out was to find that damn woman. I wanted to know what the fuck was going on with my daughter and my son. Being locked up made me realize just how much I had taken for granted. When I got out of this joint, I was gon' raise my kids, you know, actually be in they life. Hell, all I knew was this street shit, but if this was how my kids was gon' end up, then fuck it. I'd have to learn to show them how to fly right. Get an education. Play sports or music or some shit. Make it that way. Don't be in your twenties facing 101 years of nothing, just being a damn free-labor worker for the state.

I missed Trinity, too. Man, it was so much I wish I could've redone with her. I wish I coulda been a better nigga for her and the kids. She wanted to do her art shit, and I shoulda let her. She still coulda been my dime piece with her own grip. I'll admit that the main reason I never wanted Trinity to do nothing with her life was because I was afraid of her being successful. If she was successful, then I knew she'd leave a nigga like me, so I used my power and money to keep her from doing what she wanted to do. I was wrong for that.

I hadn't asked Flava about her lately, but I was definitely gonna get back to that. It was time to find out what the hell was truly going on with Trinity. Whether I missed her or not, if I found out her ass with Terrence this whole time, she was gon' wish I got that fuckin' triple cocktail concoction instead of this prison sentence. Real talk. But if I found out something happened to her, whoever did it wasn't gonna have time to worry about running from me, nor would their family members have to worry about retaliation, because I was gonna meet that person's muthafuckin' ass in the same hell I was gonna send them to. I was definitely gonna get the chair if that was the case, and I wasn't gon' mind one bit. Hell, I'd strap up in the seat and stick the needle in my arm my damn self. I'd made up in my mind that once Flava called, I was gonna hit her up about whether she'd tracked down Skeet or anybody who may have known about Trinity's whereabouts.

I looked at the clock again. I knew I had been doing too much random-ass thinking, and my attorney, Stein, was supposed to been there. Between my work on the inside and a little hookup from Skrilla, I was able to extend that olive branch to Judge Watson, so I was anxious like a muthafucka to find out the outcome. When they finally called me, I was happy as hell, but when I marched out, I saw Flava sitting there, which surprised the fuck outta me. Don't get me wrong. It was a good surprise, but I didn't take too well to surprises 'cause they were always full of shit.

"Hey, baby," Flava said, standing up and kissing me on the lips.

"'Sup," I said, hittin' her with the head nod as we sat down. "Where the hell is Stein?"

She pouted, sucking her teeth. "Yeah, I'm doing good." She copped an attitude.

"Don't get all fuckin' offended and shit. I was expecting Stein. That's all." I leaned forward, staring at her. "So, where the fuck is his punk ass?"

She pursed her lips even harder. "*Well*," she said, exaggerated.

"Don't come at me with no bullshit today, Flava. I don't wanna hear that shit. I'm telling you right now."

"Fine, then I won't tell you." She shrugged, crossing her arms.

My eyes bucked. Who in the fuck did she think she was talking to like that? This bitch done went loco for real. "What the fuck is your problem?"

"You said not to tell you—"

"Stop playing games and shit. That's your damn problem. Get to the point." Hell, I was too frustrated to be dealing with her issues today.

She smacked her lips. "Fine, Pooch. Stein ain't coming."

"What the fuck you mean, he ain't coming?" I asked angrily.

She looked around. "Can you calm the hell down? Damn," she fussed as some other people and inmates looked at us strangely.

I sat back and took a deep breath. "A'ight. What's going on?"

"First off, Stein is too scared to come back to talk to you, so he asked me to do it for him."

My screw-face expression could not be helped. "Scared? How he gon' be scared? He's my attorney."

"That might be one reason why you shouldn't be jackin' the muthafucka up by his collar and shit. You're a convicted murderer, Pooch. What you thought he was gon' do? Be cool with you puttin' your hands on him?"

Okay, she had a point. "But he still gon' be my lawyer, right?"

"Yeah, but he couldn't come here and tell you this, so he sent me."

"Tell me what?"

She took a deep breath and looked me dead in the eyes. "That fifty grand we offered Watson was a no go. He refused it."

"What you mean? That bastard wouldn't accept the money? As crooked as that bastard is, you can't pay me enough to tell me he's flyin' straight all of a sudden."

"He ain't flyin' straight, Pooch. He wants more. He said that wasn't enough."

"Ain't he a bold muthafucka? Who in the fuck puts stipulations on a bribe? Damn. He ruthless. So, what does he want? A hundred?"

"I wish, Pooch. That's what Stein offered him, since my dude Skrilla was gonna front you up another fifty Gs, but that grimy muthafucka refused a hundred. That bitch wanted two hundred."

My eyes nearly popped outta my head. "Two hundred Gs? Are you fucking shitting me?"

"Hell no. And he wanted that shit in unmarked bills. Dirty bastard."

I rubbed my face to ease the tension. Hopefully, that was the only bad news. I needed to know where that shit left me. "So, what is Skrilla saying?"

"Skrilla was willing to put up another fifty Gs, but that's it, Pooch. He said he can't take a hit like that not knowing if you were gonna get out to push the real weight to repay your debt. The only thing we have is a hundred Gs to give, and Watson wants a hundred more on top of that."

I would be in here for double murder if I could've put my hands on that damn Watson. I hated that summa bitch with a straight passion. If I couldn't get this appeal to go through or this plea bargain, I was trapped in this hellhole for life, and I simply couldn't see it. I had to give myself time to think on what the fuck other options I had, so I switched the subject.

"Did you ever find out anything about Trinity?"

"I thought you had left that broad alone."

I clenched my teeth. Now Flava was crossing the line. She may have been my number one due to my situation, but she was looking to get chin-checked for her loose lips. Number one, I was sick of her poppin' fly with me, and number two, she wasn't gon' just dog my baby mama out like that in my presence.

"First off, my reasons for wanting know about Trinity go deeper than just tryna keep up with her. We've got kids together, Flava. I want to find my daughter and son. Lastly, I'm the muthafucka that calls the shots around here, and it would be best for you to remember that shit," I said with a straight, no-nonsense tone.

She must've figured out I was dead-ass serious because she put her hands up as if to apologize. "Skeet said he's been tryna catch up with Terrence for the longest, and he don't know where he went. Everybody is either being tight-lipped about this thang, or they really don't fucking know. That's all I know."

I hit the table. "Damn," I said aloud and shook my head.

"Look, Pooch. The only thing I can suggest is to see how Stein does with the appeal. Maybe that will go through."

That wasn't an option. That appeals shit was taking too long, and I felt like I was dying in this piece-of-shit-ass place. I needed out, and I needed out like yesterday.

I leaned forward and grabbed her hands. "Do you love me?"

"I have love *for* you, yes, but if you asking me if I'm *in* love with you, then no, I'm not. On the real, Pooch, I care about you. I want you to get out because you seem like a good nigga, and I think we could really have something together, but I ain't puttin' my heart on the line for you when the only bitch you can talk about is Trinity. I wanna love you, but I need love too," she said, taking her hands away from mine and leaning back.

Now, how could I convince this bitch that I cared enough about her to ask her to put herself at risk? Flava wasn't your run-of-the-mill type of chickenhead broad. That bitch was smart, and she knew how to make chess moves. If I came at her with some bullshit, she'd smell it a mile away, call me on it, and then I'd be stuck like Chuck in this muthafucka for real. So, I had to exercise some caution. I was fucking with a heavyweight.

I leaned back, then nodded my head. "You're right." I threw my hands up. "I can't knock what you saying because you've always been real with me, Flava. That's why I've always stuck with you. We were forced together due to this situation, and I know it's hard for you to trust me because of my past with Trinity. I ain't gon' lie. I'll always love Trinity. She was my heart. But I love my kids, and she's the chick that has them, so I talk about her a lot.

I don't expect you to be in love with me because I can't really offer myself to you the way you deserve, but if I can get outta here, I'll show you that I can be that man you need in your life."

Flava looked away and swallowed the lump forming in her throat. Checkmate, bitches. I was still as smooth as Schlitz malt liquor. Damn, I'd been hanging around these old-ass cats in lockup too long with that reference. I knew I had her with that shit. For the most part, it was nothing but the damn truth, and she knew that. They say the truth shall set you free, so I was hoping like a mutha that that truth I'd just slapped on Flava was enough for her to do what I needed her to do to help set *me* the fuck free.

Obviously touched, she leaned in close and reached for my hands. "What is it that you need me to do?"

Got her. "I need for you to let Skrilla put you on the team. I need you to push that weight on the outside to get this money up real quick. I know you're risking a lot for me, and I damn sure don't want you to get caught up, but if you do this for me, I promise you when I get out it's all about me and you. I got you for life, mama."

Flava blushed. She asked, "You mean that shit, Pooch? It's just gonna be me and you? I mean, I feel you wanting to know about your kids, and I promise I'll help you find them, but no more Trinity, right?"

I crossed my toes since I couldn't cross my fingers. "Yep, no more. It'll just be Pooch and Flava, ruling the muthafucking world," I said, winking at her.

She nodded happily, but she still seemed a little cautious. "Let me think on it, Pooch. I wanna do it, but I just gotta make sure I don't end up in lockup too. Ya know."

I knew I had her, so it was time to go back to my old attitude. Good. I was done frontin' for this bitch. "I'ma call you on Monday for an answer." I wasn't playing no games. I'd thrown my best lies—and hell, best truths—at her. She had better do this.

"That only gives me one day to think on it."

"You're good at counting. That means you can be good at pushing," I said snidely. "One day is all you need, 'cause basically, either you love me enough to do it, or you don't. You've got the rest of today and all of tomorrow to make a decision. That's fair enough."

She shrugged. "A'ight. Call me on Monday."

Jackpot. I was the man again. I had this bitch wrapped around my finger now.

"Monday morning at nine a.m. Be by your phone," I commanded, adding a kiss to her lips and forehead for good measure. "I'm depending on you."

With that, I walked off. I knew she was gonna do it. She had to. If she didn't, Pit had cousins that weren't locked up who were just as ruthless as he was. I didn't want her to suffer the same fate as phone dude, but I'd do it if I had to stay in there any longer. At least it'd make me feel like I deserved to be there. Whether she wanted to or not, she'd better handle her business. As if her life depended on it.

“Men may not get all they pay for in this world;
but they must certainly pay for all they get.”

~ Frederick Douglas

Please stay tuned for the next installment of this series...

Never Again, No More 4:

What Goes Around